Praise for *I'LL NEVER TELL*

"An atmospheric thriller that takes the reader on a harrowing journey through one family's quest for the truth no matter the cost. McKenzie's characters leap from the page in this compulsive, riveting tale filled with twisty family secrets, suspect loyalties, and deadly encounters. . . . [It] will leave you guessing until the very end."

Heather Gudenkauf, *New York Times* bestselling author of *The Weight of Silence* and *Not a Sound*

"A cleverly crafted, heart-wrenching tale of obsession, regret, and the devastating effects of keeping secrets for far too long."

A. J. Banner, #1 *USA Today* bestselling author of *The Good Neighbor* and *The Twilight Wife*

"When it comes to psychological thrillers, lies and dark family secrets are the very best kind, and Catherine McKenzie handles them both with skill in *I'll Never Tell*, a riveting story of siblings linked by long-ago tragedy. Suspicions swirl, and the truth is revealed in steady, page-turning increments that culminate in a whopper of an ending."

Kimberly Belle, bestselling author of *Three Days Missing* and *The Marriage Lie*

"You can never go wrong with a Catherine McKenzie novel. Consistently superb suspense that doesn't disappoint. Stunning!"

J.T. Ellison, *New York Times* bestselling author of *Tear Me Apart* and *Lie to Me*

"McKenzie weaves a rich tapestry of flawed, untrustworthy characters, challenging the reader to solve the crime . . . a not-so-easy but spellbinding task."

Robert Dugoni, *New York Times* bestselling author of the Tracy Crosswhite series

"Secrets are the coin of suspense, and Catherine McKenzie spends them better than anyone. *I'll Never Tell* builds incredible tension in a braid of a family's past with its present, and what five siblings, set against each other by their father's last will and testament, will do to secure their future. Twisty and brilliant!"

Jamie Mason, author of *Three Graves Full* and *Monday's Lie*

"With its blend of can't-put-it-down suspense and sharp psychological insight, *I'll Never Tell* compels as both whodunit and family drama. . . . A fascinating, complicated family whose heartbreak, regret, and love leap off the page. This might be my favorite of Catherine McKenzie's books yet."

Leah Stewart, author of *The New Neighbor* and *What You Don't Know About Charlie Outlaw*

Praise for *THE GOOD LIAR*

"A riveting thriller."

Entertainment Weekly

"The questions raised . . . accumulate with every plot twist. . . . McKenzie has effected something of a Trojan Horse: *The Good Liar* is a novel of ideas in the convincing guise of a page-turner."

Montreal Gazette

"[A] complex, thought-provoking psychological thriller . . . Who the good liar may be, and what that phrase might actually mean, are questions that will resonate long after the book is finished."

Publishers Weekly (starred review)

"One of the forty hottest thrillers of 2018."

Goodreads

"With twists and turns, the lives of three women intersect in the most unexpected ways during the aftermath of a tragedy. Thought-provoking, suspenseful, and mysterious, *The Good Liar* is a true page-turner that explores the ways stories are connected and created, and what can be hidden underneath. This is a book you won't be able to put down!"

Megan Miranda, *New York Times* bestselling author of
All the Missing Girls and *The Perfect Stranger*

OTHER BOOKS BY CATHERINE McKENZIE

Spin

Arranged

Forgotten

Hidden

Spun

Smoke

The Murder Game (writing as Julie Apple)

Fractured

The Good Liar

I'LL NEVER TELL

CATHERINE McKENZIE

PUBLISHED BY SIMON & SCHUSTER
NEW YORK LONDON TORONTO SYDNEY NEW DELHI

Simon & Schuster Canada
A Division of Simon & Schuster, Inc.
166 King Street East, Suite 300
Toronto, Ontario M5A 1J3

This book is a work of fiction. Any references to historical events, real people, or real places are used fictitiously. Other names, characters, places, and events are products of the author's imagination, and any resemblance to actual events or places or persons, living or dead, is entirely coincidental.

Map illustration by Sara Heppner-Waldston

This Simon & Schuster Canada edition June 2019

SIMON & SCHUSTER CANADA and colophon are trademarks of Simon & Schuster, Inc.

For information about special discounts for bulk purchases, please contact Simon & Schuster Special Sales at 1-800-268-3216 or CustomerService@simonandschuster.ca.

Manufactured in the United States of America

10 9 8 7 6 5 4 3 2 1

Library and Archives Canada Cataloguing in Publication

McKenzie, Catherine, author
I'll never tell / Catherine McKenzie.
Issued in print and electronic formats.
ISBN 978-1-5011-7863-4 (softcover).—ISBN 978-1-5011-7864-1 (ebook)
I. Title. II. Title: I'll never tell.
PS8625.K4395I45 2019 C813'.6 C2018-905207-4
C2018-905208-2

ISBN 978-1-5011-7863-4
ISBN 978-1-5011-7864-1 (ebook)

For the Lake Lovering crew, with love

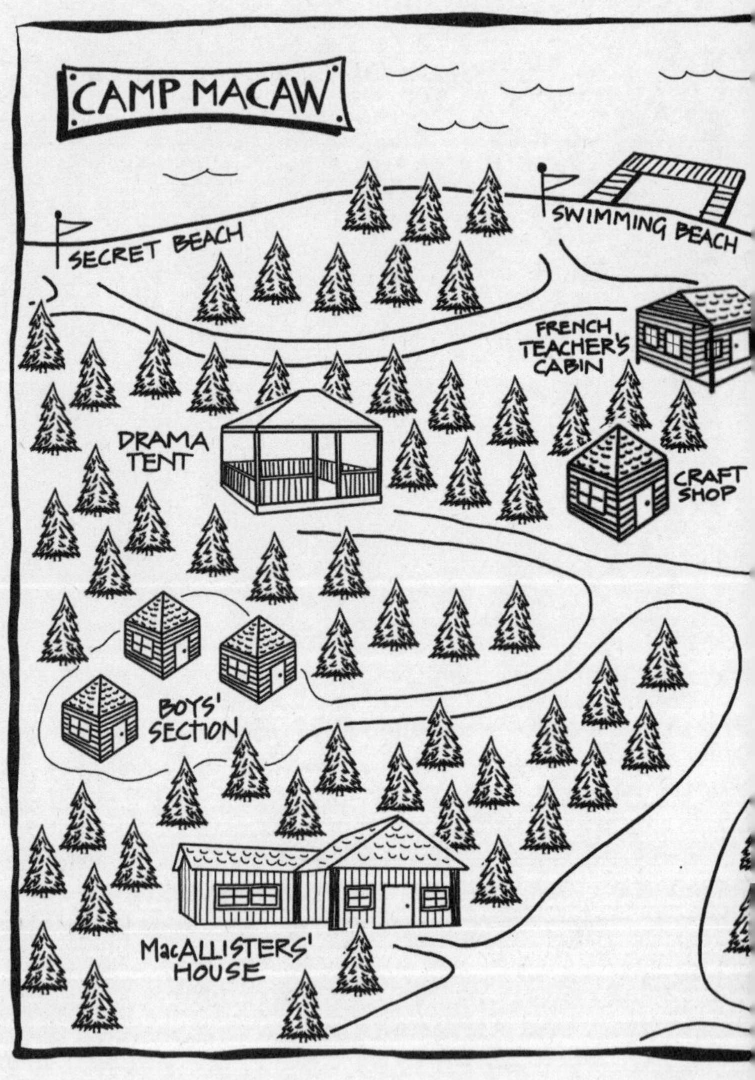
CAMP MACAW
SECRET BEACH
SWIMMING BEACH
FRENCH TEACHER'S CABIN
DRAMA TENT
CRAFT SHOP
BOYS' SECTION
MacALLISTERS' HOUSE

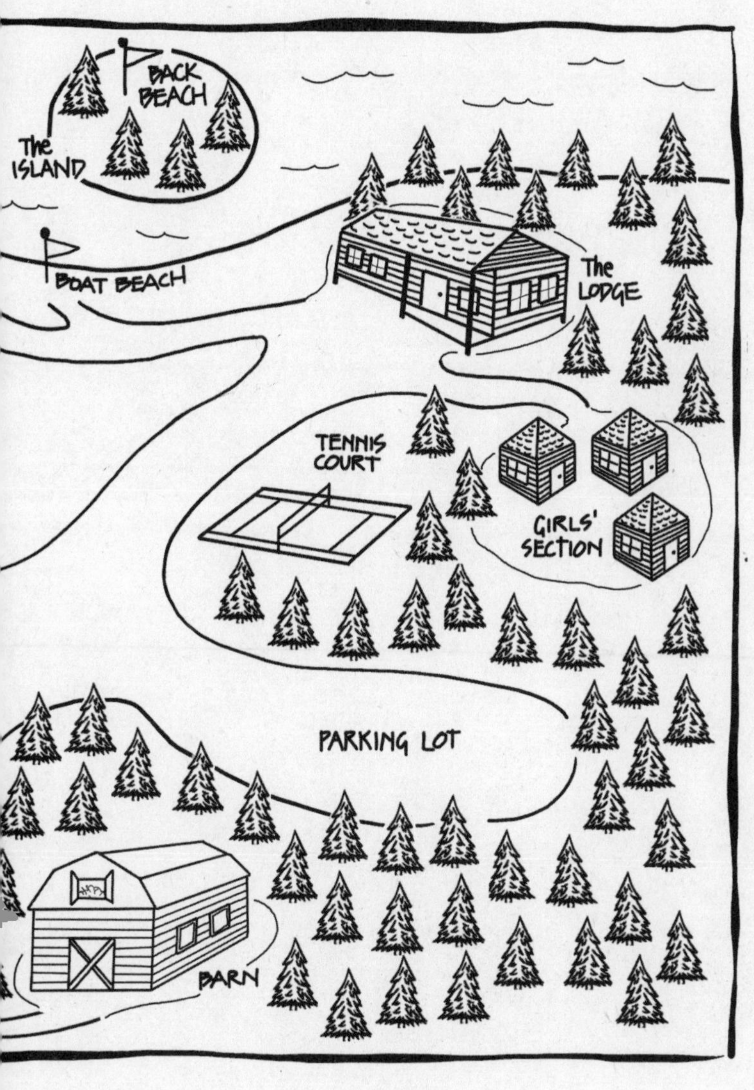
BACK BEACH
The ISLAND
BOAT BEACH
The LODGE
TENNIS COURT
GIRLS' SECTION
PARKING LOT
BARN

Amanda

July 22, 1998—9:00 p.m.

We only started the lantern ceremony my second-to-last year at Camp Macaw. Yet it's buried in my summer memories like the smell of the smoke from the weekly campfire, the game we played that made it sound as if we were caught in a rainstorm, or the call-and-response of capture the flag as we bounded through the woods. Pine and mud, sand and sunscreen.

It was a simple but effective idea: make a sky lantern out of tissue paper, candles, and wire, and then write a wish on its fragile walls. You could add your real heart's desire because within hours, the lanterns would be lit and released into the sky, floating up and away and landing on some faraway shore.

The ceremony began at dusk a few days before the end of the July session. On that last night, I held the lantern I'd built earlier away from my body so I didn't crush it as I walked to the Swimming Beach along with the rest of camp. Pebbles collected in my sandals, and my best friend, Margaux, giggled when I lifted my foot and gave it a good shake.

"Rock fall warning," she said.

"Rock-a-bye Baby."

"Rock, papers, scissors."

"Rock around the clock."

"Will you hush, you two?" Ryan said with a touch of annoyance, glancing at us over his shoulder. He was Margaux's older brother, twenty to our seventeen, a genuine adult, and the object of my penciled-in wish.

She stuck out her tongue at him, then rearranged her face in mock seriousness. As junior counselors, we were supposed to be setting an example. Mostly, we took this responsibility to heart, but we also worried our wishes wouldn't come true if we made too much noise on the way to the beach. There were rules, after all. Did the Patron Saint of Wishes care about the giddy thoughts of girls? We weren't ready to take the risk.

There were 150 of us altogether, campers and staff, holding multicolored paper lanterns—a kaleidoscope of hopes and dreams. We snaked onto the beach, our unusual silence, instead of the usual mix of French and English voices, a warning that something was coming, something important, something forever. The lake was flat the way it often was at sunset, its brackish scent so familiar we didn't smell it anymore. Ryan led us out onto the floating docks that swayed beneath our feet. There was a wisp of wind, and the rising moon was full, a flashlight on the mirrored water. Two hundred feet away, a small fleet of sailboats rocked gently on their moorings, their halyards pinging out an off-key melody.

Someone ahead of me tripped on the edge of one of the docks. Her cargo splashed into the water.

"My lantern!"

The *shhh!* of twenty counselors rippled through the night. The girl, ten, buried her face in her hands, her shoulders shaking. *She won't get her wish tonight,* I thought as I tightened my grip on the stays of my own lantern, even though I knew my own hope wouldn't come true—that the flutter in my heart was more wishful thinking than anticipation.

And yet . . .

The docks were arranged in a squared-off U; if you walked around the perimeter, you ended up back on the beach. At the halfway point, on the larger lifeguard dock, Ryan took a plastic lighter out of his pocket. The *flick, flick* of the flame lit up his handsome face. Every summer camp there ever was has a boy like Ryan, who leads the boys and has his pick of the girls. Back when Camp Macaw was started, in the 1950s, Ryan would've been holding a Zippo, a cigarette dangling from his lip. But it was 1998; we wore Tevas and board shorts, and the boys kept their hair shaggy.

A lighter would have to do.

Ryan worked quickly. We were supposed to release our lanterns as close together as possible for maximum effect. As I neared him, I turned mine around, making sure my wish was pressed against my sweatshirt because Ryan was the kind of guy who might lift it out of my hands to see what I wanted. He'd done it the summer before, in the middle of my crush. I hadn't dared write his name then. Instead I put down something silly about staying up on a Windsurfer. He'd offered me lessons, but he didn't mean it. I was only another admirer then, one of many.

Not this summer, though. I'd been bold and written down what—who—I wanted. But instead of trying to read it, he leaned in close and said, "See you on the Island later?"

All I could do was nod as my heart jumped in my chest like a frog caught on a hot road. He flicked the lighter. He lit the candle, and

I held the lantern close to me for a moment, feeling the heat seep through the thin paper. I moved forward on the dock, waiting for it to start tugging in my hands. When it did, I lifted it up and let it go, watching it join the others as I rounded the docks and stepped back onto the solid ground.

When all the lanterns were headed skyward, Margaux started singing "Fire's Burning" in her sweet alto voice. We sang both the English and French versions in a round, again and again, our voices rising and falling like the boats.

When our lanterns were a distant haze in the sky, Margaux and I walked over to Boat Beach. We carried a canoe between us down to the water, adjusted our headlamps, and climbed in.

And then we paddled to the Island.

	Amanda	**Margaux**	**Ryan**
9:00 p.m.	Lantern ceremony	Lantern ceremony	Lantern ceremony

TWENTY YEARS LATER

FRIDAY

CHAPTER 1

ROUTINE

Sean

For Sean Booth, every morning for as long as he could remember began the same way, waking up in a small room crammed into the eaves of the lodge, the cheap blankets he slept under twisted around his ankles, the sound of the breeze rushing in the trees outside his open window.

It was 6:45. It was always 6:45. He didn't have to check the time; he knew it in his bones. Sean rose immediately. He wasn't a layabout. He had his routine, and he stuck to it. One minute to take the towel off the end of his bed and wrap it around his naked waist. One more till he was in the shower at the end of the hall, first in freezing water, then letting it get so hot it almost scalded him. He believed in three-minute showers, no more, no less; anything else was wasteful. He scrubbed his short hair with a bar of Dove soap, then passed the bar across his chest and into his crevices. At forty-five, he had more of those now than he used to, but everything else was pretty much the same as it always was. He turned off the shower, brushed his teeth, and was back in his room at 6:52. He used the worn towel to rub off the water, then put on his faded cargo pants and a long-sleeved T-shirt. Then, because it was Labor Day weekend, and the morning chill would linger until later in the day, one of his two Camp Macaw sweatshirts.

It was 6:58 when his Tretorned feet hit the stairs that brought him down into the lodge's main room. The smell of scrambled eggs and slightly charred toast greeted him before he hit the last step. He waved to Amy in the kitchen, the only kitchen staff left now that the campers had all gone home. She was still there because of the guests who would be arriving soon.

He pushed open the creaking screen-porch door. The sun was bright, but there was still a touch of frost on the grass. It needed mowing, but he was going to have to wait until the day steamed the moisture away before he could climb onto his ride mower and cut it back.

He walked to the end of the wooden porch and surveyed the open-air courtyard—the tetherball court, the Craft Shop on the other end, the path to Boat Beach and Swimming Beach. The hundred-year-old pines gave it a closed-in feeling, but that never bothered him. This was the only home he'd ever known, the only home he wanted, and the thought of not having this place, of losing his routine and his room upstairs in the lodge was too much to bear. It was too much to—

No. He was getting worked up when nothing had happened yet. Mr. MacAllister had promised he'd be taken care of and, so far, everything Mr. MacAllister had told him had come true. He needed to be patient. Lord knows he knew how to do that.

He lifted his arm and took hold of the frayed bell rope. Even though there was no one left to wake, he jerked it anyway, sounding out the start of the day. He rang it eight times, once for each of them and one last time for her. The bong wormed into his head; the hearing in his right ear was diminished from having performed this task thousands of times.

But enough of this. He had work to do.

The Mackerels were coming.

CHAPTER 2

YOU CAN'T GO HOME AGAIN

Margaux

When Margaux MacAllister stopped in town at the McDonald's for a breakfast sandwich she didn't want and coffee she didn't need, she knew she was stalling. She could tell herself it was tradition all she wanted to, but something wasn't a tradition anymore if it had been twenty years since she'd done it, was it?

But her car turned in to the drive-through lane almost automatically, and her stomach rumbled because she'd left the city before she usually woke up, let alone ate, so here she was in the parking lot with the smell of grease clogging the air in her car. As she ate the sandwich, Margaux was hit with what she assumed would be the first swell of déjà vu that would soak the weekend. It was one of the reasons she'd told Mark not to come; she didn't want to have to translate the past for him or let him see the hold it still had over her. She'd learned long ago that he wasn't someone who could roll with unfamiliar scenarios. Instead, there was a constant litany of "Who was that again?" and

"How come you didn't introduce me?" The thought of it exhausted her, so when he'd offered to come along, she told him no. He was annoyed, and hadn't even turned over to say goodbye when she'd gotten up this morning, but she'd deal with that when she got back. She had enough on her plate as it was.

The view from the McDonald's parking lot was the same as always. The muddy river, the concrete bridge. The strip of tourist shops along Main Street, the greasy spoon, and the laundromat where they'd go on their days off to wash the damp out of their clothes and fill up on french fries and ice cream.

She always thought of the McDonald's as the gateway to camp because it was where Amanda's parents would stop to give them their "send-off meal" before dropping them off every summer. From the time she was ten, her parents let her stay with Amanda for a couple of weeks before camp started so she could arrive like the other campers, incognito. They never got to the McDonald's this early back then, though, so it was burgers and fries they ate, not the Egg McMuffin, hold the egg, she was eating now. And they usually sat at one of the run-down picnic tables on the rough patch of lawn, letting the early summer sun mark their winter skin.

But the view was the same, and the smell was the same, and the way the paper that covered her sandwich crinkled in her hand was so familiar it erased the smattering of red leaves on the maples in front of her, making it wholly a summer view. She could've been seventeen again, with everything that meant and everything she'd rather forget.

She finished her sandwich, crumpled up the paper wrapper, and turned her car back on. The radio station that had kept her company from Montreal was a cut-in of static, so she tuned in to the local French FM station—CIMO, it was called—its position on the dial a muscle memory. They were playing Will Smith's "Gettin' Jiggy wit It." My God. How many times had she and Amanda danced that stupid

Will Smith dance their last summer together? Too many to count. Amanda was an amazing physical mimic and danced just like him. They'd even sung it that night on their paddle to the Island, their calls of *na na na na na na na* echoing and repeating off the water.

"Bringing you all the hits," the announcer said as the song ended. "All the way back from the summer of 1998."

The tires on Margaux's car kicked up a cloud of dust as she drove down the long dirt driveway to Camp Macaw. Twenty years had passed, but nothing had changed. She was as stuck in the summer of 1998 as the radio station.

It unfolded like a slide show of her youth. There on the left was the path in the woods, where she and Amanda had shared their first cigarette and then almost got caught by her sister Mary. Mary would've told on them, too, which was why you never told her anything.

Now she was driving past the barns where Mary had come diligently every morning at sunup to muck out the stalls and exercise the horses. She spent so much time there that she always smelled faintly like horses. Mary had tried to get Margaux into riding, but Margaux was too afraid. She could fake her way through her lessons so long as they kept to the ground, but when they were about to start jumping, Margaux knew her riding days were over.

Mary had her own stable now, not far from here. She wouldn't arrive until later, after morning workout, but that was fine. Margaux wasn't ready for the full earnestness of Mary yet.

She turned in to the parking lot made up of weedy grass and the old rusted-out red truck her parents had abandoned there she couldn't remember when. She parked next to the truck and pulled out her phone to check her messages. *Shit.* She should've done that back in

Magog when she was at the McDonald's. She had two texts from Mark but no reception. They had never put in that extra cell tower on the neighboring farm, and so she might as well have been in 1998 as far as technology was concerned. Her parents had opposed the tower; they thought it was better for the campers to have a technology-free zone. Margaux agreed with the philosophy but felt antsy anyway. Mark wouldn't be happy that she was unreachable for forty-eight hours. She'd better remember to call him from the landline before he freaked out and sent the cops in to check on her.

Someone rapped on her windshield. She shrieked and dropped her phone to the floor.

"Sean! Goddammit, you scared the living daylights out of me."

He cupped his hand around his right ear, then made a motion for her to roll down her window. She pressed the button. Her window descended neatly into its slot.

"Hi, Margaux."

"You shouldn't creep up on people like that."

"No creeping. I walked right through the parking lot. Didn't you see me?"

"I was checking something on my phone."

She reached down and picked it up, wiping the muck from the floor off the screen. She needed to get her car cleaned out, as Mark often, and annoyingly, reminded her. But there she was, making him sound as if he were her enemy. She didn't know why she did that. She loved him.

"Those don't work up here," Sean said. His hands were shoved into the pockets of his cargo pants. His hair was still as red as ever, like a ripe orange, though he wore it close-cropped now. When he was younger, it had been long and curly, and the kids called him Clowney when they thought he wasn't listening.

"I noticed," Margaux said.

He shrugged but stayed where he was. She felt trapped. She wanted to get out of the car, but she didn't particularly feel like a long, winding conversation with Sean. There wasn't any helping it, though; he was as much of a fixture as the clay tennis court. Her parents had relied on him to keep the roofs from leaking and the docks from sinking, and if he gave her the willies sometimes, well, that was probably just her thirteen-year-old self remembering how he used to stare at her when he thought she wasn't looking.

"I'm opening the door," she said. He stepped back. She decided to leave her window down to air her car out. The sun was bright but not yet hot. She breathed in the scent of the pines, the dust, the tang of rusted metal. This was what home smelled like.

"Those are some bright shoes," Sean said.

"What? Oh, these. Yeah, they're ridiculous." Her feet were encased in the new running shoes she'd bought the day before. She was in the middle of a marathon training sequence, and she needed to break in these shoes before her race in three weeks. She'd waited too long, and when she finally made it to the store, all they had left in her size was a pair of bright pink shoes with orange accents. "I was hoping they'd get covered in mud so I wouldn't have to look at the color," she said.

"Not much mud this summer."

"I noticed."

He reached into the back seat and took hold of her overnight bag. It was made of battered leather, something she'd inherited from her maternal grandfather years ago.

"I got that."

"Nah. You know. Mr. MacAllister would want me to take care of you, like always."

"You can call him Pete. He told you to enough times."

"Doesn't feel right."

Margaux held her tongue. Sean's serflike attitude toward her parents was something she'd never understood, but it wasn't going to change now. She let him carry her bag and lead the way out of the parking lot.

"I'm putting you, Kate, and Liddie in the French Teacher's Cabin, if that's all right? Unless you wanted to stay in the house . . ."

"No, that's fine."

They walked through a row of tall, fragrant pines to the tennis court. The gray clay was washed out and faded from the lack of rain. Margaux's slide show started again. Up behind the court was the Staff Cabin, hidden in the woods, where she'd spent too many nights drinking and smoking and talking shit. On its other side lay the Maintenance Cabin, where the teenage boys who worked on the maintenance staff lived, a hotbed of hormones. She'd lost her virginity there to Simon Vauclair the summer she was sixteen. She'd whispered the details to Amanda afterward, breathless and a bit startled by the whole thing. Amanda had nodded knowingly even though Margaux knew for a fact that Amanda was still a virgin because she was saving it for Ryan. Margaux also knew for a fact that saving it for Ryan was a lost cause, because her brother was never going to give Amanda the time of day.

Saving it for Ryan. It sounded like the title of a cheesy B movie. But then, the first movie Margaux had gone to see after everything had happened was *Saving Private Ryan*, and she'd cried and cried. She couldn't explain why. Maybe Amanda would've understood.

It was too late to ask her now.

"Is that all right?" Sean asked. "The cabin?"

"I said it was fine."

"Just checking. Chillax."

"Chillax? Honestly, Sean, are you ever going to grow up?"

"What's that supposed to mean?"

They were on the road. Her parents' house loomed behind her, though she didn't turn to look at it. It was the last place she'd seen them, before they'd died in the spring.

"It's just . . . camp," she said. "Why are you still here?"

"I'm carrying your bag."

"No, I mean *here* here. At camp. Living here."

"This is my home."

"But it isn't."

Sean dropped her bag onto the road, releasing a small cloud of dust. "Why are you being like this? I didn't do anything to you."

Margaux knew she was in the wrong, acting like a jerk. Already this day was wearing her down. The house, her parents' empty house, was tugging at her, reaching out and making her into the person she used to be. Her summer self. That girl wasn't who she wanted to be anymore, but sometimes you don't get to choose who you are.

"I'm sorry, Sean. It's this place."

"You can't blame a place for how you behave."

"Can't you?"

He rocked back and forth on his heels. A lifetime of summers in the sun made him look every one of his forty-five years.

"Your parents were good to me, you know."

"I admire them for that."

"Only for that?"

She finally looked over her shoulder. Their house was a 1950s rancher; it never fit in with the white clapboard lodge and the dark-green cabins that were scattered over the two hundred acres of lakefront property.

"Is that what you want?"

"What?"

"The house? You want to stay here and live in their house?"

"I never—"

The blare of a car stereo being played much more loudly than it needed to be cut off Sean's words. They exchanged a glance, but they didn't need to speak to know.

Ryan had arrived.

CHAPTER 3

BACK IN BLACK

Ryan

"Back in Black." That's what Ryan MacAllister, newly forty but still able to pass for thirty-five on a good day, was blasting from the speakers of his Audi A3. He'd had the car for only a couple months, and this was the first time he'd let the sound system loose. His wife, Kerry, thought he was going through something when he'd brought the car home, a midlife crisis or whatever. But he'd leased it instead of the sensible CRV they'd agreed on because when he'd taken it for a test drive on a strangely empty highway and gotten up to speed, it made him feel better than he had in a long while. If that meant he was having a midlife crisis, so be it.

It wouldn't be surprising if he were in crisis. The last couple years had been pretty shit, what with his business partner turning out to be a criminal, and his business failing, and everything with Kerry, and then his parents dying. But this weekend, things were going to change. The will would be read and decisions would be made, and then Ryan could fix everything. Save his business. Make Kerry happy again and do some of the things she wanted—renovate their house, take a family vacation, spend less time at the office. Because that was what marriage was about, wasn't it? Adapting to each other's wants and needs? That's what their therapist told them anyway.

Ah, fuck it, who was he kidding? What *he* wanted was to put the stereo up as loud as it would go and drive his car as fast as he could away from there. It wasn't that he didn't love his family—he did—but life had begun to feel like a weight around his neck that he couldn't ever take off.

That's what camp was like too, his family, his sisters. He needed to unburden himself from all of it, all of them. Only then could he move forward. If he could break free from his past, then he'd be able to hit reset. Be a better father, husband, man.

In the meantime, didn't AC/DC sound fucking awesome through these speakers? Brian Johnson was the shit, man, he really was.

Ryan let the song end before cutting the engine. He was parked next to a beat-up old Acura, Margaux's car by the looks of it. He found it annoying that she drove around in something that battered. She was the best-looking of his sisters, but lately, these last five years or so, she'd let herself go. Not in the traditional way—she hadn't gotten fat; she ran too much for that—but in the ways that mattered to Ryan. She quit going to social events and took up with that Mark guy, a loser who'd never even make *vice* principal at the high school he taught at.

It figured that Margaux was here before him. He could've predicted that. If he'd had to place a bet, he'd guess his sisters would show up in the following order: Margaux, Liddie, Kate, and Mary. Only the first two were likely to be there on time at all.

Ryan was a right-on-time man himself. So here he was, right on time for his plan, which was to talk to Margaux before the meeting so he could get her on board and, through her, the rest of them.

Where was she, anyway?

He closed his eyes. If he were Margaux, where would he be right now?

He got out of the car and grabbed his bag from the back seat. He cut left, taking a path through the woods that brought him to his parents' house. He went to the front entrance, an unassuming door with a small concrete stoop, and let himself in with his key. The furniture was draped in sheets, as if it were something precious to be protected rather than stuff they'd have trouble giving to Goodwill. He dropped his bag in his bedroom. It was painted a deep blue and was the only room in the house where there was no evidence of his sisters.

His phone beeped in his pocket. There wasn't any cell signal at camp, but when he'd left Kerry and the girls two summers ago because he'd had to clear his head, he'd stayed here and had Wi-Fi installed with a password only he knew.

That was the summer he'd learned that his partner, John Rylance, stole their prototype money. The shittiest things always happened in summer. It got so that he started getting anxious when the days turned longer and didn't feel secure again until it was dark before he left the office.

He read the text. *Have you spoken to Margaux?* Kerry had written.

Ryan tracked down the landline in the living room and called her cell. It was an old handset, one of those ones with a rotary dial that his kids thought belonged in a museum. It took Ryan three tries to get all the way through the digits of Kerry's number without making a mistake.

"You arrived okay?" Kerry asked. Ryan could imagine her standing in their bright-white kitchen, an army of ingredients lined up on the counter. She always cooked for the week on Fridays so she didn't have to do it on the weekend. That was Kerry through and through: everything planned to the last detail.

"I did."

"Where are you?"

"In the house."

"Isn't that a party line?"

"Don't worry. Only Margaux's here."

"There's Sean, too, right? This is important. Maybe I should come down there."

"We agreed. It's my family and I'll handle it my way."

"Fine. Just don't screw it up."

Ryan lowered the receiver and tapped it against the table. He did this instead of throwing the whole phone through the plateglass window, which was what he would've done twenty years ago, when his temper felt ungovernable. This was why he'd come here when everything happened with John. Kerry had a lot of great qualities, but letting him figure out his own shit was not one of them.

"That's the plan."

"This is my life, too, Ryan. My future. Our kids' future."

"I know exactly what it is."

"Good. And don't get all broody with Margaux, either, once you start drinking."

Ryan caught sight of her as Kerry said her name. She was walking toward the cabin that overlooked the lake. The French Teacher's Cabin, they'd always called it, because one summer his parents' friend stayed there. She was supposed to teach the American campers French, but since her French was limited to ordering in restaurants, the plan failed, as had so many others his parents had tried to implement to make camp more than a shoestring operation. The friend left at the end of the summer; the name stuck.

"I'm not going to get all broody with Margaux." Drinking, on the other hand . . .

"That's what you said before the funeral too. Fast-forward eight hours and you're sitting in front of the fire, your arms around each other's shoulders muttering, 'I love you, man.' "

Margaux turned and said something to someone hidden by a tree. They stepped into view. It was Sean. Ryan wasn't surprised; Sean was always hanging around Margaux, ever since they were little. Amanda used to tease her about it and say that one day, she was going to marry him. Margaux had a way of laughing that off that let everyone know this was never going to happen, Sean included. Which was kind of shitty of her, and kind of dangerous too.

No man likes to be laughed at.

"And you're remembering wrong," Ryan said petulantly. "We never got to the 'I love you, man' stage."

"Whatever."

"You sound like the girls."

"They're infectious."

Ryan smiled for the first time since he'd turned off the AC/DC. His three daughters were the loves of his life, the reason he and Kerry stuck it out through all the bullshit. He'd do anything for those girls, though that might surprise most people who knew him. Despite the drunken *I love you, man*s that occasionally came out of his mouth, no one expected him to be sentimental.

"Only in the best way," Kerry said.

"Agreed."

"We're doing this for them."

"We are."

"Keep me in the loop."

"There's still no reception here."

"You can get texts at the house."

"How did you—"

"I noticed the signal after the funeral. Your password's weak."

"Gee, thanks."

"Change it."

Kerry insisted that they go over the plan one last time before they hung up. As she talked, Ryan watched Margaux move around in the French Teacher's Cabin. Turning on a light in the living room. Unpacking her things in one of the bedrooms. It was easier to watch her than to let himself be distracted by what lay past the cabin.

The lake. And beyond that, the Island.

Amanda

July 22, 1998—10:00 p.m.

The Island was a perfect circle of land in the middle of the lake. When you stood on Boat Beach, it seemed a stone's throw away, but it took us half an hour to paddle there and begin setting up for the overnight. The campers, and Margaux's sixteen-year-old sister, Mary, a counselor-in-training, were being ferried over four at a time by Sean, the head groundskeeper, in the crash boat.

I felt both exhausted and wired. I loved overnights when I was a kid. We'd make a campfire and roast marshmallows and torture our counselors with threats to swim back to camp. Then, the summer Margaux and I were fourteen, one of the boys' cabins raided us at three in the morning with plans to convince us to go skinny-dipping. A counselor caught us, tipped off by our loud whispering. The next morning, Mr. MacAllister threatened to call our parents and send us all home. Boys had attempted to gain access to one of his daughters in the middle of the night. This was not to be borne.

That's how he talked, half quoting stuff he'd memorized in college. He was supposed to be teaching Shakespeare, he often said, not running a children's prison. But when his father had died, when Mr. MacAllister was twenty-eight, and he'd inherited the camp, he left all that behind. He'd wanted to sell, I'd heard, but the property was locked up in some kind of trust. So there he was, stuck, I guess.

The overnights almost got canceled for good, but someone, Margaux's mom probably, intervened. Nights under the stars as mealtimes for mosquitoes helped us build character. They were a tradition. Margaux's mom was big on traditions. So the overnights continued, and the raids were planned more carefully.

Overnights were different when you were a counselor though. Sleepless nights were fine when you were twelve, but not so fine when you had to give a sailing lesson the next day at nine a.m. to a bunch of ten-year-olds who wanted to turtle their boats. Most counselors dreaded them. But that overnight—my last, as it turned out—I was excited for, because: *Ryan.*

We laid out the groundsheets, started a campfire, then helped the kids haul their bags up from the beach. The campers—ten- and eleven-year-old girls—were giddy and giggling, barely listening as Margaux traced the constellations. Once we'd waved goodbye to Sean and they were all in place around a roaring fire, we served them hot chocolate, then made sticks for roasting marshmallows with our pocketknives. I circled with a can of bug spray, taking one girl at a time away from the fire to make sure every inch of exposed skin was doused with mosquito repellant.

I did these things mechanically. All I was thinking of was Ryan, Ryan MacAllister, Ryan, Ryan, Ryan. I felt so consumed by him I was sure I'd said his name out loud, calling one of the girls Ryan instead of Claude. But Claude was the type of girl who'd shriek out at that kind of mistake instead of simply rolling her eyes when I asked her if I'd missed a spot, so his name must've only been that loud in my head. I looked across the fire at Margaux, strumming her guitar, playing a well-known French pop song, and told myself to pay more attention or I was going to get caught.

She didn't know my crush on Ryan had moved from a wish to a wish that might be fulfilled. I saw the looks she gave me whenever I brought him up. *Fat chance, Amanda Bean.* She didn't have to say it for me to hear it. I thought it too. And until that summer, she was right. Ryan never paid attention to me. I was one of his sister's annoying friends. But something had changed. He laughed at the things I said, even when they weren't that funny. When he'd danced with me one Saturday night in the lodge, he'd put his hand on the small of my back and rubbed my skin through the fabric until I felt dizzy.

And now, Ryan was coming to meet me.

To do what, I wasn't quite sure, but I knew I wanted it. I wanted it, whatever it was.

	Amanda	Margaux	Ryan	Mary	Sean
9:00 p.m.	Lantern ceremony	Lantern ceremony	Lantern ceremony		
10:00 p.m.	On the Island	On the Island		On the Island	Crash boat

CHAPTER 4

THE ONE THEY ALWAYS FORGET

Liddie

Liddie MacAllister waited until Ryan had hung up the phone before putting her own receiver back in the cradle.

She was in the basement of her parents' house, lying in the bed her father had often slept in when he couldn't be bothered to climb the stairs to her mother. She smiled to herself. She'd found some of his stash last night and smoked half a joint before falling asleep and had woken up this morning still rocking in its pleasant glow.

No one knew where Liddie was right now. She liked that feeling, the freedom of it. When she was small, one of the youngest children in a boisterous family, she'd hated being invisible. But as she grew older and understood the power of it, she'd cultivated it. You heard all kinds of interesting things when you were invisible. Saw them too. People even told you the strangest things sometimes, certain you weren't important enough to do anything about it.

Once, for instance, at a bar, when she was wearing an old man's suit she'd bought at a thrift shop, the man sitting next to her told her he was an assassin. He explained his methods, though he wouldn't say the name of anyone he'd offed, "Just in case," he kept saying, "just in case I've misjudged you." She'd listened in fascination, certain he was bullshitting her, but she'd given him a fake name when he asked and waited a full hour after he left the bar before leaving herself. She made sure never to go back to that place, worried that when "Bob" woke up the next morning, he'd regret his confidence and come looking for her.

That was the strangest night, but there had been others.

She sat up. The room was dark. The ground-level windows were covered with blackout blinds. When her father wanted to hide, he wanted to be invisible even from the sun.

Liddie thought about the conversation she'd just overheard. Ryan and Kerry were idiots, talking about their plans on an open line like that even after Kerry brought up the possibility that someone was listening. But that was Ryan. He always acted as if he were invincible, as if the usual vagaries of life couldn't affect him. Even when things had gone badly, like when he lost most of his money to John Rylance, he acted like it was happening to someone else. He even spoke about it in the third person sometimes—"When Ryan was betrayed by John"—which was just weird.

Everyone thought she was weird. With her boy haircut and her men's clothes and the fact that she'd never introduced them to anyone she ever dated. Ever since that show *Transparent* had started airing, people assumed she was trans. Before, they thought she was a lesbian. She wasn't either of those things, though she'd experimented enough along the way. But no. Dressing this way was her shield. Besides, men's clothes were way more comfortable than women's clothes and had more pockets. Liddie was sure that if more people thought about the extra pockets, they'd be more open to her way of doing things.

She got dressed and brushed her teeth in the basement bathroom, wondering all the while what Ryan thought he was going to achieve. Their parents hadn't known that they'd die together when their train derailed, but their father had apparently planned their affairs to cover every possibility. The family lawyer, Kevin Swift, had informed them after the funeral that their father's instructions were clear: Camp would continue as usual for the first summer after he died, and then, when the last bag had been packed and the final crying child was recovered by their parents, they'd gather as a family to read the will and decide what to do with the place.

Keep it or sell. That was the choice they were facing.

Her father was often disconnected from reality, but thinking the five of them could come up with a common solution about a plot of land that was worth millions of dollars was shockingly naive, even for him. Ryan's choice was obvious. Margaux's and Mary's, too. Kate was harder to read, but she was probably on Ryan's side, despite everything.

And Liddie? Well, she was going to wait and see where the wind was blowing, and then she'd decide. Or maybe she'd be the spoiler in the deck just for fun.

It wouldn't be the first time.

"My God, Liddie. You scared the shit out of me."

Liddie cackled. Ryan had actually jumped a foot in the air when she sneaked up on him in the kitchen where he was making coffee and said a quiet, "Hi."

"You should relax. You're always so tense."

Ryan pulled at the collar of his dress shirt. Had he worn a suit to camp? Was he trying to impress them, or was it simply a signal that he was viewing this as a business meeting?

"I've got a lot on my mind, all right?"

"Clearly."

"Wait . . . When did you get here?"

"Last night."

"You slept here?"

"Yeah. So?"

"It's not what we discussed."

Liddie rested against the old Formica counter. The edges were cracked and dug into her back. "Give me a break. This is my house. I can come and go as I please."

"We'll see."

"Is that a threat?"

"No."

"If you say so. I know what you're planning."

The color rose in his face. His shirt looked a bit tight on him around the neck, half a size too small. "How would you . . . You little creep. You were listening on the downstairs extension?"

"No, loser. I just know you. You can't wait to parcel this place up into a zillion condos now that we can sell the land."

"Do you know how much this place is worth?"

"I'm not an idiot. Plus, you've only been talking about it for, like, ten years."

"You don't want to sell?"

"Haven't decided yet."

"Liddie . . ."

"What?"

"We've all got to be on the same page here."

"We'll see. We don't actually know what's in the will, do we?"

He blinked quickly, a sure sign he was nervous. "What's that supposed to mean?"

"Don't be so sure that it's all going to work out the way you think."

Liddie hadn't seen the will either, but Ryan didn't have to know that. It was fun watching him squirm.

"Do you know something I don't?"

"Usually."

He was next to her in two swift steps, holding her tightly by the arm. He smelled like day-old booze and sweat.

"Ow! Let go."

"Tell me what you know."

She knew she should be scared, but all she felt was annoyed. Ryan always underestimated her and then got mad when he discovered his mistake, as if it were Liddie's fault that he couldn't figure her out by now.

"Let go, Ryan, or you'll regret it."

He laughed bitterly. "Now who's making threats?"

"I mean it. Let go of me or else."

"Else what?"

He tightened his grip.

"What the fuck, Ryan?"

She lifted her knee swiftly into his groin with as much strength as she could. She was five feet two to his six feet, but she'd taken self-defense classes and had practiced this move over and over on a large man dressed like the Michelin Man. She just never thought she'd use it on her brother.

He released her arm and fell moaning to the floor. He curled into a fetal position, his hands between his legs. He'd turned gray, and beads of sweat were forming on his forehead.

Had she used too much force? No, forget that. She was going to have bruises on her arm where he grabbed her. He deserved what he got, the stupid idiot.

"Can you talk?"

"Ice," he said through gritted teeth. "Get me some ice."

"Maybe you should feel what it's like to be hurt for a bit."

"I am feeling what it's like. Jesus."

She stood over him. He looked pitiful. She'd never used that move in real life before. "Is that why Kerry kicked you out? Because you were violent with her?"

"I've never touched her. And she didn't kick me out."

"Sure, right."

"Liddie, please. I'm sorry. I'm so sorry I grabbed you like that. It was completely unacceptable, and I don't know what came over me. Now, will you please get me some ice?"

"Fine."

Liddie walked to the yellowing fridge. It was still covered with artifacts from their childhood. Silly things they'd made in Craft Shop. Staff photos. An old list for the grocery store—*real vegetables!* her father had written, whatever that meant. The one thing missing was a photo of the entire family. There must be one of those somewhere, but she couldn't remember ever seeing one.

She opened the freezer and removed a plastic tray. The ice was half evaporated, but it would have to do. She emptied the contents onto a tea towel her mother made years ago, a rainbow pattern that always stood out in this drab kitchen. Wrapping the ice in it made her nostalgic. Not for her mother, exactly, but for the time when they were all children and the possibility of their being a happy family still existed.

"Here," she said, dropping the bundle of ice and towel in the general direction of Ryan's groin. "Is that what you wanted?"

CHAPTER 5

SECOND TO LAST

Margaux

When Margaux walked into her parents' kitchen, she found her brother lying on the ground with a wet tea towel clutched to his groin and Liddie standing over him, her hands on her hips as if she were waiting to scold him.

"An hour in and we already have an injury," she said. "Fantastic."

Liddie spun around. She was wearing a pair of boys' jeans and a plaid shirt that was buttoned at her neck. She had a tattoo on the back of each hand, and her hair was cut in a short, floppy style like Tom Cruise in *Risky Business*. Margaux never understood what dressing like that was about, but she supposed Liddie was probably looking at her own khaki pants and cashmere crewneck from L.L.Bean and thinking the same thing.

"Hey, Margaux."

"Hey, yourself. See also: What the hell?"

"I kneed him in the groin."

"What? Why?"

"Because he was being a jerk."

Margaux leaned down to Ryan. He was sweating profusely, and the smell of it was sharp, earthy, and unpleasant, like his room used to be when he was a teenager. "Man scent," she called it then. Except Mark never smelled like that. "You going to keep lying there?"

"I might."

"Suit yourself, but I thought you wanted to talk before Swift got here."

He rolled onto his back. "Motherfucker."

"She got you good, huh?"

"I may have overdone it," Liddie said.

Margaux stood up. "Looks like it."

"He'll live."

"You gonna tell me what happened?"

Liddie shrugged. "Doesn't matter."

"I'm sure that's not true. When did you get here?"

"Last night."

"Does Sean know you're here?"

"Nope."

"Why didn't you tell him?"

"He was already in bed when I arrived."

"How do you know that?"

"Because he always goes to bed at ten."

She leaned toward Liddie. She smelled like her father used to, a mix of coffee and marijuana. "Waking and baking these days?"

"What?"

"Forget it. You should've told Sean you were here."

Liddie barked a laugh. "Oh, this is rich. Do you hear that, Ryan? Suddenly Margaux cares what Sean thinks."

"Shut it."

"No, really. Please, let me hear more about what I should've done with regard to Sean."

Ryan sat up. "Enough already, you two."

Liddie looked back and forth between Ryan and Margaux. "Fine. Whatever. Take her side. What else is new?"

She turned and walked out of the kitchen.

Margaux held out her hand to Ryan to help him up. He took it and hauled himself to his feet. The towel slipped. Half-melted ice scattered across the dirty linoleum floor.

"So," she said. "This is going well."

Twenty minutes later, Margaux had removed most of the sheets from the furniture and opened the blinds on the view—pines, grass, glassy lake. The living room was the highest point on the property, so you could see all the way to the Island and the other shore behind it. It was a view she never tired of. Even so, when it came time to pick her own home and view, she'd chosen a condo downtown whose only vista was of the weather that swirled around the forty-story building. Mark had wanted a house in the West Island, a low-lying structure on a half acre of land, but Margaux put her foot down with rare determination. She wasn't going to spend two hours a day in a car so she could have a small patch of lawn to mow.

She turned away from the windows. Ryan was sitting in the faded chintz wing chair by the fireplace. The ice pack was back firmly between his legs, and he was shifting uncomfortably. She hadn't seen Ryan since the funeral. His hair was still black and his features handsome, but there was a hardness to his face that hadn't been there before. It was as if turning forty had erased the last layer of baby fat, flipped the page on his childhood. This was probably enhanced by the fact that he was, oddly, wearing a suit, though he'd loosened his tie, and the pants were now rumpled and wet.

"What did you do to Liddie?"

"Why do you assume I did something?"

"She wouldn't have kneed you in the balls if you were just being a jerk. She's used to that."

He shook his head, and Margaux knew she wouldn't get an answer out of him. Her family excelled at secrets.

"Swift's going to be here soon," she said. "You wanted to talk before he got here?"

He leaned forward and winced. "Will you vote with me to sell the property?"

"Why are you so sure there's going to be a vote?"

"Dad always said we'd inherit this place when they were gone and that it would be up to us to decide what to do with it. How else are five people going to decide to do something?"

"You don't think he might've changed his mind after all these years? You know Dad and promises."

"He hated us equally in life, so I assume he'll treat us equally in death."

"He didn't hate us, he just didn't . . ."

"Want us? He sure made that mistake enough times."

She sat in her mother's old place on the couch. The flowers in the pattern were faded, and there was a depression in the cushion, an imprint of her mother's backside. She was surprised at how well she fit into it, since she'd always thought of her mother as shapeless. What did that mean? Was she on her way to becoming her mother?

"Well, we only know for sure that you were a mistake."

He winced. One of the odd things about their parents was how they'd never hid the fact that Ryan hadn't been planned. That his unexpected arrival was one of the reasons they felt they had no choice but to come to camp and run it when Grandpa MacAllister died and Grandma MacAllister ran off to Florida with the tennis instructor.

"I think we can be pretty sure that we were all mistakes."

Ryan was probably right. "What's that saying? The one about doing the same thing over and over again and expecting a different result?"

"The definition of insanity."

"Mark Twain?"

"Einstein, I think."

Margaux wondered—were her parents insane or simply trapped by circumstance? People tended to resent the things they couldn't escape, even if those things were innocent.

"Have you ever thought about what they must've been like before all of us?"

"Not really."

"I think about it. They met. They fell in love. They were regular people once."

"And what? We made them into irregular people?"

"Maybe we did. We were . . . a lot." Margaux looked out the window again. The lake was placid. Sean was in a canoe, paddling away from shore. His arms moved fluidly as the boat sliced through the water. Margaux shivered, remembering the last time she'd been in a canoe, her frantic paddle back from the Island.

"Do you ever think," she said, "that we'll forget what happened that summer?"

When Margaux and Ryan were finished, Margaux went down to the basement. Liddie was sitting in front of an old computer screen, trolling through her Facebook feed. She'd kept most of the lights off, and the blinds were closed. Her skin looked translucent in the light from the screen.

"Since when has there been internet?" Margaux asked.

"Ryan had it installed that summer he stayed here. You didn't know?"

"Clearly. Anything interesting going on?"

"I like watching the food videos."

Liddie clicked a button. A video for Dutch oven bread started to play. It made it look easy, and Margaux thought of her own kitchen, those moments on Sunday mornings when she and Mark would make several large batches of something they could both take for lunch that week. Perhaps she could try this next. He was a big fan of country loaf, and the recipe looked foolproof.

Why am I thinking of Mark? Ah, shit. She'd never made that call.

"Do you mind if I use the phone?"

Liddie didn't respond, just nodded toward where the phone was lying next to the bed. Margaux dialed Mark's cell. He didn't pick up, so she left a message letting him know she didn't have a signal and that she'd try to call him again later. "No point in calling yourself," she said. "Hardly anyone ever picks up." She wondered if he'd let it go to voice mail on purpose to demonstrate his annoyance at being excluded.

"How come you didn't bring Mark?" Liddie asked when she hung up.

"Why would I?"

"Aren't you guys attached at the hip?"

"No."

Liddie started another video, for massive cinnamon rolls this time. "Work together, live together . . . Sounds attached at the hip to me."

Margaux was the music teacher at the high school where Mark was in charge of the math department. That's how they'd met, five years ago, at a staff mixer a few weeks after she started working there. He'd been doing impressions of the principal who'd just been fired. She hadn't laughed that hard in a while, so when he asked for her number, she'd said yes. She knew it hadn't happened quite like that, but looking back, it seemed as if there wasn't any space between that night and their moving in together. Ever since then, their lives had become so entwined that this was the first time she'd spent the night away from him. They hadn't even been separated the night of the funeral. Instead, they'd both crowded into the single bed she'd slept in as a child.

Margaux thought, sometimes, about trying to transfer to another school. It would be nice to have some hours of the day when they weren't in the same building. But the one time she'd brought it up, Mark had seemed so genuinely puzzled about why she'd want to do it that she gave up the idea. She knew people thought he smothered her, and sometimes she thought that herself. But there was a comfort in being with someone who needed her so much that he was miserable without her. The man she'd been with before Mark, the one who'd used up her twenties, had been almost indifferent to her. It was Margaux who'd adapted to his wishes and whims, she who needed him. That breakup had crushed her spirit, and she had no interest in being that invested again.

"We barely see each other all day," she said. "And the joint commute is convenient."

"If you say so."

"What do you care?"

"Wow. Major overreaction."

On the screen, the video showed the final product, a six-pound cinnamon roll. Four people dug in to what looked like enough food for twenty.

"That's disgusting."

"Disgustingly delicious. We should ask Amy to make it."

"It might be outside her repertoire."

"True." Liddie rubbed at a spot on her arm and winced.

"You hurt yourself?"

"It's nothing."

She reached over and pushed up Liddie's shirtsleeve. There were two bright marks on her forearm right below a tattoo that circled her arm like an amulet.

"Did Ryan do this?"

Liddie pulled her sleeve down. "It's fine."

"That's why you kneed him." Margaux felt shaken. Ryan had always had a temper, but he was supposed to have taken care of it. There'd been classes and medication, court ordered after he'd taken a baseball bat to a plate glass window when he was cut from McGill's hockey team. "He grabbed you?"

"Wouldn't be the first time." Liddie turned away from the computer. She looked hard, practical.

"But not since we were kids, right? Not since . . ."

Liddie stood up. "Can we talk about this later?"

"You mean never."

"If you say so."

Liddie walked around her and headed to the basement exit.

"Where are you going?"

"Kate's here."

CHAPTER 6

I HAD NO IDEA

Kate

Being on time for things wasn't Kate MacAllister's strong suit, which was why she'd arranged to get a ride to camp with Kevin Swift, the family lawyer.

She'd regretted that decision almost immediately. There might be some thirty-two-year-olds and sixty-five-year-olds who have things in common, but not many. They certainly didn't, even though Swift had been the family lawyer since her grandfather's day. So once they'd crossed the Champlain Bridge, she'd bunched up her sweater on the window and told him she was tired and would he mind if she slept for a bit? She didn't need his permission, but he'd agreed like he did with everything her family asked of him, and with the ease she'd always had, she was out in a matter of seconds.

Kate had the strangest dreams when she slept in moving vehicles, and this time was no exception. She'd been watching the latest season of *Homeland* the night before, and so now she was a spy, disguising her strawberry hair and washed-out skin with a wig and makeup that made her look dark and exotic. She tied a scarf under her chin and left her bolt-hole. Her contact was supposed to meet her in the bazaar by a fruit stand. They had a code worked out, something about lemons, only Kate couldn't remember what it was she was supposed to say.

The bazaar was loud and crowded, the air full of unfamiliar spices and the shouts of merchants in a babble of languages. She felt the panic rise within her when she couldn't find the right fruit stand, the one that sold the best lemons, or so she'd heard. Then she spotted it, and adrenaline coursed through her. There was a woman holding a bright yellow lemon, smelling it to see if it met her exacting standards. Her scarf had slipped over her face, and so Kate couldn't be sure it was the right woman, but who else could it be?

She touched her shoulder. "Are the lemons good here?"

The woman turned around. Kate's world tilted. The woman had a gash across her forehead, and her face was ghostly pale.

"Amanda."

The car jerked, and Kate's head smacked against the glass. She blinked hard, trying to orient herself.

"What did you say?" she said to Swift.

"I was asking you how well you remember Amanda."

Kate looked out the window. They were on the camp road now, a road she'd know anywhere, every tree and branch and little path into the woods; she loved all of it. Her whole life, the time she spent away from here was time during which she felt adrift, uprooted.

"Why?"

"Just curious."

She'd known him long enough to tell he was lying. Whenever Swift said something that wasn't true, his voice rose half an octave. Sentences that had been delivered at this pitch included "This is the last time they can help you out" and "It was an accident." She wondered where her grandfather had found Swift, what deal they'd struck to get such loyalty. She'd never thought to ask till now. To her, he'd always been around, like this place, like the pines. Both were tall and rustic, gnarled.

"Did you know her?" she asked. "I forget."

"No," he said, his voice that same higher pitch. "I didn't."

A few moments later, he parked the car on the gravel space outside the lodge where delivery trucks came to drop off enough food to feed more than a hundred people three meals a day. Liddie and Margaux stood in front of the porch, both with their arms crossed, as if they were waiting to lecture Kate for being late, even though she wasn't. She concentrated on them, trying to distract herself from what lay within the lodge. *Who.*

Looking at her sisters was like looking at herself if she'd made different decisions. If she'd forgone sunscreen and good hair-care products, she'd have that same blowsy look Margaux did. And if she cut her hair and wore clothes from the boys' department, she'd look like her identical twin, Liddie. Mary was the missing link, the connect-the-dots between them, but Kate could easily imagine her standing there in a pair of jodhpurs with her hair in a long braid that fell straight down her back. Margaux's hair was the blondest, Kate and Liddie had the most red, and their eyes were all the same shade of hazel. Only Ryan stood apart, with his dark hair and blue eyes, as if being the boy of the family wasn't enough to distinguish him.

She got out of the car and breathed in deeply. The air smelled different here, even from a few miles away. How did that happen?

Liddie approached her, but Margaux stayed where she was.

"You made it," Liddie said, a mimic of her own voice, like listening to herself on a recording. She pulled Kate into a hug. It was always a disorienting feeling, like hugging herself. As if she could feel her identical DNA through Liddie's tattooed skin.

"You knew I was coming," Kate said. "I texted you when I left."

"True enough. Hey, Swifty, what's up?"

Swift looked at his feet. Liddie delighted in making him feel uncomfortable in all things, and she usually succeeded.

"I believe we have a meeting scheduled at ten?" he said.

"Abso-fucking-lutely."

"Liddie!"

That was Margaux. Perhaps it was the role of all oldest girls, but Margaux often felt more like a mother to them than their actual mother had. Ingrid MacAllister had been uncomfortable in her skin, especially after it was stretched out by four pregnancies, including twins. She loved them, but she wasn't close to them. She made sure they were clothed and cared for, but she didn't get down in the dirt and play with them. Kate had wondered, sometimes, if it were a kind of revenge for what they'd taken from her, her youth. Maybe she was someone who shouldn't have had children. Or then again, it might've been Margaux's competence, even as a young girl, that made Ingrid get out of the way. Kate was surprised Margaux hadn't had any children of her own, but like so many things in her family, she didn't ask why.

"Chill, Margaux," Liddie said. "I'm sure Swifty's heard worse."

He rocked back and forth, shifting his weight from one gum boot to the other. It was an odd choice of footwear considering the weather, as was the green fly-fishing vest he was wearing over a short-sleeved white shirt, since the lake had never been good for fishing—it was too shallow.

"Is everyone here?" he asked.

"No one's seen Mary yet," Margaux said. "But the rest of us are here."

"What about Sean?"

"What about Sean?" Liddie said, her eyes meeting Kate's in the way they did when she had something more to say. Liddie loved gossip, and she often shared it with Kate, whether Kate wanted her to or not. "I might as well tell you," she often said. "Since you can read my mind anyway."

The thing was, Kate couldn't read Liddie's mind; she'd never been able to. But she didn't need to tell Liddie that, did she?

"Sean needs to be here," Swift said. "I thought you knew that."

"We don't know anything," Kate said.

Liddie scoffed. "You must know something. You spent two hours in the car with him."

"I was asleep the whole time. Plus, Swift wouldn't tell me anything he wasn't supposed to. He's a vault."

Swift looked uncomfortable again while Liddie scanned him and Kate for ten long seconds. Kate knew it was her imagination, but she could've sworn she could feel Liddie's consciousness pressing up against her own, trying to break through.

"Ah . . . Well, girls . . ."

"Don't worry about it," Liddie said. "You take everything too seriously. So where's Sean?"

Margaux's mouth was a line. "I saw him paddling to the Island."

Kate and Liddie pulled a green tarp back, uncovering a rack of battered yellow canoes. The ground was littered with dead pine needles, and the sun was completely blocked out by the heavy white pines overhead. Kate shivered, wishing she'd put on the sweater she'd slept against in the car.

"We could wait till he comes back," Kate said. "There's no hurry."

"No way Ryan can wait that long. Let's get it over with."

They worked with practiced ease to lift the canoe from the rack and carry it down to the beach. They flipped it over and slid it partly into the water. They'd had a crush on the canoe teacher when they were kids and had even rowed in junior regattas between the ages of ten and twelve. Then Kate had wanted to quit, and Liddie, for once, let her have her way.

"I'll get the paddles and life jackets," Kate said.

"Cautious Kate."

She found the key to the paddle shed hidden under the rock where it had always been and opened the door. She grabbed two paddles and orange life jackets that smelled of mildew. She thought the shed was creepy, but that might've been because Liddie locked her in here once when she was mad about Kate getting the Camper of the Week Award. Liddie hadn't even been punished for that, because two kids had been caught having sex on Secret Beach the same day, and Liddie's sin paled in comparison to that kind of camp-ending disaster. That's what their dad had called it, a "camp-ending disaster," only he seemed excited by the possibility, not terrified like Kate was.

When she got back to the beach, Liddie had rolled her jeans up past her knees and was standing in the lake. Her legs were white against the black water.

"How cold is it?"

"Not too bad for Labor Day weekend."

Kate slipped off her boat shoes and considered whether she should take off the khaki skirt she was wearing until she realized she didn't want Sean to see her in her underwear. She put her life jacket down on the seat and tossed the other one in the boat. Liddie pulled the boat into deeper water, then climbed in.

"I'm paddling on the right," Kate said.

"Only on the way there."

"Fine."

They quickly found their old rhythm. Their paddles sliced soundlessly into the dark water as the prow cut through the light chop that had started up in the time it took them to push off. The weather could change on the lake in an instant, and Kate wished she'd checked the forecast. The Island was about a mile away, a swimmable distance that some of the campers did every summer. When Kate and Liddie were doing junior triathlons, they used to swim it every other morning, Margaux their lifeguard in the rowboat.

"Remember how we used to swim to the Island in the dark?" Liddie asked.

"You don't need to remind me."

"Fine, then, I won't."

They paddled twenty strokes in silence. *Let me in,* Kate thought, but nothing happened.

"You still dating Owen?" Kate asked. She watched a blush color the back of her sister's neck.

"Off and on."

"You going to let the others know?"

"Maybe."

"You can tell everyone else you're straight, you know. It's no big deal."

Liddie turned around.

"You can tell everyone you're gay, you know. It's no big deal."

"I don't like labels."

"Just on your clothes."

"You're such a bitch sometimes." Kate turned her paddle and flapped up an arc of water, soaking Liddie's right side.

"What the fuck?"

"Careful, you're going to tip the boat."

"You are so dead, you know that?"

"This is probably not the best place to make threats like that."

Liddie put her paddle back into the water. Another minute of silence brought them close enough to see Sean's boat propped against the rocks and Sean himself sitting next to it, watching their progress.

"Why the hell did he come over here?" Liddie asked.

"You know why."

Amanda

July 22, 1998—11:00 p.m.

The night crept by. I can't tell you how many times I looked at my watch, flexing my wrist so the light on my Swatch lit up the screen. Margaux kept asking me what I was waiting for, some "hot date, ha, ha, ha." I told her I was tired and we should get the kids to bed.

"We're not going to get any sleep either way," she said.

"At least we'll be lying down."

"You feeling all right?"

"I'm fine. Just tired, like I said."

I stood up from my perch on a log around our campfire. Margaux had been playing songs on her guitar, camp favorites, and then taking requests. She had a pretty singing voice and the ability to play anything she'd heard once or twice. Mary sang along with her. Their voices blended well, like one of those all-girl singing groups from the sixties.

"All right, kiddos," I said. "Bedtime."

"Ah, man! Already?"

"You can talk till your flashlights run out."

"Awesome!"

I snapped my headlamp back on, and we coaxed the girls into their sleeping bags. When everyone was in place, I volunteered to take the water cans down to the beach to fill them and douse the fire.

"I can do that," Margaux said. "You rest."

"It's fine. I want to do it."

I thought I might have to fight her for this thankless task, but then one of the kids called out that her flashlight was broken, and Margaux went to deal with it. I breathed a sigh of relief, but then my heart thumped loudly. Maybe Ryan was just messing with me? Maybe he wasn't going to be able to make it? How would I ever face him again if that happened?

I walked to the water—not the beach we'd arrived at but the one on the other side of the Island; Back Beach, it was called. I walked along the dark path through the woods, looking for the signposts I'd marked earlier when I'd been collecting deadfall for the fire. This broken tree branch. That notch in a soft birch. There was light up ahead, the full moon bright enough to act as a night-light. The water slapped gently against the rocks. I could hear the girls in the distance, laughter, the snap of the fire, the creak of the trees. The lake smelled like rotting seaweed, and I knew my hair reeked of campfire smoke. Not the most attractive combination, but there wasn't anything I could do about it.

I checked my watch again. It was past the time we'd set to meet. Where was Ryan? If he'd actually paddled over, he wouldn't just leave again without waiting for me, would he?

"Boo!" someone said into my ear.

My heart stopped.

	Amanda	**Margaux**	**Ryan**	**Mary**	**Sean**
9:00 p.m.	Lantern ceremony	Lantern ceremony	Lantern ceremony		
10:00 p.m.	On the Island	On the Island		On the Island	Crash boat
11:00 p.m.	Back Beach	On the Island		On the Island	

CHAPTER 7

THE ISLAND—PART ONE

Sean

Sean watched the twins paddle their way across the lake. He figured they were coming for him, but he wished they'd leave him alone. Leave him to his routine, his memories. This place. His island. *His.*

He loved the Island. It was his favorite part of camp. After what happened twenty years ago, it had been off-limits for several years. He'd missed coming there, enough to defy the MacAllisters once or twice. When they'd lifted the ban, they made the overnights co-ed, attended by twice as many counselors who worked in shifts and pairs. No one was allowed to be alone. Nothing untoward could happen. If one kid stepped out of line, they'd ruin it for everyone, forever. That's what Mr. MacAllister had said, roving back and forth in front of the lined-up staff as if he were a drill sergeant at morning inspection.

Everyone took him seriously. Mr. MacAllister wasn't always the best manager, but he had the staff's respect. He kept camp going through thick and thin, and he knew how to pick leaders, making sure that the staff coordinators each year were popular and well liked. No one wanted camp to close, least of all Sean.

But even so, enforcing group togetherness was a waste of the Island. It was the perfect place to be alone, an actual circle of serenity on the lake, equidistant from both shores, so thick with trees that unless you were right on the rocky beach, no one could see you.

No one would even know you were there.

Everyone needs a place like that sometimes.

The campers called the Island haunted. They told ghost stories and scared themselves into near hysteria around the campfire. But to Sean, it was a churchyard, a memorial to the childhoods everyone but him seemed to have left behind. He couldn't imagine his life without this place, and he shouldn't have to.

He reached down into the cool water and picked up a stone the size of his palm. It was black and smooth, the perfect weight. He tested it, moving his hand up and down. The twins were almost to him now. He could make out some of their words, though not exactly what they were saying. He stood and turned his back to them, walking swiftly along the edge of the forest to Back Beach. There was a cairn on the edge of it, a memorial made of rocks. Sean put his rock on the top and said a small prayer under his breath, then turned away and walked until he arrived back where he'd been as the twins' boat scraped onto the shore.

"Hey, girls," Sean said. "What's up?"

"You're needed back at the house," Liddie said. "Let's go."

CHAPTER 8

WE ARE GATHERED HERE TODAY

Ryan

Nothing about this day was going as Ryan had planned. He should've obeyed his first instinct: turn up the AC/DC and drive on down the road. But instead, here he was sitting in damp pants with his nuts still throbbing from the knee he'd received from Liddie. He deserved that knee; he could admit that. He was ashamed he'd grabbed her that way, strong enough to scare her. He'd worked hard to control his temper, been to therapy and anger management classes, and usually it was in check. But he could feel it loose now in his body, roving through his stomach, expanding into his chest. It had been a long time since it was this palpable, probably since the cops had arrived at his offices to search for evidence of John's fraud.

Fucking summer. It really was the worst.

He reached into his coat pocket and pulled out a bottle of powdery pills. He was trying to cut back on the Klonopin, but he needed it today. Losing his temper for real could be disastrous. He cracked the cap, put one on his tongue, and let it dissolve, the bitter taste already having a placebo effect. He stowed the bottle as Swift and Margaux entered.

"You look like shit," Margaux said.

"Thanks so much."

Swift sat down on the couch. It sagged under his weight, looking as tired as Ryan felt. Swift took a handkerchief out of his pocket and wiped at the sweat on his brow. He was wearing gum boots, jeans that looked fresh from the store, and a fishing vest. Ryan wanted to make a joke, but he couldn't quite get the thought fully formed.

"Everything all right?" Margaux asked Swift.

"Oh, it's fine, fine," he said, panting slightly even though he'd only walked from the parking lot. "I'm used to working behind a desk, that's all."

Ryan hadn't seen Swift since the funeral, but not for lack of trying. Swift had been putting him off for months, saying Ryan would learn everything he wanted to know when they met at camp on Labor Day weekend, as per his father's instructions. Ryan was frustrated, but what else could he do? He knew that somewhere his dad was sitting there laughing at them all, waiting for this silly meeting that reminded Ryan of one of those mystery books his dad was always reading. Agatha Christie or Rex Stout. A gathering of the family and then . . .

Ryan pushed the thought away. He had to let the pill take effect and wait for the rest of his sisters to arrive, and then he'd know everything he needed to know, just like Swift had promised.

"You need to take better care of yourself," Margaux said. "Use a treadmill desk or something."

"Perhaps, perhaps."

"Why don't I get us some drinks?"

Ryan felt a spark of hope, but all Margaux brought back were several glasses of iced tea made of that sugary mix their mother liked so much. Ryan drank it down, wishing he'd planned ahead and brought a flask, but that would've been a terrible idea. Alcohol didn't equal calm. Maybe Kerry was right and he did need her to pull this off.

"What's with all the doom and gloom?" Liddie said as she, Kate, and Sean entered smelling like the lake. "You'd think this was a funeral."

"Liddie!"

"What, Margaux-Mommy? The funeral was months ago. This is supposed to be the celebration."

Margaux frowned. Everyone knew that she hated it when Liddie called her that, which was exactly why Liddie did it.

Kate waved her hands. "Ignore her. You know she's only looking for attention. As always."

"Oh, touché," Liddie said.

Sean went to the kitchen and came back with a glass of iced tea.

"You could've asked us if we wanted some," Liddie said. "We're thirsty too."

"I'm fine," Kate said.

Sean returned to the kitchen and brought back two more glasses.

"Thank you, Sean," Margaux said. "You didn't have to do that."

Sean shrugged and perched on the edge of the couch. That was typical of him, Ryan thought. He never did anything that might make someone think he was acting like he was one of the family. They all treated him like that, Ryan knew, but what he didn't understand was why Sean put up with it. Were there people who *wanted* to be the heel on someone's boot?

Kate and Liddie sat on the other couch, leaving a cushion of space between them.

"Let's get this show on the road," Liddie said.

"We can't start till you're all here," Swift said. "Those are my instructions."

"Oh, hell," Liddie said. "Where's Mary? Has anyone heard from her?"

"She told me she'd be here," Margaux said. "But you know she's never on time for anything."

"We should call her," Ryan said.

"She doesn't have a cell phone. And she never picks up her landline."

"So what? We just have to wait?"

No one answered him. Instead, they all turned and looked at the front door as if their collective will might make Mary suddenly appear like something that had been summoned at a séance.

Like a ghost.

Amanda

July 23, 1998—6:00 a.m.

There's this line at the end of *The Great Gatsby*—the famous one about boats against a current—that gave me the shivers the first time I read it in school. It made me think of camp, about how much of my time there was spent in one kind of boat or another: a sailboat, a canoe, the water-skiing boat—I was like the Forrest Gump of boats. I loved being out on the water, the way I knew instinctively how to stand with my feet farther apart so I was balanced. "Sea legs," they called them, and I had them.

I always felt saddest when we pulled the boats from the water at the end of summer and put them in their dry cradles for the winter. I didn't want to be away from camp for that long, a whole fall and winter and spring. Sometimes, when I dreamed about the future, it involved sailing around the world or living somewhere where I could be on the water year-round. Half-formed thoughts for a half-formed girl.

You see, I thought my life would *start* on the water, not end. I didn't know—how could I?—that the last boat ride I'd take would be unknown to me, unknowable. How I'd be splayed out on my back, my boat beating against the shore of Secret Beach, waiting for someone to find me. That the current would take me there, then hold me in place.

How it seemed like forever before someone came.

	Amanda	Margaux	Ryan	Mary	Sean
9:00 p.m.	Lantern ceremony	Lantern ceremony	Lantern ceremony		
10:00 p.m.	On the Island	On the Island		On the Island	Crash boat
11:00 p.m.	Back Beach	On the Island		On the Island	
6:00 a.m.	Secret Beach				

CHAPTER 9

HIGH JUMP

Mary

The thing about jumping a horse, Mary MacAllister always said to her students, was knowing when to give the right signal. If your timing was even a little off, then you'd crash.

Life was like that too, she found. Timing was everything. She was bad at it, she knew, when she wasn't on a horse. Often late, sometimes missing events altogether. It didn't matter, mostly. She was never late with the kids she gave lessons to. She wasn't late for the horses; she rose at dawn every day without an alarm in order to make sure they were fed and watered and exercised. It was the rest of it—the details of life that seemed to occupy others—that she never seemed able to nail down.

She'd meant to be punctual today, but one of her horses had thrown a shoe and another had a hot foreleg and honestly, what did it matter? Part of her was probably enjoying the thought of them all sitting there, waiting for her, knowing that their greedy plans couldn't be put into motion until she showed up.

Mary had never fully understood the trust that tied up camp. The technical details didn't matter. What they all knew—because her father railed against it with the frequency and tone of Mrs. Bennet in *Pride and Prejudice* whining about "the entail"—was that so long as their father was alive, the property couldn't be sold. "It'll be up to you, kids," her father used to say, "to figure out what to do with this place."

And then her parents had died, and they'd gotten their first surprise. Her father wanted them to keep camp going for one last summer. Swift wouldn't tell them anything more, other than the fact that they'd get more information on Labor Day weekend, but it made Mary wonder. Had his complaining simply been the way he expressed his love? Or had he come to love what he used to refer to as "his prison," a type of Stockholm syndrome brought on by forty years of laughing children and the quiet beauty of the lake?

She'd find out soon enough.

When she was finally ready to go, she decided to ride there. She hated the confinement of cars, and there was a public path through the woods from the farm she'd bought four miles away. It was already past ten when she saddled up Cinnamon and led her out of the barn. The path was as pretty as she remembered, all dappled light and views of the lake through the trees. She loved the silence of it, how the only sounds were the ones she and Cinnamon made, their matched breathing, and the occasional buzz of a motorboat from the lake.

She knew some of her siblings would want to sell the property, take the money and run. But that was a crime. One she'd survive, perhaps, but still. Was there anything she could say that would convince them to leave well enough alone? She'd thought and thought, but she never seemed to know the right buttons to push with them.

The path gave out near the Craft Shop. Mary tied her horse to the porch banister, patting Cinnamon down and bringing her one of the large tins of water that sat outside every building on the property—a simple fire extinguisher even a kid could use—for her to drink from. She wanted to stay with Cinnamon or get back on her and ride away, but she knew this would only postpone the inevitable. So she cut through the woods and took the back stairs up to the deck of her parents' house.

She looked through the sliding glass doors into the living room. There they all were, her family, and Sean and Mr. Swift, sitting on the couches her parents had inherited from her grandparents, watching the door like they were in a play waiting for someone to enter. *Waiting for Godot.*

But no.

Me, she thought. *They're waiting for me.*

This gave her a thrill. No one ever used to wait for her; she felt like she'd spent her childhood running after one sister or another. The only time she felt present, waited for, expected, was at the stables.

She watched them. They looked like they'd been arranged in a tableau, sitting for a painting. It would be a shame to disturb it. But disturb it she must.

She rapped on the glass.

"Now that we're all here," Swift said five minutes later, when the general dismay at Mary's tardiness had subsided, and she had her own glass of iced tea clutched in her hand as she sat on the sofa between the twins, "we can get to the matter at hand."

Swift stood up and pulled a document from one of the pockets of his fishing vest. It was folded into thirds and had an official-looking seal on it.

"A bit of background, though I suspect you know most of this already. Before your grandparents died, they transferred the land that the camp sits on into a trust. Your father was given the custody of the property, and I was the trustee. The trust was to stay in place until he died, and the land couldn't be sold for any reason before that time. Because none of you were born when the trust was set up, your grandfather gave your father the right to decide who the property would go to when he died."

"Which he did," Ryan said.

"Which he did," Swift agreed. "Which brings us to today. This is your father's will. It contains some provisions that are . . . unusual." He cleared his throat. "And I want to let you know that I . . . Well, I tried to discourage him from this idea, but he was adamant."

"Tell us already." That was Liddie; that was always Liddie, but in this instance, Mary couldn't help but agree. Why was there so much drama? It was her father's worst characteristic, his flair for the dramatic. Even the simplest of things had to be acted out. No, worse. *Staged.*

Swift coughed, his throat rattling.

"Your father left the property in co-ownership to his children with one, um, unusual exception, which I think it's best if I leave to your father to explain."

He took another piece of paper out of his jacket. "He set it all out in a letter." He started to open it but then dropped it. He picked it up, his face flushed, the sweat back on his brow. "Sorry, sorry."

He unfolded it. "Ahem. Here we go.

" 'Children, this may come as a surprise to some—or all—of you, but this property that you're sitting on means the world to me. That might not always have been so; I've been a reluctant lover, so to speak, but it's true now. As I write these words, your mother's outside photographing the lilies in her garden. It's dusk, and the light on the lake is like nothing I've ever known. It's odd to think that I'm both here as I write this and, when you hear these words, gone. But alas, that is man's fate. To be fleeting. To be impermanent.

"'My father wanted this place to be permanent. He tied it up so I didn't have any choice but to stay. And while that ended up being the best thing for me, I doubt you can all say the same. So as much as I might want to keep you tied to camp, I'll make a different choice from my father and let you choose your own destiny.

"'Choices are important. Some more than others. Leaving you with no guidance would be wrong. But there is, as you all know, more to the story than that.

"'Camp Macaw suffered a terrible tragedy twenty years ago. The police consider it unsolved. Over the years, however, I've come to believe that it was perpetrated by one of you. This hasn't been an easy thing to accept—that one of our children could be responsible for what was done to that innocent girl—but accept it I must. You'll again have trouble believing this, perhaps, but I've struggled for a long time, trying to decide what to do with this knowledge. I had to be sure, you see, and even now I am not. That's a tough position to be in, and there's no perfect solution, alas, so this is what I've decided.

"'Ryan, I believe that you're responsible. I'm not certain, but certain enough. The police may have cleared you, but they didn't have all the facts. I don't understand why you did it, but if you're hearing this, then I've lost the chance to ask you.

"'Girls, because I can't be entirely sure that I'm right, I'm leaving this in your hands. If you think I'm wrong—that your brother is innocent—then you can agree to let him share equally in the property. So this doesn't persist too long, you'll have to vote forty-eight hours after Swift reads you this letter. First, whether Ryan gets his share, and then, whether to keep the place or sell it. The decision about Ryan will have to be unanimous, and it will be irrevocable.

"'Whatever you decide, my hope is that you'll keep camp going. It's an amazing place. We were a true family here, the best version of ourselves. It would give me enormous peace to think of it being handed down from generation to generation, unceasing. But I've left that decision in your hands as well. I can only hope that you'll keep my wishes in mind, and that they become your wishes too.

" 'And finally, Ryan, this might be hard to hear, but I'm doing this out of love for you, and also out of respect and love for Amanda. I cannot know what you're feeling right now, but please believe that you have my compassion. Perhaps I should've confronted you while I was still living, but my lack of certainty held me back. And for that, I'm truly sorry. If I'm wrong about you, I ask your forgiveness and trust that your sisters will do the right thing.

" 'Good luck to you all.

" 'With love, Dad.' "

There was a full minute of silence when Swift stopped reading, the only sound that of him folding the letter back into squares and tucking it into his pocket.

"What. The. Hell?" Kate finally said. "That's so messed up."

"That's it?" Ryan asked. "What does that even mean?"

"I'm sorry to say this, Ryan, but unless your sisters agree, you don't inherit."

"How does that work?" Mary asked.

"Your father has left the property to you four girls and to me in co-ownership. If you decide that Ryan should inherit, I'll transfer my share to him."

"You can't be serious," Ryan said. "Is this even binding?"

"I assure you that it is."

Liddie, Ryan, and Kate all started speaking at once. In the jumble of voices, it was hard to make out what anyone was saying, but it wasn't hard to imagine. Mary heard the word *outrage* more than once. She met Margaux's eyes across the room. She was crying. This surprised her. Margaux didn't usually show her emotions openly, but she'd been close to Amanda. Perhaps this absurd situation was bringing all that up again. You'd think that twenty years was enough time to get over something, or at least through it. But other people were never on her timeline.

She tried to speak, but no one could hear her. After a moment of frustration, she put her hand up in the air, the method they always used at camp to get silence in the room. They followed suit one by one, a reflex adult life hadn't erased. Sean was the first; Ryan was the last. Only Swift kept his hands at his sides, looking puzzled.

"What happens if we don't agree to give it to Ryan?" Mary asked Swift when the room was silent. "Or if it's not unanimous? Does that mean we're stuck owning the property with you?"

Swift's eyes darted to the left, and Mary knew the answer before he said it.

"No, I'm simply an interim step. If you can't agree on Ryan, then I'll transfer my share to Sean."

CHAPTER 10

LEFTOVERS

Margaux

The summer Ryan left his family, Margaux had gone to visit Kerry and her nieces to check in. It was Maisy's sixth birthday. Kerry had invited her whole class and set up a bouncy castle in their backyard. The party was loud and lush, overcompensation for the fact that Ryan wasn't there. Except he was. He arrived as if he were one of the guests, a few minutes after Margaux, with a large pink package under his arm. Maisy and Claire and Sasha were ecstatic to see him, jumping on his back and into his arms, dragging him into the yard. As she watched them, a pileup of a happy family, Margaux wondered if she should leave. She'd come as a stand-in for Ryan, but now that Ryan was there in the flesh, she felt superfluous.

But leaving would mean explaining to Mark why she'd come and gone so quickly, and this after making a big deal about his not coming along. The truth was, she and Mark always ended up fighting after they were around other people's children. He wanted a baby; she didn't, but she hadn't made that clear to him, not yet. She didn't know how to navigate this role reversal, and she wasn't sure it was a firm decision, not back then at thirty-five, and not even now at thirty-seven, though she understood nature might soon make that decision for her if it hadn't already.

So she stayed. Her parents were there, though she hadn't expected them either. The Mackerels (a nickname the campers had given her family years ago that stuck to them like glue) weren't hands-on grandparents. And even though they ran a camp for children, they seemed out of place at the party. Some of that was how they looked. Her father kept his hair long and in a ponytail and was wearing a T-shirt with Che Guevara on it. Her mom had let her nearly white blonde hair turn actual white, and she wore it in one long thick braid that she wrapped around her head like her Swedish milkmaid relatives must've done generations ago. Her clothes were made of natural fibers, which only enhanced her earth-mother vibe.

Watching them across the lawn, it crossed Margaux's mind that if she saw them on the news as the leaders of some doomsday cult, she wouldn't bat an eye. They certainly stood out in the taupe-wearing crowd. Neither of them approved of Kerry, who "came from money," her dad always said, and enjoyed spending it. But now there was money trouble, and Margaux wondered how they were even affording the party. Perhaps Kerry's parents were kicking in. They were standing next to the punch bowl wearing matching Calvin Klein.

Margaux girded herself and joined her parents as they watched the children bounce in the plastic house. She hadn't seen them in a while. Mark didn't feel comfortable around them, and something about his unease made her see their flaws in ways she hadn't since she was still spending summers at camp. She was resolving to try to do better when Sasha, the youngest, came up and slipped her little paw into Margaux's.

"Painting?"

She dropped down. "What's that, honey?"

"Grandma bringed paints. You help me."

"Which grandma?"

Sasha pointed to Ingrid.

"Should we ask her to paint too?"

"Okay."

Sasha tugged her over to Margaux's mother.

"Come," she said, grabbing Ingrid's hand and pulling them along with her to a small craft table. There was a new set of watercolor paints, creamy paper, and a pristine set of brushes.

"What shall we paint?" Ingrid asked. She dropped elegantly down to the grass and readied a bowl of water.

"Party?"

"Absolutely."

Ingrid went to work as Margaux and Sasha watched. The party quickly took shape under her skilled hand, and Margaux had a flash of memory, of her and her mother creating something with similar paints, preserving a moment. Somehow, she'd forgotten.

"Shall we do the people?" Ingrid asked after she'd drawn in the lawn, picnic tables, and the bouncy house.

"Fambly," Sasha said.

"You got it. You want to help, Margaux?"

Margaux smiled at her mother as she reached for a brush. She was glad she'd come. Maybe she should save this and get it framed . . .

Ryan burst into the backyard with a girl under each of his arms.

"Bouncy house time!" he bellowed, dropping the girls and launching them toward the entrance.

Sasha was up like a flash, the painting forgotten.

"Me too, Daddy! Me too!"

Ryan basket-tossed each of his daughters into the castle, their yelps filled with sugar-fueled glee, their matching pastel dresses little hot-air balloons around their waists. They'd always been rambunctious, wild even, but this was something else. They were performing for Ryan, Margaux realized, trying to show him what he was missing by being away. Her heart broke at the thought.

"Someone's going to get injured," Ingrid said, as shrieks emerged from the bouncy house. It was hard to see what happened, but after they'd been in there for less than a minute, the other children started pouring out as if they were escaping a war zone. Only Ryan's girls remained inside, jumping higher and higher with determination on their innocent faces. A few minutes later, when the castle had been collapsed and Kerry asked them for an explanation, there was a chorus of denials. But Margaux knew the look in the eyes of the fleeing children.

It was fear.

"Did Mom know?" Margaux asked Swift.

"What?"

"The letter was only from Dad. So I want to know, did my mom know about this? Is this what she thought also?"

Swift rubbed at his chin. Sweat was gathering at his collar. "No, I don't believe she did. Your father left two sets of instructions; if he died first, then she'd get a life interest in the camp before it passed to you. If she died first or they died together, well . . ."

"We know what fucking happened then," Ryan said through clenched teeth.

"Yes."

"This is such bullshit."

Ryan raised his arm and threw his glass of iced tea toward the plateglass window. It smashed above Swift's head with a report that sounded like a shot. Everyone but Sean froze. He zipped across the room and had Ryan pinned against the wall before anyone had time to react.

"Get the fuck off me!" Ryan said.

"Not until you calm yourself."

"How am I supposed to do that with you manhandling me?"

He held Ryan more tightly as Ryan struggled against the wall.

"Stop it, Ryan," Liddie said. "You know he's way stronger than you. Always has been."

Mary walked up to them. She put one hand on Sean's shoulder and another on Ryan's. She spoke in low tones, saying, "Steady, now," soothing them like she did with her horses. It worked. Ryan stopped struggling, and Sean's arms relaxed. Mary spoke again, and he released Ryan, taking a step back. Ryan sank into his chair and looked at the ice scattered at his feet. Kate left the room and returned with a towel and a broom, quickly cleaning up the mess. Liddie went to help her; only Margaux and Swift stood still, frozen.

"All right now?" Mary said to Ryan and Sean, her hands outstretched from her body, her palms facing them.

They nodded.

"Why don't we sit back down and talk about this?" Mary said. "Okay, Mr. Swift?"

Swift snapped out of his reverie. "Yes."

"Margaux?"

"Yes?"

"Are you okay?"

"I'm fine."

"You know you've been standing in the same place for five minutes?"

Margaux shook herself. Everyone was seated and yet, yes, there she was, still standing. She wasn't quite sure what was going on. Was it simply the shock? This had happened sometimes when she was young. She'd get stuck in her head and wouldn't notice that the world was moving around her. But she'd been snapped out of that when she was seventeen, and it hadn't happened since. Until now.

She sat down. "I was waiting for everyone to calm down."

Mary gave her a look but didn't say anything. No one else seemed to be paying any attention to them. All eyes were on Swift.

"Okay, Swifty," Liddie said. "You have our attention. Do you mind explaining all of this?"

He cleared his throat. "There isn't much to explain. Your father's wishes are clear. Ryan will only inherit if you all agree that he should. If you don't, then Sean will get the fifth share in the property and you'll have to decide what happens to it."

"Do we have to be unanimous about that also?" Margaux asked.

"No, that decision can be taken by simple majority since your father only specified unanimity for the decision about Ryan."

"What do you mean, 'Do you have to be unanimous about what happens to this place?' " Ryan asked. "Have you already made up your mind that it's Sean and not me?"

"I'm just trying to understand."

"I can't believe this is happening," Ryan said. "I'm sure if I talked to my lawyer—"

"And tell him what?" Kate said. "That Dad thought you hurt Amanda? That you *did*?"

Ryan paled. "I didn't do anything to her."

"That is so fucking sick," Liddie said. "Not even Ryan deserves to be treated this way."

"Liddie," Mary warned.

"What? I mean, what's going on here? Some kind of restorative justice?"

"Stop it, Liddie," Margaux said. "Just stop."

Kate put her hand on Liddie's arm, and some silent communication passed between them. Liddie harrumphed but didn't continue.

"This is a game, isn't it?" Margaux asked Swift. "One of Dad's jokes? We'll spend the weekend trying to make this decision, and then there'll be another letter telling us that he was 'just joshing' and sorry if we didn't enjoy his last bit of fun."

"That's possible, I suppose, but I don't have another letter."

"What happened to Amanda wasn't a joke," Sean said. "That girl was innocent."

"Not that innocent," Mary said.

"What's that supposed to mean?" Margaux and Mary locked eyes. Margaux had heard this kind of thing about Amanda before, and it always made her angry. *If Amanda hadn't snuck away . . . If Amanda had been doing her job . . . If Amanda, if Amanda.* "What happened to Amanda wasn't her fault."

Mary looked away. She never stood her ground about anything, which was something Margaux kind of despised about her. You had to stand up for yourself sometimes in this world.

"Are we supposed to vote now?" Margaux asked.

"In forty-eight hours. That's what the letter said. So, on Sunday, after the memorial, I guess," Kate said.

"So Ryan has forty-eight hours to convince us he's innocent?"

"Or to convince us to look the other way and let him inherit anyway," Kate said.

"I told you this was sick," Liddie said, then turned back to Swift. "This is so typical. How long? How long ago did he set this up?"

"Ten years ago."

"Ten? *Ten?* You mean, after . . ."

"Yes."

"But that was an accident."

"Perhaps your father didn't think so."

"Clearly. Fantastic, Mary, way to go."

Mary stared back placidly. "I hardly see how I'm to blame for that."

"Because you never see. God, I'm so sick of the lot of you."

Liddie turned on her heel and stormed out of the room. Kate stood to go after her.

"Don't, Kate," Margaux said. "Let her blow off some steam."

"But what if she leaves?"

"She won't."

Kate sat back down. Margaux watched her siblings. Ryan was sweating and rubbing his arm where Sean had pinned him against the wall. Kate was biting at the nail on her thumb. Mary was sitting tall, as if she were on her horse, setting up for a jump. And Sean was bumping his leg up and down, which he did, Margaux knew, when he was excited.

Whether there was another letter coming or not, this really was a terrible joke.

Margaux walked Swift back to his car after the family meeting broke up. "Sorry about all that," she said when they reached his car. "I'm not sure what came over Ryan."

He wiped at his brow with a handkerchief he pulled from his jacket.

"Hold still." She took the handkerchief and used it to brush him off. There were fine flecks of glass on Swift's shoulders.

"There was glass," she explained.

He didn't say anything, just took the handkerchief and shook it out. She thought about suggesting that he check in with his doctor—make sure his heart was operating on all cylinders or valves or whatever it was that made hearts go other than love—but decided not to. Swift wasn't her problem. At least, not in that way.

"I tried to talk him out of this," he said.

"I'm sure you did."

"It doesn't give me any pleasure to have to deliver this message."

"I believe that."

"What do you think will happen?"

"Honestly? I'm not sure."

He wiped at his brow again. "Families are complicated."

"I'll say. Did he ever tell you why he was so sure it was Ryan?"

"I couldn't say."

"Are you going to go to the police?"

"What would I tell them?"

She stared at the line of trees that blocked the view to the lake. The wind had picked up. She could hear the floating docks banging against one another.

"You know what's funny?" she said. "I always thought my parents held me responsible for what happened."

"Why's that?"

"I was one of the last people to see her that night. Doesn't that make me a prime suspect?"

Amanda

July 22, 1998—11:00 p.m.

When that terrifying voice whispered in my ear, I'd been so certain it was Ryan. But it took only a second after I turned around to realize it wasn't and for me to start to feel foolish.

"Margaux!" I said, ashamed and confused that I could've mixed up the two. "Shouldn't you be with the kids?"

Her hands were on her hips. "I was about to ask you the same thing."

She was dressed all in black—black hiking pants, black sweatshirt; even her hair was slicked back so it didn't reflect light the way it usually did. When she'd changed into this outfit earlier, I hadn't thought much about it, but now I realized that it was how she dressed when we'd go on midnight raids in the boys' section. All that was missing was the black mascara she usually wiped under her eyes like a football player.

"I got distracted," I said.

"Really?" She was swinging her flashlight back and forth by its lanyard. An arc of light hit the rocks on the beach, then the trees behind her.

"What's with the tone?"

"Oh, I don't know. You were acting strange all night, and then you said you were going to get water to put out the fire, and instead, here you are, pacing the beach, clearly waiting for someone. So what's going on? Who are you meeting?"

"No one."

"Puh-lease. It's Simon, isn't it? That's why he stopped talking to me."

She meant Simon Vauclair, a fellow counselor who also happened to be the person Margaux had lost her virginity to the summer before. He'd dumped her about a week after, and she'd been devastated. She wasn't always rational about him, but the accusation felt like it came out of nowhere. Though I'd known Simon as long as Margaux had, we'd never gotten along, which she knew.

"You think I'm waiting for Simon? That's nuts."

"Why? You danced with him last week."

"Once. And he only asked me because he was in the bathroom when everyone partnered up, and he was trying to avoid Tracy."

"That's not what it looked like to me."

"Why do you care? You told me you hated him."

She flinched. She'd tried to convince everyone of that, but deep down she still wanted him. I knew it; he knew it. He treated her like shit anyway. It was one of the reasons I hated the guy.

"So you *are* meeting him," she said. "You've been acting weird all day."

"I have not."

"You have so."

My chest felt tight. We'd never had a fight before, not in the ten years we'd known each other, and now here we were, fighting like six-year-olds.

"This is stupid. You know I don't like Simon."

"If you say so."

I watched the flashlight arc back and forth, getting higher each time. When the light reached my eyes, I turned away.

"If you're here," I said, "who's with the kids?"

"They're fine. Mary's there."

"Dammit, Margaux, we're not supposed to leave them alone with her. We better get back before someone gets injured."

"But what about Simon?"

"I'm not meeting him. I told you."

"What are you doing here, then?"

I didn't want to tell her, but I didn't seem to have a choice. "It's Ryan."

"Ryan?"

"Yeah, you know, your brother. Ryan."

"Ryan's meeting you."

"Yes."

The flashlight dipped toward the ground. I knew she wasn't going to believe me, but she seemed to be thinking it over. Testing it out.

"Huh."

"What's that supposed to mean?"

"It's nothing. I'm just surprised. Wow. Okay. Interesting." She stepped forward and hugged me unexpectedly. She smelled like the campfire and marshmallows. "Be careful, okay?"

"What?"

She let me go. "With Ryan. Don't let him break your heart."

"He's probably not even going to show."

"I bet he does."

"We should go back."

"It's fine. You stay here. I got this."

"What about the kids?"

"It'll be fine." She bent down and took the fire cans from where I'd left them on the ground. "I better go before they notice that they don't have any adult supervision."

"You're sure?"

"I am."

"Thanks, Margaux."

"Of course. And, I don't know. Have fun. Okay?"

I watched her walk into the woods, her words echoing in my head. *Have fun?* Somehow, I'd never thought of that. I'd always been so nervous around Ryan that it never was fun. Exciting, yes. Pit-of-the-stomach feelings, for sure. Maybe that's what I was missing out on. The fun.

When she disappeared in the trees, I turned back to the water and scanned the horizon. I couldn't see anything, but I could hear it.

Oars.

Ryan was coming.

	Amanda	Margaux	Ryan	Mary	Sean
9:00 p.m.	Lantern ceremony	Lantern ceremony	Lantern ceremony		
10:00 p.m.	On the Island	On the Island		On the Island	Crash boat
11:00 p.m.	Back Beach	Back Beach		On the Island	
6:00 a.m.	Secret Beach				

CHAPTER 11

JOHN DEERE

Sean

Sean was doing what he always did when he needed to think: riding his mower, taking down the grass and letting it collect in the bag attachment he'd repaired so many times over the years that he'd lost count. That clean cut–grass smell and the look of it after—he loved those things. It was so easy to keep on going until you hit the woods; he always wished he could go a bit farther. Mowing felt like church to him, what church was supposed to feel like, anyway. Solemn. Peaceful. His sermon was nature and a job well done.

But today it wasn't working like it had in the past. Course, he'd never had to face this kind of possibility before, that he might finally get what was coming to him. That he could have a real say in what happened to camp and whether it would continue on as it should.

Only, it was conditional. Just like everything Mr. MacAllister did for him, come to think of it. He could work at camp, but he couldn't be a counselor. He could be Mr. Fix It, but he wasn't a real member of the family. Everything had a catch. He searched for the right words in his mind, but ah, hell, he never was any good at this sort of thing. He only knew that Mr. MacAllister had said one thing—he'd be able to stay on at camp as long as he wanted—and it turned out that what that meant was he'd be able to stay only if the others wanted him to.

Sean's throat felt tight at the thought. He didn't know where he'd go if he had to leave. What would he do? His whole adult life had been given to this place—he didn't know how to do anything else but be at camp, work at camp.

Would they ever choose him over Ryan, their own brother, even if most of them didn't like Ryan? Was that a possible outcome? And how did they feel about him? He'd never been able to tell if he was someone they put up with or if there was more to it. As he understood it, if they couldn't agree, then he'd get in there anyway, the default option. That was clever on Mr. MacAllister's part. They'd never all agreed on anything in their whole lives. And he wanted to be fair to Ryan. That was right for a father to do, wasn't it?

He didn't have a father, none he knew about, anyway, because his mama, herself a faded memory, never told him anything about the man who got her pregnant. That was okay. Real family seemed like a lot of trouble—all the feelings you had to take into account, the people you had to accommodate. Half family was enough for Sean.

Just so long as he could stay at Camp Macaw.

CHAPTER 12

RUNAWAY

Liddie

When Liddie left the house, she went down the stairs and then turned and went into the basement through its separate entrance. There was a grate down there that allowed you to listen to conversations in the living room perfectly. She'd found it the summer she was eight, and she'd used it to discover any manner of things. Mostly, she listened to the Sunday night staff meetings. Liddie gathered all kinds of useful information during those. The names of the kids who'd been caught having sex in the woods, or smoking pot, or anything else you'd like to know. Most of the kids were naive enough to think that the Mackerels weren't aware of what was going on in camp. Liddie knew they were wrong and used it to her advantage.

She'd never gotten used to how strange it was, though, to listen to a conversation you'd just left. There was always a risk you'd hear something about yourself you wished you hadn't. Take today. Liddie didn't like the tone Margaux had used, so certain Liddie wouldn't leave, but she did like that Kate wanted to come after her. That was her biggest fear: that she might one day say she was going to do something dramatic—kill herself, for example—and Kate wouldn't stop her. She'd have to go through with it, then, or be humiliated.

The rest of the meeting was boring. There was a lot of yelling, mostly by Ryan. Then Ryan got morose, professing his innocence, saying over and over again that he'd had nothing to do with what had happened to Amanda. It was kind of sad. Then Swifty left with Margaux, and she heard something even more upsetting: Ryan working on Kate to get her to vote for him. Kate didn't say much. Liddie could imagine her face as she listened to Ryan, struggling to avoid his charm. Liddie knew what would happen. Kate was so straitlaced, so buttoned up, particularly around her family, that she wouldn't do anything to rock the boat. If everyone else agreed, Kate wouldn't be the one to spoil the plan. It was brilliant to go to her first, actually. Liddie would've done the same. Because if Kate thought it was okay, *if even Kate thought it was okay*, then it must be the right thing to do.

When she heard Kate say, "I hadn't thought about it like that before," Liddie couldn't stand to listen anymore, so she changed into her running things, grabbed her phone and headphones, and left. She was sweating hard by the time she got to the main road, but she knew that once she crested the hill, she'd have a clear signal.

She dialed the familiar number.

"Hey, babe, how's it going?"

She felt relieved. Talking to Owen always calmed her down. He was steady and unflappable, a perfect counterpoint to the wildness that lived inside her. Which was funny, given what he did for a living. But that matched her too. Neither of them was what people expected from their outsides.

"It's a shitshow."

"Are you running?"

"Yep."

"Things must be bad, then."

Though the hilly terrain was taxing, she filled Owen in. How she already regretted coming to camp. How she could see the weekend unfolding. How she wanted to go home.

"I'll come get you if you want."

He'd dropped her off the night before, leaving her at the top of the road because she wanted a day to settle in without anyone knowing she was there.

"Isn't it some kind of Palooza tomorrow?"

Owen was, for want of a better term, a rock star. Not a headliner, yet, but about to become one.

"I could blow it off."

"I thought you needed the money to fund your next album, since you're leaving the label."

"I could find it elsewhere. Do a GoFundMe or something."

She'd been amazed to learn how easily fans gave up money to support whatever project their favorite artist was working on. Fund My Film! Fund My Book! As far as she knew, no one had tried Fund My Vacation!, but she was sure someone enterprising would get to that soon enough. So long as it was for a legitimate project, Owen had no qualms about doing this. Liddie was embarrassed for him at first, but when she saw how excited the fans were for the perks—a Skype call from Owen, a signed picture, even a "date" if you donated enough money—she reconciled herself to it, though she'd insisted on rules for the "date." Harder to accept was the way strangers felt like they could intrude on their private time in restaurants, theaters, on the street.

"Okay, but no date with you this time."

"Babe, you're adorable when you're jealous."

Liddie pumped her arms and crested another hill. She stopped to catch her breath, staring at the placid cows grazing in the field behind a thin wire fence.

"You still there?" Owen asked.

"Still here."

"Should I come get you?"

"I'll be okay."

"And what about Ryan?"

"What about him?"

She'd left out Ryan grabbing her arm. She knew if she told him that, Owen would come down in a flash, and she wasn't ready to have her Owen world collide with her Macaw world. Not yet.

"He's dangerous, isn't he?"

"Of course not."

"But if he was the one who did that to . . . What was her name again?"

"Amanda."

"If he was the one who did that to Amanda . . . You guys should go to the police."

"He's my brother."

"What's that got to do with it?"

Liddie looked at the animal closest to her. Its life was so simple—stand in a field and eat grass all day, not even aware that he was being fattened up for the slaughter. Or was it the women cows who got eaten? That would figure.

"I'm not in danger, and no one's going to the police. Besides, they already investigated all of this when it happened."

"But they never charged anyone."

"There wasn't enough evidence to go forward. That's what they said. I think."

"You think?"

"I was twelve. I didn't really know what was going on. None of us did."

Liddie thought back to her sessions with the detectives. How her parents needed to be there because she was a minor. How it all felt like a game, one she was winning because secrets were her thing. *Where were you that night, Liddie? Were you with Kate the whole time? How did you feel about Amanda?*

"Not enough evidence to go forward against who?" Owen asked.

Liddie didn't want to talk about this anymore. What she wanted to do was run.

"Liddie? Are you still there?"

She held the phone away from her and spoke loudly. "Owen? I can't hear you. It's a bad connection. I'll try again later."

And then she hung up.

Amanda

July 23, 1998—6:00 a.m.

It was the twins who found me.

I don't know what they were doing at Secret Beach. Later, they'd tell the police, under the watchful eye of their parents, that they'd been out looking for flowers for a project they were working on in Craft Shop. It was weird, though, those two, up before the wake-up bell, scurrying around in an area they weren't supposed to go to unless they were with an adult. But they were twelve and the owners' children, and this immunized them from too much scrutiny.

I could hear them. Not the words but their voices. Panicked whispering. The brush of their legs through the long grass near the beach. Then I heard the word *trouble*—I think it was Kate, but that might be because it makes the most sense that it was Kate—and in my helplessness, I felt angry. That they cared more about getting into trouble than saving me, someone who'd been like a sister to them, or so I always thought.

Then one of them said something about *dead. Dead body* or *Dead girl.* And I screamed, *I'm alive,* but that was in my head, and they couldn't hear me. *Help yourself,* I thought. *Do something.* But everything was in pain and frozen. *Move something. Move something.* I concentrated as hard as I could and managed to move my hand. To me, it felt as if I were waving frantically, but I know that can't be right because then I heard them quite clearly.

"I saw her hand move!"

"What? No, dummy, you're imagining it."

"Am not. I mean it, Liddie. She moved."

"I'm going to check if she's breathing."

"How?"

"Shhh!"

A hand pressed over my face, right over my mouth, making it even harder to breathe than before.

"What are you doing?"

"I don't feel anything."

Oh, the pain, the pain. *Move, move, move.* I moved my hand again. Someone screamed. The hand over my face fell away, and then everything was black.

	Amanda	Margaux	Ryan	Mary	Kate & Liddie	Sean
9:00 p.m.	Lantern ceremony	Lantern ceremony	Lantern ceremony			
10:00 p.m.	On the Island	On the Island		On the Island		Crash boat
11:00 p.m.	Back Beach	Back Beach		On the Island		
6:00 a.m.	Secret Beach				Secret Beach	

CHAPTER 13

STORM COMING

Ryan

Ryan had never been so mad and scared in his life. Equal parts mad, equal parts scared. It was an odd seesaw of emotion. Normally, when he was angry, he couldn't sit still. He'd pace the house, the yard, the streets for miles if it was particularly bad. Kerry understood that, and she'd rather he walk a hole in his shoes than punch one in the wall. But this new anger, this anger/fear, had him paralyzed. What was he supposed to do now? How was he supposed to make this come out right? What the hell had his father been thinking?

He was punishing him, obviously, but for what? For all the trouble he'd caused in the family? Despite what his father had written in that terrible letter, he still couldn't believe it. Didn't he deserve the chance to defend himself? If his father had told him of his suspicions, he could've explained so much better now than when everything happened, when he was twenty. Instead, he had to convince his sisters—a group of people with their own interests and no reason to rule in his favor.

He'd tried talking to Kate, but that had been a mistake.

"Come on," he'd said when they were alone. "You know I had nothing to do with what happened to Amanda."

Kate sat there on the couch, her hands playing with the ends of the pink sweater that was tied over her shoulders. Even that sweater made him angry; she didn't play tennis and it wasn't the eighties—she must barely even remember them—so why was she dressing like that? What part was she playing now?

"Are you sure about that?"

"Why are you saying that?"

"You know why, Ryan."

He shivered, though the house was still warm from the meeting; all that body heat and anger almost fogged the windows.

"You mean . . . Because I was on the Island that night?"

He'd never understood how the police knew he was there, even before he'd confirmed it. Maybe it was just a cop's instinct. They'd been aggressive, trying to get him to confess. All their questions, their fear tactics—they'd worked. He'd been terrified. *We know you were the one who hurt her, Ryan. This would be much easier if you told us the truth.* Over and over. Somehow, he held fast—he'd been there, but he'd left, and he hadn't seen anyone else—and when they asked him what he thought had happened, he mentioned the houses on the other side of the lake. There had been a group of guys staying there that summer, guys in their twenties who drank on a pontoon boat and who used to come a bit too close to the beach during free swim when Amanda and Margaux were lifeguarding. *You should check those guys out,* he told the police. *They were always whistling and catcalling* . . . They'd taken notes, they'd written it all down, but did they actually look into it? They weren't about to tell Ryan that. Besides, they had their man.

Then the questions stopped. There were a few anxious weeks when nothing happened and Ryan felt like a pendulum swinging. The police had closed their investigation; all the notes, he imagined, were packed up in a series of boxes marked UNSOLVED. If you'd asked him back then, he would've told you his parents paid someone to make it all go away, or they'd had Swift do it because that's what people like Swift were for. And that's what happened to his kind of people, wasn't it?

He knew now that this was impossible—his parents might run a camp for rich kids, but they were far from rich themselves. And maybe it was possible to get the cops to look the other way if you were, say, a Kennedy. But a MacAllister? No way.

So he didn't know why the police had given up, and it had never occurred to him until then that if his father *had* paid someone off, it was because he thought he'd done it.

"Ryan?"

"What?"

"Are you going to tell me what happened?"

"What does it matter? If I tell you everything, are you going to believe me?"

"I might." Kate stood up. "I don't want to hear your confession."

"I'm not confessing anything. I'm just asking you . . . where you stand, I guess."

"I don't know. I only know you've been lying all this time, and that must be for a reason. If there was nothing to hide, you would've told the whole truth."

"People lie for all kinds of reasons, Kate."

"I hadn't thought about it like that before," Kate said sarcastically.

"You should try though. Life isn't so binary."

She gave him a look that reminded him, again, of Liddie. "That could be true, but you're a liar just the same."

CHAPTER 14

FUSS

Mary

Mary unhooked Cinnamon's reins from the porch rail and led her up the road to the stables. The horse nuzzled her neck, blowing out through her nose in a way Mary knew meant she was content.

She felt surprisingly content too, but my goodness, what a lot of fuss her father was causing. And all because of that girl Amanda, who her father hadn't even liked because he thought she was a bad influence on Margaux.

Mary remembered that night on the Island well. She'd been excited because it was her first overnight as a counselor-in-training, and also because it was with Margaux. She and Margaux were close in their other lives, their winter lives, which took place in Montreal. They always arrived back in town two weeks after the school year started, and this had cemented their reliance on each other when they were small. Friendship groups were formed in those first anxious hours in the schoolyard. By mid-September, no one new was going to break in. But at camp, Margaux didn't need Mary. She belonged automatically, and she had Amanda, so Mary was cast off like last year's fashion.

They'd had a fight about it that night, when Margaux had left her in charge to go check on where Amanda had gotten to. "She's probably waiting for some boy," Mary had said. "She'll be fine."

"What boy?" Margaux had asked, frowning. "You don't think . . ."

"What?"

One of the kids near them coughed, and Margaux stopped. She wiggled her sleeping bag closer to Mary. "Did you see her dancing with Simon last week?"

"Maybe?"

"They were dancing real close."

"Simon's a jerk."

"That's not the point. Friends don't date exes."

"I don't think Amanda cares about Simon."

"Really?"

"You know she only has eyes for Ryan."

Margaux laughed quietly. "That's true. Poor Amanda."

Margaux unzipped her sleeping bag.

"Where are you going?" Mary asked.

"Watch the kids. I'll be back in a few minutes."

"Margaux . . ."

But she hadn't listened.

Mary walked past her parents' house. After the kids had all graduated from high school, they'd sold the house in town and moved out to camp permanently.

Mary thought about the last time she'd seen her parents, two months before their deaths. Her mother had been chipper; they were taking a train across the country and wasn't that wonderfully old-fashioned of them! They were going to see something, see the country, see it the real way. Mary should consider coming along. When was the last time she'd taken any time off?

"Six days on a train?" Mary had said. "No."

"Why not?"

"I'd feel cooped up. Have you seen how small those rooms are? They make the rooms above the lodge look ginormous."

Her mother had given her an unfocused look. She wasn't fixated on the details of the plan but on the plan itself. The grandeur of telling her friends at the bridge club that they were going on a journey. Mary felt small for feeling any kind of contempt about it. Her parents worked hard and made little money and weren't often able to take a trip. She should be encouraging them, not running them down.

"Sorry, Mom."

"What for, dear?"

"I'm glad you and Dad are going. It's not for me, but I hope you have a great time."

"Why, thank you."

She'd spent the rest of the visit acting the part of the dutiful daughter. She helped prep dinner and cleaned up afterward without being asked. She asked her father about the latest environmental disasters that were playing on the news: ice caps melting and tornadoes and the fires in California. She showed her mother how to look up the places they'd be visiting and promised she'd come over for a slideshow of the pictures her mother would take on the trip. She didn't check her watch once and let them determine when it was time for her to go. When her mother mentioned bed, she kissed them both goodbye, feeling as if this might be a new chapter, that perhaps they'd turned a page and she could relate to them as adults, the way people were supposed to with their parents, not that lingering relationship formed when she and her sisters were teenagers.

She never got a chance to find out. Her parents' train had derailed after colliding with a large moose somewhere in Ontario. The first-class cabin had survived intact; the conductor and the first two berths in the second-class cabin weren't so lucky. Mary wondered whether she would have survived if she'd gone on the trip. Would she have paid the extra money to be in the larger—and safer—car? Would she have upgraded her parents as well? Stupid, errant thoughts were better than the sense of . . . well, there was no other way to put it but *relief*.

Because Mary knew deep down that it wouldn't have been any different between them. For that to happen, she'd have to have been different. She'd have to care enough to try and change. Was it her fault she didn't, or theirs?

"Mary, wait up."

It was Kate, trotting up the road, the muscles in her thin legs well-defined from a lifetime of competitive sports. That was one thing about the MacAllisters—they were all active. A childhood of outdoor activity burned into their DNA.

Mary stopped, holding Cinnamon's head steady.

"You walk fast," Kate said, slightly out of breath.

"Sorry."

"It's fine. You headed to the barn or back to your place?"

"The barn. For now."

"Mind if I walk with you?"

"You don't need my permission."

Kate frowned. Her face didn't carry the lines that Mary's did, wind-whipped and sun-scarred. "What the hell, Mary? Will you talk to me or not?"

"Sorry."

"It's okay. This stunt of Dad's has us all out of sorts. I was just talking to Ryan and—"

"He was trying to convince you to vote for him?"

"Well, not exactly. He was more feeling me out, I guess, wondering which way I'd go."

"Which way will you go?"

"I want to hear what other people think first."

Mary wasn't surprised. Going along with what others wanted was kind of the leitmotif of Kate's life. How else did you end up with a pink sweater tied around your neck?

"So what do you think?" Kate asked.

Cinnamon tugged at her bit. Mary patted her nose, calming her. "I don't know, to be honest. The whole thing is kind of nuts. I guess it all depends on the outcome you want."

"If I want to be an owner with Ryan?"

"What do you want to happen to camp? Ryan wants to sell; that's obvious. He needs the money, right? Sean, on the other hand, wouldn't sell this place if his life depended on it."

"Is that how you're going to decide? I don't think that's fair to Ryan."

"Why not?"

"That means we think he did it."

"Why does it mean that?"

"If he didn't, then he should get his fair share like the rest of us. He should get a say."

They arrived at the barn. It was large and red, the upper level filled with the hay that got loaded in for winter every August. They hadn't canceled the order for this winter, since they didn't know what was going to happen with camp. The barn was ten years past when it needed a coat of paint, but it had been built a hundred years ago of solid posts and beams. Everything else would fall down around them before it would go anywhere. Unless everything on the property was bulldozed for condos. Though maybe they'd keep the barn for authenticity's sake. They could hold weddings there or old-timey gatherings that used dried grass for table decoration.

"But then we'd still have a fight about what to do with the place," Mary said. "Is that what you want? A fight?"

"I only want what's fair."

She wrapped Cinnamon's reins around the hitching post. She didn't want Kate to come inside with her. Kate was allergic to horses, and though it wasn't her fault, she found the way Kate was constantly sneezing and apologizing annoying.

"If you're looking for fairness, you're looking in the wrong place."

"Probably." Kate scanned the barn and up to the paddocks behind it. "Did you ever wish you could see what this place would look like if we had enough money to do it right?"

"No."

"That's pretty definitive."

"It's fine the way it is."

"It's falling apart."

Mary glanced at her sister, trying to figure her out. Kate was pretty, like all of them, and nondescript, which was like all of them but Margaux. Put her in some different clothes, and she could pass for one of the counselors still. She'd been the last of them to leave camp, and then only because their parents had made it clear they weren't going to let her take over while they were still around.

"It's always been like this," Mary said.

"But it could be so much better."

"So that's your vote? Keep it and spruce it up? With what money?"

"We could sell off Secret Beach. That would still leave us with a hundred and fifty acres—plenty of room. And then we could invest the proceeds into getting this place up to standards, which would allow us to charge more and make a profit. For everyone."

"It wouldn't be the same if we did that."

"It would be better."

Mary patted Cinnamon's head, as much for her own comfort as for the horse's. "You've never gotten this place, have you?"

"Of course I have. I love it here."

"You love what you think it could be. But ask anyone else. Ask the staff who are coming on Sunday for the memorial, the lifers, whether they want the kind of changes you're talking about. I'll bet you a million dollars they'll tell you to leave well enough alone."

"If you had a million dollars."

Mary smiled. "That's right."

"So we'll just sell it? No way those guys want that either."

"True. But it's not their decision to make, is it?"

Kate looked downcast. Mary knew she should feel bad about this, but she couldn't muster up the necessary emotion. She felt like throwing herself on Cinnamon's back and returning to her own stables, where everything was arranged exactly the way she wanted it to be. But she couldn't gallop away from her family, not right now, maybe not ever.

"It shouldn't be ours either," Kate said.

"Probably not."

"Did you know Ryan was there that night?"

"Where? The Island?"

"Yes. He confirmed it to me just now."

Mary was both surprised and not. It would explain the reason for the police's interest in him all those years ago. When she'd asked her parents about it then, she was told to stay out of it, that it didn't concern her. And then, when the investigation had closed, it had seemed beside the point. She'd let it go, and she'd thought everyone else had also.

"I didn't, no."

"Well, he was. So he could've done it. Dad might be right."

"There were a lot of people on the Island that night, Kate." Mary didn't wait for her to reply, she just unlooped Cinnamon's reins and walked into the cool of the barn.

Amanda

July 22, 1998—11:30 p.m.

This time, I was the one who did the surprising.

I watched as Ryan rowed slowly to shore, looking over his shoulder to make sure he hit the sweet spot between the rocks. I was perched on another rock, crouched down, hoping my toes wouldn't cramp as they often did when I was in this kind of position. It happened to me when I went windsurfing: horrible cramps that left me clutching my toes, trying to tread water, hoping not to drown. Ryan had rescued me in the crash boat and told me I looked cute almost-drowned.

I couldn't believe he'd actually showed. My heart thudded in my chest, my breath a thread. Ryan was here. Ryan was here for me. What did that mean? Was this where it was finally going to happen? On a rocky beach with him having to put a hand over my mouth to muffle the sound of . . . what? Oh my God. I'd been reading too many romance novels. He wasn't going to ravish me on the rocks. Maybe he'd kiss me or put his hand under my shirt. Or maybe he'd be one of those guys who expected me to give him a blow job, pushing the top of my head down instead of asking for what he wanted.

The only guy I'd ever kissed had been like that. As if the fact that I let him put his tongue in my mouth meant I wanted to take his penis in my mouth as well. He'd gotten kind of aggressive about it when I'd said no, and then—

I stopped myself. I was always doing that. Dredging up the past instead of living in the moment. Why was I even thinking of that idiot in the first place? Oh yes. Ryan!

He was almost to the rocks, stabbing the oars into the water to keep himself from hitting the shore too hard. I heard him swear as one of the oars fell out of its slot and splashed into the water.

"I got it," I said, and Ryan jumped.

"Amanda?"

"Were you expecting someone else?"

"No, I . . . It's getting away."

I walked into the warm water, my Tevas slipping on the rocks, the edges of my cargo pants soaking up the water. I reached out and grabbed the oar by the neck; it was slippery, and chipped. A piece of it caught in the webbing between my thumb and forefinger.

"Shit."

"You okay?"

"I got a splinter."

"Help me bring the boat up, and I'll take a look."

I sucked at my hand and put the oar on the ground. Then I turned and grabbed the prow. Ryan was on the other side, a foot away, and close enough for me to smell his sweat and the lake on his hands.

"Ready? And one, two, up!"

We lifted the boat together. It was heavy, and when I looked, I could see that the back had filled with water. Mr. MacAllister talked about fixing this rowboat every year but never did. We carried it two feet up the beach so it was safe, then laid it on the ground. Ryan grabbed some larger rocks and shoved them under the prow so it could drain. Then he pulled the plug out of the bunghole, and the water started to whoosh out.

"I should let this thing sink," he said.

"How would you get back?"

"Good point."

He took the bow rope and tied it with a bowline to a tree, securing it tightly. "My dad is such a fucking cheapskate."

"Mr. MacAllister is?"

"Haven't you noticed? How everything is falling down around us?"

"I love camp just the way it is."

He grinned. "Yeah, truth be told, I kinda do too. Don't tell Margaux."

Did he mean about the fact that he loved camp or that he was here with me? Better not to ask. I nodded instead. "It'll be our secret."

"Exactly." He patted his pocket. "Just like this."

He pulled out a flask of something.

"What is that?"

"Jack Daniel's. Have you had it before?"

"Someone gave my dad some once."

Dad had called it "hillbilly whiskey," but I didn't think Ryan would appreciate that. Besides, my dad was a snob about most things.

"It's strong," I added.

"That's the idea."

He twisted the cap off and handed it to me. I took a small sip. It tasted awful, like cough medicine.

I handed it back. "I shouldn't drink much. The kids."

He took a long pull. "Sure, the kids."

"Who's looking after your cabin?"

"Ty."

Ty was his best friend.

"So he knows you're here."

"He does."

"With me?"

Ryan gave me a slow smile. "With someone."

My stomach clenched. Did I want him telling Ty that we were hooking up? Probably not. But did the fact that he didn't say who he was meeting mean he was playing with me? Did I care? At least then, if things didn't work out, I wouldn't have anything to hide. But now Margaux knew and Ty knew (if he knew Ryan was on the Island, he knew it wasn't to hang out with Margaux or Mary), which meant that by the time we sat down to breakfast tomorrow, everyone would know . . . what?

"You going to come closer?" Ryan asked as he sat down on the rock I was perched on before.

I sat down next to him. The rock was cool and rough, but the side of my body that was touching Ryan's felt like I had a sunburn. Ryan looked at my hands, twisting between my knees. He reached out and took one of them. He had a row of multicolored bracelets on his wrist—the kind girls weave in Craft Shop from embroidery thread—that I'd never noticed before. But I knew what they were. Conquest bracelets, a rainbow of all the girls he'd been with before me.

What color would I be?

I looked up. He was smiling at me, his teeth white in the night.

"I want to kiss you," he said.

And then he did.

	Amanda	**Margaux**	**Ryan**	**Mary**	**Kate & Liddie**	**Sean**
9:00 p.m.	Lantern ceremony	Lantern ceremony	Lantern ceremony			
10:00 p.m.	On the Island	On the Island		On the Island		Crash boat
11:00 p.m.	Back Beach	Back Beach	Back Beach	On the Island		
6:00 a.m.	Secret Beach				Secret Beach	

CHAPTER 15

ANGER MANAGEMENT ISSUES

Margaux

After Swift left, Margaux wasn't quite sure what to do with herself. She went back to the French Teacher's Cabin, and when she saw the time and the phone, she decided to call Mark again. He answered but sounded annoyed. Margaux wasn't in the mood to placate him, so she let him know she was okay, then said a hurried goodbye. She went out onto the deck overlooking the lake and tried to read the book she'd brought with her, but she couldn't sit still. She'd never been able to do that well, just sit, always feeling as if she needed to be doing something, to be useful. Liddie could lie around in bed all day. She'd always been envious of that ability.

After ten pages she didn't absorb, she put on her running things. She had a long run to do this weekend; might as well get it over with. She filled her water bottle from the tap in the sink, her face curdling at the odor of rotten eggs. The water was perfectly good to drink, but it smelled like Hades.

As Margaux jogged up the road, she wondered what the property was actually worth. They'd all said, her whole life it seemed, that her parents were sitting on a gold mine, that if only the trust didn't exist, they could sell it and live like kings. But what if that wasn't true? Sterling Lake wasn't that popular a destination. It was small compared to Lake Champlain or Memphremagog, both of which straddled the US-Canadian border and therefore had two countries clamoring for lakefront. And the boat restrictions meant that only small motorboats and party boats were allowed. The lake was nine miles long and two miles wide, and much of it was relatively unoccupied. Perhaps that was because of the two other camps on it, the ones they'd, oddly, never had much to do with. But it might also have been because it was that much farther off the beaten path, that much longer from the highway. That much less desirable.

Wouldn't it be funny, hilarious in a way, if regardless of what they decided, they were stuck with camp after all?

She reached the road and checked her pace. For these longer runs, she liked to stick to ten-minute miles, walking for thirty seconds in between in order to drink some water and stretch out her bad knee. She never used to think about her knees, pushing through injuries and warning signs, because running was her salvation. Ever since she'd joined the cross-country team in high school, it was the way she got herself right when she had things to work out in her head. But in this last year, there'd been physical therapy and discussions about surgery and long stretches when Margaux couldn't run. Those had been torture, sitting in the PT's office, hooked up to enough machines to make her feel like if the wrong switch was flipped, she'd end up some kind of mutant. What would her life be like, she wondered, if she couldn't run at all?

She pushed that thought aside, then turned right onto the highway, toward Mary's farm, knowing this stretch of road would be less occupied by cars. She'd almost been driven off the road the last time she'd gone running out here, an experience she didn't want to repeat.

Her cadence was steady now, her brain on autopilot. Three miles passed without a thought to cloud her mind. Her watch beeped to remind her to stop and walk. As she took a swig of stinky water, she noticed that there was someone ahead of her, running like her. Running too much like her. Liddie.

She picked up her pace and caught up to her in a few easy minutes.

"Boo."

Liddie leaped and darted to the side, almost tumbling into the ditch. She ripped her headphones from her ears.

"Margaux. Shit." She leaned over her knees, rubbing down her right leg. "Damn. I think I turned my ankle."

"I didn't see your headphones. I thought you must've heard me."

"Well, I didn't."

Liddie sat down in the grass. She was wearing long surf shorts and a basketball singlet, and her socks were those cheap, ribbed white ones boys wore in high school gym. Did she own *any* clothes made for women? Margaux knew she wasn't supposed to ask such questions these days or think such thoughts, not unless Liddie brought it up, but she wished her sister could confide in her. Margaux wouldn't judge, but she was sick of all the things that were hidden in her family.

"Are you okay?"

Liddie pulled off her shoe and sock and wiggled her ankle. She winced, but it didn't look like it was swelling.

"It hurts."

"Sorry."

"Run's over for today, that's for sure. Dammit. How are we supposed to get back?" Liddie pulled her iPhone out of her pocket. "No goddamn bars."

Margaux looked around. There was a run-down building up the road.

"Twilight."

"What?" Liddie turned her head. "Oh, man, that place?"

"Doesn't look like we have many options."

"I guess."

"Here, I'll help you."

She held out her hand. Liddie stuck her sock back on and shoved her foot into her shoe like a slipper. She took Margaux's hand and stood.

"Can you put weight on it?"

"I think so. But: ouch."

"Lean on me."

Liddie put her arm around Margaux's shoulder, and Margaux put hers around Liddie's waist. She couldn't remember the last time they'd been this close, maybe never, though surely as children they'd at least tumbled around the grass together. Margaux couldn't help but notice that Liddie even smelled a bit like a man; was that the same shampoo Mark used?

"Ready?"

"Ready."

They hobbled down the road like contestants in a three-legged race till they got to the Twilight's parking lot.

"I count eight cars," Liddie said. "And my guess is no men at the bar."

This was a game they'd played when they were staff. Twilight was rumored to be the local whorehouse. The cars outside never matched the number of patrons at the bar.

"I say one man at the bar."

"One tall beer?"

"Deal."

They hobbled in. The bar was empty of men. There was a ragged-looking woman standing behind the counter and two others in their midforties sitting on barstools wearing men's work shirts and heels and nothing else.

"Looks like the beer's on you," Liddie said.

"Looks like."

She led Liddie to a table and went up to the bar. The bartender wasn't anyone she knew; it had been years since she'd been a regular patron. The staff used to come here some nights after the kids were in bed—downstairs only, if you please. Her name tag said her name was France.

"Can I use your phone?"

"You buying something?" France spoke in a voice scarred by cigarettes.

"Two tall Budweisers, two bags of salt-and-vinegar chips, and two Mars bars."

"That'll be twenty dollars. The phone's on the wall over there."

Margaux fished her emergency twenty out of the inside pocket of her shorts. It was sweaty, and France gave her a disgusted look as she took it by the edges of her chipped red fingernails. Margaux went to the phone and made a collect call, which she was half amazed still worked. They'd be picked up in twenty minutes.

When she was done, France was bringing their loot to the table on a beer-stained tray.

"Chips and Mars bars, too. Fantastic," Liddie said.

She ripped open one of the Mars bars with her teeth and wolfed half of it down. "I'm starving. Should've eaten something before I went out."

Margaux's own stomach rumbled in response. She hadn't had anything to eat since that breakfast sandwich at McDonald's, which was stupid of her. If she hadn't stopped when she caught up to Liddie, she probably would've bonked in a couple of miles. She sat down and ripped open her Mars bar, biting into its soft center. She'd forgotten how sweet these things were. And how delicious.

"God, that's good."

She picked up her beer and took a long swig. Budweiser was her camp beer. It tasted like her youth, like things best forgotten.

"This is fantastic."

"And how," Liddie said, clinking her bottle against hers.

"Sorry I screwed up your foot."

"I'm sure it'll be fine tomorrow."

Margaux took another drink. She could already feel the beer's effects. Or maybe it was this place, and she was placebo drunk. Memory drunk.

"We should train for something together," Margaux said. "What about the half marathon in October?"

"Now you want to run with me?"

"It could be fun."

"I'm already signed up for it, actually."

"Perfect."

"I'm running it with someone else." Liddie looked into her bag of chips as if she were expecting to find a prize inside.

"Do I know her?"

"Why do you assume it's a her?"

"I wasn't . . . I . . . Who is it?"

"Owen."

"Who's Owen?"

"You know Owen."

"The only Owen I know is Owen Bowery."

Liddie popped a chip into her mouth.

"Oh, wow."

Margaux worked the thought of Owen, the cute camper who'd turned into a sort of rock star, and her sister she assumed was gay, or at the very least asexual, around in her mind. Liddie looked shy, not herself. Could she have been wrong about her all these years? Or did the fact that she was transgender mean she was, in some sense, gay? Margaux felt stupid and confused but still smart enough not to ask these questions out loud.

"Have you been in touch with him all this time?" she asked instead.

Liddie shoved a few more chips into her mouth. "We ran into each other a couple of years ago. And then I designed the cover for his album."

"You did?"

Margaux wasn't up on all the latest music, but working in a high school kept her more exposed to modern culture than she might otherwise have been. She'd heard of Owen's band, Free-fall, and when she realized she had a connection to it, she'd started following their career. She could even sing some of their big hit, "Another Round, Another Town."

"Yep."

"Wow. You're dating a celebrity."

"Don't you be like that. You've known him since he was thirteen."

"Sure, but that was before."

"Before he was famous?"

"Exactly."

Margaux opened her bag of chips and ate one. She started to cough. She felt as if the first layer of skin had been scraped off her tongue.

"These are crazy strong," she said once she'd rinsed her mouth out with beer.

"Right?"

"So . . . Owen. How long have you been seeing him? You are seeing him, right? Not just running with him."

Liddie nodded. "A couple of years."

"Wow."

"Will you stop saying that?"

"Sorry, it's just . . ."

"You thought I was gay?"

"Maybe?"

"Or trans, right? That fucking show."

"I didn't know what to think, Liddie. You never told us anything."

"You never told me you were straight either."

"One doesn't though."

"Exactly my point."

Margaux picked up her beer and took another long drink. "I guess you're right." She put the bottle down. It made a hollow sound on the table. "My beer's empty. How did that happen?"

"Magic."

She started to giggle as the front door banged open.

Liddie turned to look. "You called Sean?"

"Who did you think I was going to call?"

Liddie tossed back the rest of her beer. She stood up and held her arms out to Sean. "All right, Prince Charming. You going to carry me or what?"

CHAPTER 16

SOMETHING'S COOKING

Kate

If the wind had been strong enough, Kate might've gone for a sail. Take one of the Lasers out by herself and sail down to the other end of the lake, where she could be anonymous. That was the problem with camp. Everywhere and everything was memories. Whether they were your own or other people's. You couldn't escape them. The person you were, the person you used to be, it didn't matter. All that mattered was how others saw you.

Good girl. Together. The even-keeled one who always went along with everyone else because that was easiest. She knew what people thought of her.

She *was* that girl, but she hated how it defined her. She had other sides—hidden sides—that no one ever gave her any credit for. Which meant she never got to be anyone else when she was around her family. Only good ol' reliable Kate.

And yet, here she'd stayed, long past the others, every summer starting in May with precamp, then setup. Painting cabins and pulling mattresses out of storage. Clearing brush and debris and the leftover leaves. Through the staff arrival, and then the campers, right on up until mid-September, pulling it all apart again, a LEGO set being put back in its box. When you worked at a camp, you couldn't have a normal job. Even in college, she'd spent the fall semester catching up on the classes she missed. It had seemed worth it to Kate because she was going to—someday soon, her parents kept assuring her—take over the running of Macaw when they finally retired.

Only they didn't. Instead, on her twenty-seventh birthday, they'd sat her down to a special lobster dinner that she'd had to share with Liddie, like everything, and told her they'd decided she wasn't going to get to run camp after all. They didn't think she had it in her. She was too accommodating, too nice. People would take advantage. The whole time they were telling her this, Liddie was cracking the claws of her lobster, prying the loose meat out of the carcass, methodically, as if she were conducting an autopsy. Oblivious to the fact that Kate's life was being equally dissected, bit by bit, across the table.

At least she hadn't begged and pleaded with her parents. She had that point of pride. Instead, she'd pushed her plate away and left. She'd called a friend, and they'd gotten drunk on sugary margaritas at a taco joint in Saint-Henri. Later, Kate had kissed a boy for the first time since high school. It felt dangerous and stupid, which matched her mood.

She'd woken up alone and with a splitting headache. It was the first of May. Normally, she'd be heading off to camp. Her bags were already packed for the summer. But that was all off. She'd had to find something else to do. Her parents said she could continue as she'd been, working alongside them, doing all the real work without the decision-making power, but that was too humiliating.

The funny thing was, mostly, once she got used to it, she didn't miss camp. It was weird that first summer, when the days warmed up, not to be on the lake, living in a musty cabin, ignoring the news. But by then she was working at an organic grocer's, helping out on their farm on the weekends. She made some friends her own age. She took an interest in things other than the social sphere at Camp Macaw. She certainly didn't miss her parents. When some of the counselors invited her to come to their annual Thanksgiving dinner, she declined. She was okay. So long as she stayed away.

That was the rub, as her father might say.

She didn't miss it if she stayed away.

But now that she was back? She missed it like crazy.

Feeling restless, Kate went to visit Amy. She'd been putting this off, the way you do sometimes with the thing you want the most so you still have the anticipation of it.

Kate found Amy where she always was—working in the kitchen. Amy hadn't been the chef when Kate was small. She joined the kitchen staff the year Kate worked as a kitchen helper. She'd gone by "Aimee" then, and her English had been as broken as her spirit. She'd been twenty-five to Kate's sixteen. She'd escaped a bad marriage and had a young kid in tow. No hard skills except the ones she learned growing up helping her mother take care of a large family. Kate's parents had a habit of taking in strays—like Sean—and Amy certainly fit that bill. That first summer, you could still see the bruises along her collarbone until changeover.

She'd been hired on as an assistant to June, the long-term chef who'd been around Kate's whole life, and had taken over when June finally retired.

She and Kate had clicked from the start—could they both tell, then? Something about each other that neither could yet admit? Kate often wondered. She spent hours with Amy, always speaking in English, even though Kate was bilingual, because Amy insisted she needed to learn, to be perfect, "So I won't be stuck anymore," she said. Two summers later, when Amy was making her come for the first time with her fingers down the front of her shorts and up inside her underwear, her back pressed against the hidden side of the nurse's cabin, Kate didn't care. Amy's tongue was hot in her mouth, and she wanted that mouth sucking and licking every inch of her.

Afterward, when it had started to rain, she and Amy slipped into the back room of the nurse's cabin, taking a risk but not a huge one because it was the nurse's day off, and no one was sick. She'd slipped off her shorts and guided Amy down her body, pressing up into her while her own fingers sought out Amy's hard nipples. She'd come so hard that time it hurt, and she knew then she was lost. Lost to whatever Amy wanted from her, or anyone else who could make her feel like that.

Amy had been scared though. Scared they'd get caught, that she'd lose her job, which was the only security she had for her son. She'd withdraw until Kate almost had to beg for it, beg to let her reciprocate. In those months when she wasn't at camp, Kate would seek out that high elsewhere, always looking for the intensity of that first time as they lay damp and groaning on a cot bed while rain spat at the windows.

Except for briefly at the funeral, Kate hadn't seen Amy in five years. Her break with her parents had brought about a final break with the woman who held sway over her sexual happiness, and most of the rest of her happiness, too. She hadn't wanted to leave Amy behind, but it was the only way she could move on.

Kate watched Amy as she moved about the kitchen. She was in her early forties now, and time had not been kind, though she was still beautiful to Kate. Amy wore her dark hair short, like Liddie, more comfortable in her identity since Kate wasn't there to blow her cover. The ties of the apron she wore hugged her waist, cinching it in, and when Amy turned and saw her, something in Kate let loose. The years and resentments fell away, and all that was left was bare, naked want.

CHAPTER 17

DINNER BELL

Ryan

Ryan hardly knew how he spent the afternoon. Mainly he played the conversation with Swift over and over in his head, then tried to think of how he was going to tell Kerry about all of this.

And then he went and got drunk.

His dad might've had cheap taste in liquor, but who cared about the good stuff when your life was draining away before your eyes?

After he found a bottle of bourbon in the liquor cabinet, Ryan settled into his father's favorite armchair and turned it so it looked out at the trees, the lake, all that should be his, one-fifth of it anyway, ready to be cut up and parceled off to the highest bidder. And now?

All those expectations, all those plans. Lost. Gone. And for what? An accident. An *accident*. Because it was the accident that had made his parents suspicious. That's what they said, or Swift said, or someone said. It was said. One mangled girl they were prepared to ignore. But two? That was a pattern.

The thing was, part of him understood their reasoning. The cutting-him-out part, at least. If you thought you had a serial harmer of women in the family, then disinheriting him was the least you could do. But the rest of it? Putting his fate in his sisters' hands? What was the point of that? They should've just turned him in to the police and let the chips fall where they may. The chips, the cards, playing out the deck.

Lord he was drunk.

And then Ryan must've drifted off, because the next thing he knew, the bell was ringing.

It was time for dinner.

Like Mary's hand-raise during the meeting with Swift, the sound of the bell invoked its own Pavlovian response in Ryan. Sean must've been ringing it; it was always Sean who rang it, those firm, even pulls, the last one extra long. Eight pulls, eight bongs, more than enough to get the message across.

Despite the nap, Ryan was still drunk, and now hungry, a bad combination. He'd better get some food in him. He went into his bedroom and rooted around in his bag for a fresh shirt and pants, feeling the ache in his balls from Liddie's knee when he took off his pants, and again when he put on the fresh ones. He added a sweatshirt for good measure, an old one from camp days that he'd packed in a fit of sentimentality.

His phone beeped from the pocket of his pants. He didn't have to look to know it was a text from Kerry.

What's going on? Did they agree to sell?

Ryan concentrated hard to make sure there were no typos in his response.

I'm working on it.

Should I come down? My mother will take the girls.

No, I'm handling it. Got to go. Dinner.

He could see the bubble of Kerry's next text, but he put his phone down before he read it. If he didn't read it, then he didn't have to respond. She'd be pissed, but less so than if she knew the truth, and he didn't trust himself right now not to tell her or tip her off in some other way. Kerry knew him too well.

Ryan placed his hand over his heart; it was still there ticking, beating up against his chest. Why did it feel as if it were missing? Was that simply the space left by his flown-away dreams?

He went to the bathroom, brushed his teeth, and rinsed out his mouth. He patted down his hair with a wet hand and squinted at himself in the mirror. *Close enough,* he thought, if he didn't look too hard. He grabbed a couple of bottles of wine and left.

Outside, dusk was descending. The days were already shorter, the sun down over the lake by the time he got to the lodge. Sunsets were always beautiful at Macaw, but he'd check it out another day. Or maybe not.

Inside the lodge, half the tables were stacked on top of each other along the wall, like they used to be for dances. A table was set in the middle of the room, a bench on either side. One table was all they needed now that it was just the nuclear family and Sean. Always Sean.

"You made it," Margaux said.

Ryan focused on her. "Everyone needs to eat."

"Don't be that way."

"What way?"

She motioned for him to sit next to her. Sean, Liddie, and Mary were sitting on the other side of the table. Kate was in the kitchen helping Amy.

Ryan plunked the bottles of wine he'd snagged from the house on the table.

"Anyone got an opener?"

Mary wrinkled her nose. "Smells like you've had enough to drink already."

"It's fine, Mary," Margaux said. "I could do with a drink."

"The big beers at Twilight weren't enough?"

"How did you . . . ?"

"Sean told me."

"Right. Of course."

Liddie reached for a piece of bread. "White squishy store bread," they'd called it when they were kids, slathering margarine on it in thick layers.

"We had a beer in the middle of the day at the Twilight," Liddie said. "So what? Not the first time."

"How's your ankle, Liddie?" Margaux asked. Ryan wondered what she was talking about. Wasn't it her arm he'd grabbed? Yes, it was. Something else had happened this afternoon while he was brooding, like a TV show that continued when he wasn't there to watch.

"I'll survive."

Ryan grabbed a piece of bread, rolled it up, and ran it into the tub of margarine.

"Gross, Ryan," Margaux said. "Use a knife at least."

He ignored her and stuffed the bread into his mouth. God, that tasted fantastic. He hadn't had a piece of white-flour bread in years. And margarine . . . He wasn't even sure Kerry knew what that was.

Kate and Amy came out of the kitchen carrying a tray of fish sticks and tartar sauce, mixed vegetables, and potatoes. The traditional Friday camp meal, never to vary, no matter what, even when it was only them. Friday fish. As if they were Catholics instead of heathens. Celebrants, instead of sinners.

"This looks great, Amy," Margaux said. "Will you join us?"

Amy blushed. "Oh no, that's fine."

"Please do," Kate said. "You're family."

Amy blushed again, and Ryan got the distinct impression she'd rather eat in the kitchen. But Kate sat down next to Margaux and made space for her, so she took off her apron and joined them.

Sean took his penknife from his pocket and used the corkscrew to open the wine. Everyone passed up their translucent plastic cups, and he poured it out, Ryan noticed, like it was his fucking bottle and not Ryan's.

"You can always count on Sean to have the right tool," he said.

"Oh, hush, Ryan. Honestly," Mary said. "Thank you, Sean."

Liddie stared down into her glass. "What should we toast to?"

"Mom and Dad," Margaux said. "Come on, guys, one last time."

They raised their glasses, knocking them against one another, the plastic making a hollow sound. "To Mom and Dad."

Ryan took half the glass down in one swallow. It was awful. It must be that wine his father had started making from those kits you could get at the wine store. "I can make a whole bottle for twenty-five cents!" he'd told Ryan once, as if that were something to aim for in life. When Ryan was living with them that summer, he'd gone to the wine store and stocked them up properly because spending a summer with his parents and shitty wine was too much.

"What happened to your ankle?" Ryan asked Liddie.

"I twisted it running when Margaux scared me."

"What is it with this family and people sneaking up on each other?" Mary asked.

"That's from Dad," Kate said. "Remember how he used to wait in your room so he could leap out of the closet and get you to jump?" She looked at Amy, nudging her arm. "You remember, Amy. He used to do it to you, too."

Amy looked at her plate. "He used to hide in the food shed."

"That's just bizarre," Liddie said. "A grown man, acting like that."

"He liked his bit of fun," Kate said.

"Look at you," Liddie said. "Defending him."

"Why shouldn't I?"

"Because they used you as cheap labor for ten years, then pulled the rug out from underneath you. For starters."

"Seems like a pattern, doesn't it?" Ryan said. He could tell he was slurring his words, but he didn't care.

No one had anything to say to that. Ryan finished his glass of wine and reached for the second bottle. He was beyond caring what it tasted like.

"So which of you think I did it?"

"Ryan!"

"What, Margaux? Are we supposed to sit here and pretend that it's not what everyone's thinking about?"

"I wasn't thinking about it."

"Right."

"I was thinking about *Amanda*, Ryan, you asshole. Not everything's about you."

Margaux looked as if she was going to cry. That got to him. His whole life, the only thing that ever upset him was a woman crying. Or a girl.

"I'm sorry, okay, I'm sorry."

"Is that a confession?" Liddie asked. "Because that would make everything a whole lot easier."

Ryan caught Amy's eye. She colored again and looked down at her plate.

"You know what's going on, Amy?" Ryan asked.

"Leave her alone," Kate said.

"I'll take that as a yes. Fantastic. Should we let everyone know? Send it out in the next newsletter? Instagram a photo of the letter? I know, let's tell everyone at the memorial on Sunday!"

"Cut it out."

"No, Margaux. I'm allowed to be angry. So yeah, for those of you who didn't know, I admit it, I was there that night, on the Island. We hooked up. Amanda and me. But I'm not the reason she ended up in that boat at Secret Beach. She was alive and well when I left her. I was back in my bunk by one, and Ty can vouch for me. Ty did vouch for me. It's possible to have been with Amanda that night and not be responsible for what happened to her, right, girls?"

He looked back and forth between the twins. They were staring at him with identical looks—dread, anger, guilt.

"We were twelve, Ryan," Liddie said.

"So?"

"You really want to go there?" Liddie said.

Kate reached out to Liddie. "Hush, Liddie. Don't play his game."

"This isn't a game," Ryan said. "This is my life. My future." He pushed back the bench, almost sending Margaux flying to the floor.

"What the hell?"

"You guys should vote," Ryan said.

"What?"

"Now. Vote now."

"We're supposed to vote on Sunday," Mary said.

"So what? You've all made up your minds, haven't you? Let's vote and get it over with so I can go."

"You'd leave?" Kate asked. "Before the memorial?"

Ryan ignored her and stormed into the office. There was a heavy old desk in there, full of colorful Craft Shop papers. He even found a pair of scissors and a box of Sharpies.

He left the office and returned to the table. "You can do it anonymously. No one has to worry about me hurting their feelings. I mean hurting my feelings. Whatever." He picked up the scissors and quickly cut four squares of paper. He gave one to each of his sisters with a Sharpie, then went to the wall near the door and lifted the mailbox off it. "Just write 'guilty' or 'not guilty' on the paper, fold it, and put it in the box. Write it in block letters so I don't know who's who."

"Ryan, come on," Mary said. "Calm down. Eat your dinner. We don't have to do this."

"But we do. We do have to do this. This is what Dad wanted, so let's get it done."

"I'll do it," Liddie said.

"I knew I could count on you. How about you, Kate?"

"I'd rather wait until Sunday."

"Course you would," Liddie said. "How can you make up your own mind if you don't know what everyone else is going to do?"

"Fuck off."

"That's my girl."

Kate grabbed her Sharpie. "Fine, I'll do it. Are you happy?"

Ryan looked at Mary. "Mary?"

"Sure."

"That's it?" Margaux said. "Sure?"

"It's about him, Margaux. He should be able to decide."

"This only works if you all do it, so what do you say, Margaux?"

Margaux looked uncertain.

"Go on," Sean said. "It's for the best."

She picked up her Sharpie. Ryan felt a tight bundle of nerves in his stomach, the liquor and red wine roiling around in a toxic brew. He grabbed a fish stick off his plate and shoved it into his mouth.

"I'll be out on the porch. Call me back in when everyone's votes are in the box."

He picked up his plate and carried it and the second bottle of wine through the screen door. He sat on the rough wood bench against the wall. He ate the rest of his dinner rapidly with his hands, both starving and knowing he needed a layer of food to soak up the alcohol. He'd always hated this dinner. Go figure it would probably be his last one at camp, maybe his last dinner anywhere once Kerry was through with him.

He put his plate down and looked up at the sky. It was fully dark now, and the stars, the stars were amazing.

"Ryan!"

He couldn't tell which of his sisters was calling him back. He stood up, wobbled, steadied himself on the wall. He paused in the doorway, looking at his family. The twins with those same identical looks on their faces. Margaux, resigned. Mary, impenetrable. And the two outsiders, who he knew as well as the rest of them, Sean and Amy. What were they thinking? He met a guy once who worked as a jury consultant, someone who could tell from micro-expressions what decision a person had made before you heard the verdict. But he didn't have that kind of training. He only had his gut telling him that he was out.

He stepped inside. Sean rose and handed him the mailbox. He looked down through the slot. He wondered what had happened to all those letters he'd put through it to his grandparents, deliberately leaving off a stamp or getting the address wrong just to piss off his parents. What a little shit he was. Maybe he did deserve this.

Except he didn't.

He handed the box back to Sean. "You read them."

"You sure, man?"

"Yeah."

Sean opened the lid and pulled out four pink folded pieces of paper.

Kate buried her face in her hands.

"Feeling guilty, twin?" Liddie asked.

"No, I just don't want to look."

Amy patted Kate on the back in a gesture that was both maternal and familiar.

"Read 'em, Sean."

"Read 'em and weep," Margaux said. "Sorry, sorry, old habit."

Sean unfolded the first one. "Guilty."

Ryan felt the bile rise in his throat. The fish sticks were going to taste even worse coming out than they did going down.

"Guilty," Sean read again.

Two down, Ryan thought.

"Guilty."

Kate was crying now, and Ryan felt tears pricking his own eyes. This was it, then.

"There's one more," Mary said.

Ryan unfolded the final piece of paper.

"Read it already," Liddie said.

"Not guilty."

"Oh," Margaux said. "Oh."

"What, Margaux?"

"We're not unanimous. This didn't solve anything."

Ryan sank to his knees, his strength leaving him like when Liddie had knocked him in the balls. No one rose to help him. No one said a word.

The only sound was that of Sean ripping the votes into confetti and the moths, drawn to the ceiling light, hitting the bulbs over and over because they didn't know any better.

SATURDAY

CHAPTER 18

HANGOVERS AND OTHER MIRACULOUS CURES

Margaux

Margaux woke on Saturday morning with a splitting headache to the sound of her cell phone buzzing insistently on the nightstand.

She grabbed it without checking who was calling.

"Hello?"

"I thought you said there wasn't any cell reception?"

She cursed under her breath. It was Mark, because he couldn't trust her, apparently, to tell him the truth. And here he was, being proven right by some errant pocket in the cell network that had allowed his call to come through. She felt angry with both of them, but most of all with herself. For leaving the phone on, for answering it, and for that third bottle of wine she'd retrieved from her parents' stash and drunk after the votes had been tallied. That had been a mistake, but not as big as the fourth bottle had been.

"Normally, there isn't."

"Oh, normally . . ."

"What's that supposed to mean?"

She pushed herself up, and the world started to spin. The sky was barely light outside the gauzy curtains. What time was it, anyway? She checked her watch. It wasn't even seven.

"Nothing, nothing."

"What's going on, Mark?"

He sighed, a long, slow sound she knew too well. She could picture him, sitting at their kitchen table with the phone tucked against his shoulder. He was probably wearing the same shirt he wore to sleep in most nights, full of holes and soft to the touch. When they'd first started dating, she used to steal that shirt, wear it around the house for an entire weekend, happy to be encased in his smell. At some point she'd stopped doing that. And then, a few years later, she'd asked him to throw it away because why did he need to wear a shirt full of holes? He could afford a new one. One that wasn't so bound up in the past.

She had to break up with him, she realized. All she'd been doing since yesterday—no, scratch that, since longer than she could remember—was criticizing and cringing about the most basic aspects of him. His favorite shirt, for Christ's sake. The thing he felt most comfortable in in the world bothered her. That wasn't fair to him, or to her either. But good lord, how was she ever going to do it?

"I miss you," he said.

"I only left yesterday."

"So you don't miss me?"

And then there was that, too, because she didn't. She used to. She used to be the one who would ask him to admit he missed her, who'd get annoyed when he'd smile and be coy about it and say *may-be*. She'd punch him in the shoulder and tell him he was being mean, and then he'd do something, like rub the crick in her neck when she was grading or bring her a cup of tea, that made her know he did miss her, that they were even in their relationship. Where had that feeling gone? Because right now she felt as if she didn't care if she ever saw him again.

What had happened to them?

"I do," she said, because it was easier to lie than to start pulling everything apart. "It's just chaos here."

"Ryan wants to sell?"

"It's more complicated than that."

She got up, thunking her head against the sloped ceiling. "Dammit."

"What happened?"

"I knocked my head."

She rubbed at the spot on her skull that was already rising. She felt an uncharacteristic urge to cry.

"Ouch," Mark said.

"Yeah, ouch."

"Why don't you let me come get you? You don't need to stay there."

"The memorial's tomorrow."

"I'll stay for that, and then we can leave and, I don't know . . . go somewhere."

"Where would we go?"

"How about the Gaspé? We always talked about taking a trip up there."

She put the phone on speaker and put it down on the bedside table. She had one bar of signal. One bar that flickered when she took her hand off the phone, then stabilized. She was naked except for her underwear, her clothes in a rumpled mess on the floor next to the bed. Her head was pounding, from the knock and the alcohol. She felt like shit.

She rummaged in her suitcase for a clean pair of underwear.

"Margie?"

"I'm here."

"You sound far away."

"I put the phone down for a minute."

She swapped out her underwear and slipped on a clean T-shirt.

"What?"

As she picked up the phone, she thought she saw movement outside her window. *What the hell?* She leaned forward to pry it open. She needed both her hands to do it; the window was caked with years of paint. She tucked the phone under her chin and used all her strength to push it up and open. It gave way with a *crack*. She stuck her head outside and looked around. No one was there, though the trees were rustling despite the lack of wind.

"Margie? What's going on?"

"It's nothing. Sorry, I got distracted."

"What about the Gaspé?"

She tried to concentrate on the conversation at hand. Maybe it had been Sean or one of her sisters. No big deal. But yet, with everything, it still sent a shiver down her spine.

"A trip now? We have school."

"We could play hooky for a couple of days."

"You've never played hooky in your life."

"There's always a first time."

She heard another noise outside and froze. She felt exposed, standing there in her underwear and a T-shirt that didn't cover much. She tried to listen past the fuzz in her ears, but once again there was nothing. It was probably one of her sisters, moving around in her sleep. But it didn't sound like it was coming from their room.

It was outside. Definitely outside.

"Marg?"

"Still here."

"It seems like you're a million miles away."

"I've got a lot on my mind."

"What?"

She wanted to end the call, but she knew Mark. The easiest way to get rid of him would be to fill him in and assuage his fears. When all this was done, when it was decided what was happening with Ryan and Sean and the property, she'd end things. Or, she didn't know . . . Did she have to be that drastic? Maybe they could go to therapy and work on it. Figure this out, because that's what people should do when they've spent five years together. Right?

So she told him about the day before, her father's ridiculous letter, the fights, and the vote. She left out the bottles of wine she'd shared with Sean and Mary, sitting around the stone fireplace in the lodge while Sean fed logs one by one into the fire. That was precisely the sort of thing that would get Mark to climb into his ten-year-old Prius and drive to camp, which despite her early morning confusion was the one thing she knew she didn't want.

"You were the not-guilty vote," he said when she finished.

"Yes."

"But he did it, didn't he?"

"No one knows for sure."

"Someone knows."

She chewed at the end of a strand of hair. It smelled like cold fish and bad wine. God, she was hungover. She hadn't had that much to drink in years, and she should've known better, but that was the thing about alcohol, wasn't it? Half a glass of anything bleached away your memories of the last time you drank too much, even if it was the night before. And the other half made the next drink beckon like a fresh lover.

"I guess."

"You should find out. You know, investigate."

"Why?"

"So you can make the right decision."

"I already made my decision."

"You should reconsider. I mean, if Ryan's responsible . . ."

She grimaced at herself in the mirror over the beaten-up dresser she hadn't bothered to put her clothes into. She looked old and worn out, but she was clear enough to know what he was getting at. He'd never liked Ryan because Ryan was the kind of guy who'd probably tortured Mark in high school. But why did Mark care if Ryan got a piece of camp or not? It didn't affect her portion either way.

"You want me to sell this place, don't you?"

He was silent. The birds called to the morning sun, but all Margaux wanted to do was shut it out.

"Jesus, Mark."

"Think of what we could do with the money."

"Ryan's the one who wants to sell. Not Sean."

"Sean will do whatever you ask him to."

She put the phone down again and stared at it. This was exactly why she didn't want to have anything to do with this decision. Why she'd wished for years that her father had extended the trust that had bound him to it and took the decision out of their hands. Instead he'd dropped them all into an Agatha Christie novel, but there wasn't any Hercule Poirot to help them. Not even a Hastings in sight.

Mark's voice continued to rise from the phone.

"You could quit teaching . . ."

She cupped her hand over her mouth. "Mark?"

"I'm here."

"Mark? I'm losing you . . ."

"I'm here; I'm here."

"The signal . . . cutting . . . later . . ."

She reached down and ended the call. A moment later, the bell started to ring.

Amanda

July 23, 1998—Midnight

When Ryan finally broke the kiss, my lips felt bruised. He'd started off slow, we both had, but before long I was pressed up against him, his fingers inside my shirt rubbing the fabric of my bra, then pushing it aside. And then I was in his lap, my legs straddling his hips, feeling his erection through my pants. I didn't feel like myself, and I didn't care. I just wanted this feeling to go on forever.

He laid his head against mine. We were both out of breath.

"I wasn't expecting," he said. "I didn't . . ."

My faced flushed brighter than it already was, and I climbed off him. My underwear felt wet and tacky. I was worried he could smell me, that he'd be disgusted by it. I moved down the rock from him and stared out at the inky lake. The numbers on my watch glowed. It was midnight. It had been half an hour since Ryan arrived. It had taken only thirty minutes to turn me from an innocent girl into a slut. I could hear Margaux's voice telling me not to think of myself that way, but I couldn't help it. My mom would kill me if she knew about this.

Kill me dead, as Margaux and I used to say. Like there was another possible result of killing.

I kept waiting for Ryan to say something, but all he did was pick up a rock and toss it into the water with a sideways throw that sent it skipping once, twice, and then a third time before it sank. I felt like that rock. Tossed aside. Every part of me wanted to sink from view. Maybe the water could take away the heat that was all over my body.

"You okay?" Ryan asked eventually.

"Yes." My voice shook, and I hated myself. This was what Margaux had been warning me about this whole time. Caring about Ryan was a fool's choice, and I'd been fooled.

He came closer to me and lifted a piece of hair away from my neck. "I like this part of you."

He brushed his hand along my skin. I could feel the goose bumps rise under his fingers. Why couldn't I control myself around him? Would I get better at this as time went by?

"Don't worry," he said, his breath tickling me. "We don't have to do anything you don't want to."

I turned. He looked so perfect sitting there, so exactly like I'd imagined him all those nights in my bed, the palm of my hand pressed between my legs, that it didn't feel real.

"That's the problem," I said, more candid than I wanted to be. "There's nothing I don't want to do."

	Amanda	**Margaux**	**Ryan**	**Mary**	**Kate & Liddie**	**Sean**
9:00 p.m.	Lantern ceremony	Lantern ceremony	Lantern ceremony			
10:00 p.m.	On the Island	On the Island		On the Island		Crash boat
11:00 p.m.	Back Beach	Back Beach	Back Beach	On the Island		
Midnight	Back Beach		Back Beach			
6:00 a.m.	Secret Beach				Secret Beach	

CHAPTER 19

MARY, MARY, QUITE CONTRARY

Mary

Mary was in the barn when the bell rang. That same, sharp eight beats Sean had been sounding out for as long as he'd been at camp. It felt as if it were ringing in her head. That was because of the alcohol. She didn't drink much these days, never had. But last night, she'd felt like drinking. Felt like being someone other than herself. Doing something different. Sitting there in the lodge, with Margaux and Sean, watching the fire: that had been almost perfect.

She'd woken without the need of an alarm, long before the bell, years of training overcoming the lack of sleep. She'd dressed silently in the house, Ryan's snores loud enough to cover the quiet tread of her feet. She walked up the tranquil road to the barn. These early mornings were one of the things she loved about riding. The need to rise. The way the day greeted you. The fresh smell of the hay in the barn.

Cinnamon was glad to see her, eager for her morning exercise. She could easily imagine the same scene at her own barn, a few miles away, where the camp's eight horses were now stabled for the winter. She'd brought them over to her barn last weekend. She'd asked a stable hand to look after them for the weekend so she didn't have to go back and forth. Next week, a truck was coming to collect and move the camp hay.

She watered Cinnamon, saddled up, and climbed on. They'd taken the old path up behind the barn. It hadn't been cleared properly this year, and so they'd picked their way through it, ducking under low-lying branches and skirting downed logs.

She turned around on instinct when they reached the boundary line. The land next door was still a working farm, one of the last in the area. The Carters would have a fight similar to theirs when the next generation inherited.

Though not quite the same. No, the MacAllisters had always done things differently.

She still couldn't quite believe the steps her father had taken. To have thought that all these years about Ryan, and to have never said a thing. Had Ryan always been their prime suspect? Or had they gone through all of them, one by one? Swift had said that her mother didn't know about the plan, and Mary could believe it. Her mother was too watercolored to have turned her mind to such a gory topic. "It's easier to ignore than to engage" had been her mother's sage advice when Mary was being bullied in elementary school. As if you could control whether you were bullied or not by having the will to ignore the taunts. She didn't blame her mother though. Being invisible had worked well for her. Why not her children?

The barn came back into view. Traditional, red. Raised by some long-forgotten farmers whose names were faded entries on the property register. Inside were generations of carvings from her family and those who came before. Names in hearts. Declarations of independence. An honor roll of winning show horses. Faded ribbons from the events she'd attended so many years ago. Her mother had introduced her to the love and care of horses in this barn. How to brush a coat. How to gentle. They'd spent hours together here, mostly quiet, away from view.

Being invisible.

Maybe that's why she was the only one of them who was close to their mother growing up. Her parents were of the generation that didn't believe in being friends with your children. They were there for support and discipline, and whether they liked you or not was not part of the equation. Though it had frustrated Mary at times, it had never bothered her the way it did the rest of the kids. It was only as an adult that she'd had regrets; too late to change now. Perhaps if she'd known her father better, if they all had, he wouldn't have felt able to punish them in this way. Even though it was Ryan who was on the outs, they were all being put on trial. What kind of father would do that to his children?

But of course she knew what kind of father he was: the kind who'd raised someone who could take a blunt instrument to Amanda's head.

Mary guided Cinnamon into the last paddock before the barn. When they were halfway through it, something spooked her. Cinnamon reared up and almost spilled her to the ground. She gripped Cinnamon's mane, her heart pumping.

"Shhh, girl. Shhh."

She patted her neck and spoke softly as the horse pawed at the ground. There was something by the fence that she didn't want to go near.

"Is someone there?" Mary called out, but the only response she received was the slight echo of her own voice against the red broadside of the barn. When they were small, before the twins followed them everywhere, she and Margaux used to run through the building, calling each other's names and laughing as the barn answered back for them.

She slid off Cinnamon's back and lifted the reins over her head so she could lead her on foot. She patted the white blaze above Cinnamon's muzzle. "It's okay, girl. No one's there."

But even as she said this, the hair on the back of her neck stood up. She was so used to being alone that she had a sixth sense when someone else was around, as if she could feel the displacement of the air, the extra mass of another person.

"Ryan?" she asked the fence. "Sean?"

Because it was a man she was sensing, that earthy smell they seemed to have, still clinging to them from when they were boys, tickling her nostrils.

Cinnamon neighed behind her, egging her on.

"Come on, whoever it is, this isn't funny."

Mary was up on her tiptoes now, tensed and ready not to react when whoever it was jumped out of his hiding place. A MacAllister family specialty, that was. The terrifying of one another. She never understood the appeal.

She reached the fence. The buzz of crickets filled her ears. She felt almost dizzy. The grass was long up against the barn, bleached out by the summer, the kind of rough you'd lose a thousand golf balls in. She stood as still as she could. She knew someone was there; she could swear she could hear him breathing. But where was he? What was he doing? Why wouldn't he show himself?

Cinnamon neighed behind her again, louder this time, a warning. There was a sound like a shot behind her. She turned on instinct, but again, nothing. She took another step forward, and now she was at the fence. She held it with shaking hands and swung it open. *Swoosh!* A large bird took flight, its wing brushing against Mary's face. She muffled a scream. She felt her knees buckle. She leaned against the fence, closing her eyes. It was okay. It was nothing. Only a bird, a bird.

She regulated her breathing and opened her eyes. There was a dog standing there, its tongue out, a white spot around its left eye. *Buster.* Buster, her parents' half-feral dog. He must've been what Cinnamon was reacting to, the breathing she'd heard earlier. She recognized it now, that half pant, half wheeze that had led her parents to put him out of doors in the first place because her father claimed he couldn't sleep with that sound in the house.

Mary brushed the grass off her riding pants, her hands unsteady. Terrified by a bird and the family dog.

What was this place doing to her?

Maybe I'm lonely, Mary thought as she walked down the road after stabling Cinnamon, her riding boots kicking up dust. It wasn't something she thought about often, other people, what she was missing keeping to herself. Especially these last few years. She had her horses and her students, the occasional talk with a parent who wanted a detailed update on how their precious daughter was doing. That felt like enough contact most of the time.

But then last night, staying up late, talking to the two people who knew her best . . . that felt like something else. Like something reminding her of what her life could be, rather than what it was.

She wasn't sure why she deprived herself of other people. She and Margaux used to be as close as they were in age. "Irish twins," people called them, until the real twins came along and ruined everything. But that closeness had evaporated over the years. Maybe it was Mary's fault, maybe Margaux's.

Probably Mary's. After all, she could hang out with Sean whenever she wanted; he was only a few miles away. But she'd trained herself not to think of that, to ration out her contact with him.

And there, as if she'd conjured him with her thoughts, was Sean, standing on the porch, the gong of the morning bell still clinging to the air. Even though he was dressed like he always was, he looked older than forty-five. The years between them somehow felt larger than they ever had when they were all at camp together.

Sean saw her and waved. She waved back. Had she said something last night she regretted? Her memory was hazy.

She didn't go to him. Instead, she turned left toward the Craft Shop. She wasn't sure what drew her there, other than that it was the place she'd spent the most time in outside the barn. They all took after their mother this way, drawn to the arts. She liked working with paper and glue, the colors that could take shape with a bit of application.

Like the rest of camp, the building was made of thick plywood. Not a building that was palatable anytime but summer. She flicked on the lights. One side was devoted to crafts, the floor covered with a confetti of paint. On the other wall was a long row of rough bookshelves. Generations of paperbacks and hardcovers, leftover books from childhood tossed together with the leavings of forty years of leadership groups. Grisham mixed with Rowling. *Robinson Crusoe* and *A Is for Alibi*.

She ran her hand along the spines, feeling the words through the covers. Here was her favorite book, one she'd read countless times as a child. *The Secret Garden*. She'd always felt an affinity for strange little Mary Lennox. She was strange little Mary MacAllister, "Mary, Mary, Quite Contrary," as Margaux called her when she was annoyed with something Mary had done.

The door creaked behind her. This time, she knew who it was without looking.

She was both scared again and not.

CHAPTER 20

I SPY WITH MY LITTLE EYE

Kate

Liddie and Kate were rummaging around their parents' basement when they heard the eight clear gongs of the morning bell.

Liddie had pulled Kate from bed before the sun was up, tugging her like she was a small child who had to get to school on time. Shoving clothes at her and telling her to "Hurry up" and "Keep quiet" so they didn't wake Margaux. Kate didn't think that was possible given how much Margaux had had to drink the night before. She'd heard Margaux rattling around the cottage when she'd come in, around one, the time of night at camp that Kate always thought of as the witching hour. It was hard to explain, but Kate never saw two a.m. here. You either went to bed at one or you were up at three; two was as mythical as the lake monster that people had claimed to be spying since the 1950s.

Kate was pissed that Margaux had woken her. She was a light sleeper, a troubled sleeper, and nighttime disturbances usually led to several hours staring at the ceiling. Last night, those hours ended up being a reminder that she wasn't where she wanted to be, in bed with Amy. She knew Amy was sleeping upstairs in the lodge, in one of those small cells with a single bed down the hall from Sean, but she didn't care. It wasn't like her bed in the French Teacher's Cabin was so comfortable or welcoming.

She'd tried to pull Amy aside last night after the fracas with Ryan. She suggested they visit their old haunt, the nurse's cabin, but Amy had refused. She was tired, she said. She wanted to sleep. And "there's no use in starting all that again." Amy had never told her no before, not a definitive no like that. But she supposed she deserved it for the way she'd left after her parents had rejected her. She'd tried to convince Amy to come with her, back then, to move to Montreal, but she had her son and her family nearby and, ultimately, they were "something that only worked at camp." Kate hadn't fought her. Instead, she'd left and never called again, and so there she was, alone, awake, full of regrets.

Then morning. Then Liddie. Kate's breath had fogged around her face as they walked up the road in the semidarkness. It started getting cold at night in mid-August. Kate cursed herself for not bringing warmer clothes. Then again, she didn't know she'd be creeping around before the sun was up, though she should've guessed. It was par for the course with Liddie.

The light was pearl gray, the evergreens a dusky black. High, thin clouds wisped through the sky, signaling the near certain arrival of rain.

Liddie held a finger to her lips when they got to the house, mumbling something about Ryan and "even though he's probably passed out for the day," they'd better not take any chances. She tried to get Liddie to tell her what was going on, but Liddie tugged her arm again, and then they were inside, surrounded by the smell of old smoke and dank basements. Liddie snapped on the desk lamp, one of those kitschy lava lamps from the sixties Kate had always hated. It made a wavy pattern on the wall that made her feel queasy.

"What are we going to do with all this stuff?" Kate asked. "I doubt even Goodwill would want it."

"I'm thinking 1-800-GOT-JUNK."

"Don't you want to keep anything?"

"Do you?"

She wished she could say yes, that there were memories here she wanted to hold on to. There probably were, but she wasn't willing to sift through the 99 percent of it that she didn't want to find the pearl. She wasn't a discount shopper—she couldn't stand to spend hours riffling through rows of clothes that might be a great deal but were mostly a load of crap. She'd rather one-click her way through her favorite online stores, the slight updates in style enough change for her.

"I guess not."

"I'm sure the others will agree." Liddie walked to the wall of cheap bifold doors and pulled them open, revealing a barely contained mountain of boxes and file folders. She reached in and took out a stack.

"What are you doing?"

"Looking for Dad's case files."

"His what?"

Liddie gave her a look. "You know, the files he put together on the things he was investigating."

Kate had a flash of memory—coming downstairs late at night in search of her father to ask him a question about something to do with the staff. He was sitting at his desk, his face blued by the lava lamp, then purpled, like a quickly advancing bruise. There were pictures tacked on the wall over his desk and a large piece of paper in front of him that contained an elaborate diagram. Names and places in circles and stars. Arrows and deeply pressed lines pointing out connections. When she'd spoken, he'd turned the page over and had acted as if what Kate had seen was normal. She'd done what she always did, brushed it off, asked her question, and went back to Amy without giving it too much thought.

That was probably a good summary of her life, her epitaph: *Kate MacAllister. She never gave anything too much thought.*

"You think he investigated what happened to Amanda?"

"Didn't he say he had in that letter?"

Liddie put the papers down on the floor. The pile slid and spread out across the dingy carpet like a deck of cards. She ran a hand through her short hair, already sticking up and out like a fan.

"This might take a while."

Kate sat next to the pile of papers. The basement smelled vaguely like pot, a smell she'd never liked and appreciated even less at six a.m.

She picked up a file folder. *Stephanie* was written on the side in her father's oddly formal block lettering. "Are these camper files?"

Liddie glanced up from the file she was looking through. "I think so."

She opened the folder. It contained a picture of a girl she vaguely remembered who'd spent two summers at camp before getting expelled for repeatedly being found in the boys' section late at night. This must have been one of her mother's pictures. Her mother was the family photographer, and she kept an archive of the photographs she took every summer, her own set of much more neatly organized files that were in the metal cabinets under the stairs, ordered by year.

Kate held up the picture. "Do you remember her?"

"Stephanie Stephens, right? She was screwing Jack Cider and his friends. That's why she got kicked out."

"I don't think that's why."

"That's totally why. They had a threesome or something. It was pretty fucked up because some other kid was watching."

Kate scanned the notes her father had left, and yes, that's what had happened. And even though it seemed to Kate that Stephanie was a victim, not of rape, technically, but certainly of gross manipulation, she was sent home along with the boys because they were afraid the story would get out and circulate among the campers.

"How did you know that? We were, like"—she checked the date—"eleven when this happened."

"How did you *not* know?"

"Because I didn't hide under the stairs to listen in on people."

"Don't judge me."

"I'm not judging."

"Of course you are. You always do."

Kate looked away. Why did things have to be like this between them? It was like fighting with yourself. Other twins she knew still dressed the same as adults, but her whole life, she always felt as if Liddie was trying to get away from her, deny their shared DNA except for when it suited her purposes, like getting her to participate in one of her stupid schemes. Once, after they'd watched this documentary about how people who thought they were identical twins were wrong, she'd even wanted them to take a DNA test. "Maybe we're just *fraternal* twins," she'd said. As if that would be a good thing.

"Why would Dad keep all this stuff?"

"Who knows."

Kate turned a page. The top of the sheet read *Timeline*. It started the year Stephanie came to camp and ended when she left. "It's like he was investigating her, even before this happened."

"Maybe he was."

"Gross."

Liddie shrugged. "Dad was kind of gross sometimes. Didn't Amanda say that she'd found him peering into her cabin once?"

"When did she say that?"

"That summer, I think."

"Why wouldn't she tell anyone?"

"She was telling someone."

"Who, you?"

"Mom, I think. Sean might've been there also."

"That's weird."

"Please. He was always following her and Margaux around."

Kate thought about it. Was the memory she had of Sean lurking on the fringe of the duo Margaux and Amanda formed something she'd created at Liddie's suggestion or a real memory? "Yeah, that rings a bell."

"Rings a bell? God, you're so weird sometimes. It's like you weren't even at camp even though you were always at camp."

"Just because I focused on other things . . ."

"Whatever." Liddie stood up and went back to the closet. She started pulling out more boxes. "We should get rid of all this stuff."

"Probably."

"Enthusiastic much?"

"Quit it, Liddie."

"You're so sensitive . . . Aha. Bingo."

Liddie pulled out a box from the back. It was heavy, and she half dragged it along the floor. Kate could see the name *Stacey* scrawled across the top.

"Who's Stacey?" Kate asked, feeling stupid. Maybe Liddie was right. She was supposed to be the one for whom camp was inevitable, a part of her skin. And yet, try as she might, she couldn't think of a single camper who was ever named Stacey. It had to be her parents' fault. The shock of their betrayal must've erased her memories, created something like a blackout. How else to explain the gaps in her knowledge, the things Liddie took for granted? Or the lingering sense that she had something to hide?

Liddie was looking at her as if she were losing her mind. And she might be, because the last thing she expected Liddie to say was:

"Stacey Kensington. Jesus, Kate. Don't tell me you've forgotten the girl Ryan killed ten years ago?"

CHAPTER 21

HANGING AROUND, DOWNTOWN BY MYSELF

Ryan

That name—*Stacey Kensington*—got Ryan's attention. It had been both a long time and no time at all since he'd thought about her. She lived with him, haunted him, the way nothing else in his life did, even Amanda.

He'd come to that morning in his parents' bed rather than his own, flat on his back, still in his clothes, to the loudly ringing bell, and then to the sound of his sisters talking. That felt like the default setting of his life—his sisters' voices, always one of them speaking, often several of them at once. Now they'd been replaced by the voices of his daughters and his wife. A lifetime surrounded by women's voices; you'd think he'd be used to it.

He'd known, somehow, when he and Kerry decided to have kids that he'd have daughters, and he was good with that. Kerry had wanted boys; she thought they'd be easier, safer. She'd been disappointed when they'd learned the sex of each of their girls, doubly so when Ryan had put his foot down after Sasha was born and said that three was enough. He wanted to be able to focus on each of them, both because they were his daughters and he loved them, and also because, goddammit, he was going to be a better father than his own.

He wanted the best for his daughters for many reasons, but one of them was Stacey.

That was probably warped—ensuring three good lives to replace one life taken—but he didn't know what else to do. He couldn't change what had happened. Life didn't work like that.

He lay there and listened to his sisters talking in the basement. He could hear them clearly through the grate above the bed, something he never knew before, but it explained a lot. All his life, his parents had this way of knowing things they weren't supposed to, especially during the summer. Ryan had always thought they gleaned their information from counselors. Stoolies. But if they could hear what was going on in the basement this whole time by simply lying in bed . . . Ryan's stomach rolled over at the thought of his parents listening in on some of the things he'd gotten up to in the basement. Jesus.

"The girl Ryan killed ten years ago . . . ," Liddie said. That came through clearly and drove him up and out of the room. He nearly didn't make it to the bathroom in time, the vomit barely contained by the hand he'd slapped against his mouth.

He raised the lid on the toilet bowl and hunched over. Everything he had inside left as he heaved and heaved. When he was finally done, he felt weak in the knees. He sat on the edge of the tub and watched his hands shaking. A mistake, a mistake, a stupid mistake.

Will I never be free of this?

He was still sitting there twenty minutes later, when he heard his phone buzzing from the bedroom. Kerry. While he wasn't in control of most of the details in his life these days, he did know one thing: ignoring her was a bad idea.

He pried himself off the floor and padded down the hall. His head was pounding, and he felt embarrassed by his own smell. He needed to make a change, a serious one. Stop drinking, at the very least, but probably something more fundamental.

The text was floating on his iPhone's screen.

Call me.

He reached for the landline. It was off the hook. He had no recollection of having done that. Perhaps he'd knocked it off in the night.

"What's going on?" Kerry said before the phone had even completed its first ring.

"I'm getting a late start."

He looked at the clock. It was only seven thirty. He picked up his iPhone. He'd missed four texts from Kerry. No wonder she was in a panic. He both loved and hated his phone. Mostly, he wished he could have both its access to the internet and be free from the constraint of people knowing he had it with him at all times.

"I mean, early."

"What are you talking about? I texted you a million times last night. And then I called and you hung up on me."

"I did?"

Ryan had no memory of talking to Kerry. The last thing he remembered was the vote. Oh God. The vote. Fuck. He was completely fucked.

"Someone did, anyway. The receiver picked up, and then it was put down and no one was there."

"I'm sorry, I don't know what happened. It was . . . a rough night."

Kerry's tone softened. "I knew you'd go all, 'I love you, man.' "

"Ha. Yes. You were right. You know me too well."

Ryan's brain was whirring. He knew how to do this: make up to Kerry after he'd been bad. *Ask her what she's wearing. No, wait. Ask her how she is.*

"How are you?"

"What?"

"How are you? What are you and the girls up to today?"

Kerry paused for a moment, and he could tell that she was wondering if this was a trap. A diversion. "They have that water park thingy for Maisy's friend's birthday."

Ryan reached deep for a name.

"Cristal?"

"That's right."

"Do they all want to go?"

"They're dying to."

"Are you talking to Daddy? I want to talk to Daddy!" Maisy's voice was as loud as the bell Sean had pulled with extra force that morning. Ryan winced, but his heart warmed at the thought of her. He'd done something right in this world. One thing. Three.

"Maisy wants to talk to you."

"Put her on."

"Hi, Daddy!"

"Hi, sweetheart. How are you?"

"We're going to the water park!"

"I know. That sounds like super fun."

"It's going to be super fun. Only, Daddy?"

"What is it?"

"Mommy said I couldn't wear a two-piece bathing suit, and all the other girls are going to be wearing them, and I don't want to be a freak."

"Holy shit." That came through the grate, loud and clear. Ryan could only imagine what they were getting up to down there. What they were discovering.

"You said a bad word!"

"I think that was one of your aunts."

"I bet it was Aunt Liddie."

"What makes you say that?"

"Mommy always says she's up to no good."

Ryan smiled, both at the image of his daughter doing a dead-on impersonation of his wife and the truth of it. The normalcy. On Thursday—less than forty-eight hours ago—he'd woken up with two of the girls in the bed between him and Kerry, and they'd had a goddamn *tickle fight*. He'd felt so happy then, so sure everything was about to be on track. He should've known better. It wasn't the first time his life had changed in a flash. A bang.

A scream.

"Put your mom back on the phone."

"You'll ask her about the bathing suit?"

"We'll see. But listen to what she tells you."

"Oh-kay."

"I love you."

"Love you more."

"Not possible."

Maisy giggled and handed off the phone.

"She can't wear that bathing suit," Kerry said.

"I know."

"I don't know what's wrong with the other mothers. I never wore a two-piece until I was in college!"

"You looked great in it though."

Ryan could remember it exactly, that first summer he'd met Kerry. It was family day, and she'd come with her parents to visit her younger brother. They'd had a swim race to the Island, and Kerry had stepped right out of her dress, revealing a black two-piece that fit her nineteen-year-old body perfectly. She dove into the water with grace and came in second, right behind Ryan. Later, after the bonfire, he'd snuck her into the woods and kissed her against a tree until she complained about the dents the bark was leaving on her back. She was the first girl he'd done anything with since Amanda.

But not the last.

"Oh, stop it."

"It's true. You still do."

He heard his sisters again in the basement. Less distinctive this time. He needed to get off this call and find out what they were up to. But it was nice lingering with his family for a moment, remembering what he was fighting for.

"How is everything going there?" Kerry asked.

"No surprises."

"Really?"

"Nope."

"So how is everyone going to vote?"

"Vote?"

"On whether to sell the property? Hello?"

"Right, sorry. About how you'd expect."

"Mary, no. Margaux, maybe. Kate, no. Liddie, yes."

"That's about right."

"So it's not happening."

Kerry sounded strangely defeated. Ryan's heart squeezed. He reached up and rubbed his chest. He could fix this. He could.

"I'll convince them."

"You will?"

"Yes. I have to, right?"

"We'd be okay if you don't. My parents could help."

He closed his eyes. He felt strangely like crying, something he hadn't done since Maisy had broken her arm in two places at her birthday party the summer he wasn't living at home. She and the other girls had been so wild in the bouncy castle they'd rented, and then there was this sickening shriek. He'd stayed calm through the whole thing, though he felt sick to his stomach at the sight of her arm so out of whack. Then afterward, when her arm was set in a white cast, and she held it out to him to sign it, that was when he lost it.

"You know I don't want to have to rely on them."

"That's what family's for, isn't it?"

Ryan sat there in silence. Could he do this? Could he take money from Kerry's parents and simply forget about camp? No, he couldn't. They'd constantly remind him of the loan, making him feel like a failure. He had to fix this on his own.

"You all right?" Kerry asked.

"Sure."

"Maybe less drinking today?"

"Less drinking definitely."

The twins were talking again. Ryan strained to hear what they were saying. Were they still discussing Stacey? What else was in that basement?

"I'll talk to you later?" Ryan said.

"You promise?"

"Of course."

What was one more broken promise, anyway?

CHAPTER 22

CRAFTING

Sean

"Hi, Mary," Sean said as he entered the Craft Shop. Though he said it quietly, he saw Mary's shoulders twitch. Why was this everyone's reaction to him? Even after the closeness of last night? Why was his existence always such a *surprise*?

"Hey, Sean."

She turned. She was in riding clothes. Tight suede-colored pants, tall brown boots that shone with care, a white polo, and a loose jacket. Her uniform. He always thought of her this way, though he knew she wore other clothes. The one thing that was different from usual was the color of her skin. Mary was generally as tanned as he was, and he could've sworn she was yesterday. But today, she looked pale. Like she'd been indoors all summer, or ill.

"You feeling as rough as I am?" he asked. Truth be told, he'd had trouble making his routine that morning. He'd woken at 6:45 as usual, but his tongue felt thick in his mouth despite the vigorous brushing he'd given his teeth the night before. He'd felt like turning over and going back to sleep, but he'd made it. Rung the bell on time, greeted the day with regret. He needed to start exercising, he thought. Do something to push back against the number fifty, which was closer than he liked to think. He didn't have a father to model himself on, as far as what could happen to his body if he didn't take care of it. It was better if he erred on the side of caution.

"I'm fine," she said, though her lips were cracked and still slightly stained from the red wine.

"I'm impressed."

"Thanks."

She was holding a book. *The Secret Garden.* He recognized it right away. It was his mother's copy, or one that looked exactly like it. She'd tried to get him to like that book, but it was a "girl book," he'd said. He still regretted telling her that.

"I bet Ryan's a mess," Mary said. "And Margaux."

"It was stupid. We shouldn't do that again."

"I had fun," she said, jutting out her chin. The long blonde braid of her hair was hanging over her shoulder. When she had her back to him, she could've been fifteen again. But front-on, she was the one who'd aged the most of them. Or maybe that was him. Why was he up in his head so much this morning? It had to be the alcohol, still working its way through his system.

"What about you?" she asked. "Did you have fun?"

"It's always fun to hang out with you guys. You know that."

Mary frowned. Sean was pretty sure he knew why. He never used to notice her much; growing up, his attention always pulled to Margaux. Was that a mistake? Mary was much more like him. Compact. Quiet. Maybe they could've—

"You don't have to say that."

"I mean it."

"No, you don't, but that's okay. You got to hang with Margaux, right? That must've been nice."

Sean felt the heat rise in his cheeks. Did everyone know, then? What was in his heart? What he'd wished for for so long? What he'd risked everything to get?

"Has it been weird for you, living here without them?"

Sean considered her question as he watched her hands on his mother's book. She'd been so mad at him when he'd refused to let her read it to him. *I don't want to hear about stupid Mary and her garden!* Those were maybe the last words he'd said to her.

They'd been living in what must've originally been a garden shed in the back of the Twilight. There were places like that in small towns all over Quebec, ones they'd visit every three months or so, as his mother shifted through the circuit. She'd always measure his height right when they arrived, searching for the mark they'd left the last time.

Sean hadn't understood it at the time, their peripatetic life. That was the word Mr. MacAllister had used—*peripatetic*—and Sean had had to look it up. "Traveling from place to place, especially working or based in various places for relatively short periods." That's what the dictionary told him. And he supposed that was right, once he pieced his childhood together. All the seedy bars they lived near or above. His mother's odd wardrobe, made up mostly of fishnet stockings and long white shirts. How there was always mascara in the corners of her eyes even if she'd just taken a shower. That smell that clung around her like a perfume, only it was skunky, masculine.

And the men. Always so many men.

"Sean? Did you hear me?"

"Yes, sorry. It's been different, that's for sure."

"You miss them."

"Is that so weird?"

"No, it's the rest of us who are weird."

"You don't miss them?"

"Honestly? No, not exactly. That's pretty awful, isn't it?"

"I've never understood you kids."

"We aren't kids anymore."

"What's that got to do with it?"

He was angry now. The MacAllister children were a bunch of . . . selfish . . . ungrateful . . . This was the kind of language his mother had always used. His mother, the prostitute. It made him sick to think of her that way. To imagine all the men who'd used her, and the awful truth that he was probably the reason she needed to do that in the first place. And then to be confronted with the fact that Mary and the others couldn't care less about what happened to camp. It was too much.

"What did you want to say?" Mary asked.

"It's nothing."

"No, come on. You want to say something, I can tell."

Sean looked down at his hands. They were balled into fists, the knuckles white on the outside.

"I just don't understand you. You grew up in this great place and went to good schools, and your parents, they weren't perfect, but they did the best they could. They stuck around. They fed you. They loved you. And you'd have thrown that all away, all of you, to have different parents. Just because your dad was weird sometimes, and maybe your mom wasn't the most maternal person. Yeah, I know what you all thought about them. They did too, you know? And it hurt them. You hurt them."

Sean felt out of breath but exhilarated. He'd wanted to say something like this for so long. And Mary's reaction—eyes staring out of her head—was also worth it. He was only sorry that everyone hadn't been around when he finally let go. He wasn't sure he could get the words out again.

"Tell me how you really feel," Mary said quietly. "Don't hold back."

"I'd like my book back."

"What?"

"That book," he said, pointing to *The Secret Garden*. "That's mine."

"This is mine from when I was a kid."

"No. It was mine first."

He crossed the distance between them in a bound and took it from her hands. This felt good. He should've done this years ago. Decades.

"See?" He flipped it open to the cover page where his mother's name—*Dorothy*—was written in faded ink. Someone had crossed through it and written the name *MacAllister*. Of course they had. That's exactly what had happened to him.

Crossed out and replaced by a MacAllister.

"Who's Dorothy?"

"That's my mother."

"Oh," Mary said, and Sean knew that someone had told her all about his mother, the thing he thought no one knew except for Mr. and Mrs. MacAllister, who'd saved him when she'd died in one of the squalid rooms above the Twilight, a needle in her arm, vomit trailing down her chin.

Sean had found her like that, early in the morning, when he'd awakened in the garden shed and hadn't been able to find her. He hadn't woken up anyone else in the building, hadn't called the police, even though his mother had told him to always find a grown-up and how to dial the numbers that would bring help if he needed it. Instead, he'd taken off running down the road and had almost collided with Mr. MacAllister's car.

"She was a good person," Sean said.

"I didn't know her."

"She was a good person. And this was hers."

Sean was standing too close to Mary now. She smelled like the barn, like hay and horses and manure. It wasn't unpleasant, not to Sean, but there was something else mixed in that hit him like a gut punch.

Fear.

CHAPTER 23

BINGO

Liddie

"Ryan's up," Kate said, about half an hour after the morning bell had rung.

Liddie stopped what she was doing and listened. Kate was right; she could hear the murmur of Ryan's voice through the grate in the ceiling.

"Who's he talking to?"

"Kerry, I think."

Liddie walked over to the phone on the desk. She lifted it gently. This was one of the bad things about cell phones; the opportunities to listen in on other people's conversations were greatly diminished since everyone had given up their landlines.

"Liddie!"

"Shhh!"

Kate made a slashing motion across her throat, then mouthed, *Cut it out.* Liddie mouthed back, *What?* Kate took the receiver from her hand. She put in back in the cradle gently.

"Why'd you do that? Now we won't know what he's saying to Kerry."

"We're not supposed to know. It's private."

"Please."

"We should get out of here."

"But we haven't found what we're looking for yet."

"I think I found it," Kate said. She went to the box she'd been looking through and pulled out a file that was thick with newspaper reports and the distinctive color-coded stickies their father used to note important facts. "Everything in here is about Amanda. Well, and the rest of us, it looks like, but lots about Amanda."

"Why didn't you say so before?"

"I didn't have time. Anyway, let's go, okay? I don't feel like talking to Ryan right now."

Liddie couldn't help but smile. "Are you scared of him?"

"No, not exactly."

"You are."

Kate grabbed Liddie's arm and tugged her toward the exit. An hour ago in reverse. They were the inside-out of each other, for good or for bad.

"That hurts!"

Kate kept pulling, so Liddie had no choice but to follow her or twist away like she'd been taught in her self-defense class. She'd already used a self-defense move on one member of her family this weekend; two in two days seemed excessive.

When they were outside, Kate let her go. It was already much hotter than an hour before, a blast of Indian summer. But were they even allowed to use that term anymore? Liddie didn't know and didn't care.

"If I'd known you were this assertive this whole time, I would've used you more."

"Used me more for what?"

Something caught Liddie's eye. She looked up. Ryan was standing in the window, shirtless, looking down at them. She waved out of instinct, then dropped her hand.

"Come on, let's get out of here."

They headed for the Craft Shop but stopped short and hid behind a tree when first Sean and then a few moments later a shaken-looking Mary emerged.

"What do you think that's about?" Kate whispered into her ear.

"No idea."

"Why are we hiding?"

"I don't want to get into it with them."

They stayed quiet, watching Sean walk toward the beach and Mary into the lodge. When everyone was out of sight, they scurried to the Craft Shop. Liddie felt like she used to when they were kids and she was dragging Kate around camp during off hours to get up to some harebrained scheme. Like the morning they found Amanda in the boat on Secret Beach. Working on a craft project was what they'd told their parents and the police they were doing, but that wasn't the truth.

It was cooler in the Craft Shop; the bare bulb in the ceiling was still on. Liddie shivered. A ghost walking on her grave. That's what they used to call it. But there weren't any ghosts. There were only the things you couldn't leave behind.

"Everything okay?" Kate asked.

"It's fine. Let's do this."

"What is *this*, exactly?"

She looked at the box Kate had placed on the floor. Newspaper clippings; photographs; colored pieces of paper; thick, official documents. Where to begin?

"Dad used to look for patterns. Maybe if we tack all this stuff up, we can figure out what he saw?"

"Like on *CSI*?"

"You have a better idea?"

"Nope."

"I guess we have a plan, then."

Liddie began clearing a space on the wall, taking down leftover finger paintings and intricate macramé wind catchers that might've been in place since they were children, based on the faded shapes left on the wall.

Maybe there were ghosts, after all.

"Can you find some thumbtacks?" she asked Kate, who was standing in front of the bookshelf. "The Bookshelf of Lost Books," they called it when they were children, because it was a collection put together from all the books other kids had left behind over the years. Nothing was new, they always said. Nothing was only theirs. They always got the leftovers. The things left in the lost-and-found.

If Liddie wrote a biography of her childhood, it would be called *Nothing Was Ever Mine*.

Kate brought over a rainbow container of thumbtacks, and they started pinning random pieces of paper onto the wall. As Kate had said, the files weren't exclusively about Amanda, at least not obviously. There was information about all of them. Liddie pocketed a couple of pieces of paper that surprised her while Kate was riffling through the box. She wanted time to decide what to do about them.

"Look," Kate said as she tacked up an article about Owen to the board.

"That's Owen."

"You gonna marry a rock star?"

"I don't know, maybe."

"What does he have to do with any of this?"

"Nothing. He didn't even come to camp till the summer after."

Liddie met Owen when they were thirteen. She'd followed him around like the snoop she was, sensing even then that there was something exciting about him. Something from the future, though she would've killed anyone who said that out loud, including herself. In fact, once she'd had that thought, she spent the next three summers deliberately not talking to him, because if she talked to him, then maybe he'd know how she felt or Kate would or, worse, Margaux or Mary, and that wasn't something she could tolerate. So she stayed out of his way and watched him when no one was looking. Most of the time, she was sure he didn't know she existed.

He'd worked one summer as a groundskeeper, and then moved on. *That's that,* Liddie thought as she watched the staff bus drive off and tucked him away.

The next time she'd seen him was years later in Grand Teton National Park. It had been a weird day; two strangers had offered her leftover items of food as they were packing up their camps. Some garlic butter, cheese, mayonnaise. That was one lady. Then lighter fluid from a grungy guy who was driving a $120,000 camper van. She felt weird taking the things—what was this, a commune?—but did it anyway because it seemed like the right etiquette. And then, when she was sitting by Jackson Lake, the air full of the smell of melting snow, staring at the most amazing view she'd ever seen in her life, she'd heard her name.

"Liddie MacAllister. No way."

She'd shielded her eyes, certain she was dreaming. It was Owen. He looked the same, only grown up. Long limbs. Russet hair that half covered his eyes in the same surfer-dude cut he'd sported at fourteen. He was standing on a paddleboard that was gliding toward her, which did nothing to diminish the dream effect.

She'd stood, wishing for once in her life that she wasn't wearing men's clothing.

"If it isn't the famous," Liddie said, her heart knocking, "or should I say infamous . . ."

He grinned and walked off the end of his board effortlessly. It came to rest on the rocks, vibrating gently. When she thought back to that moment, she could've sworn she fell into his arms right then, which was ridiculous. That hadn't happened till six hours later, high on red wine and campfire smoke and all the memories he seemed to have of her.

That was two years ago. These last twenty-four hours were the longest they'd been away from each other since. She didn't know why she'd told Kate anything different, that lie about how they were "off and on." Sometimes lies came easier to her than the truth, even when the lies were easily discovered.

"So why did Dad have him in his file?" Kate asked, breaking into her thoughts.

Liddie stood back to look at their work, trying to find a pattern. There were clippings about each of them and the people they were connected to. Sometimes it was simply a printed-up copy of a tweet or a Facebook post. Other times—like with Owen—it was a concert review that had been in the paper, a show Liddie had attended, the first.

She shuddered. "I think Dad was spying on us."

She and Kate looked at the wall again. Liddie was sure they were doing the same thing: searching for the oldest entry.

She followed the trail back and back, a flip book of her life in reverse. She watched the years peel away, like one of those shots in a movie of the pages flying off a calendar, only backward in time. Backward through her life. All the way back to 1998.

Her father had been spying on them.

All of them.

For twenty years.

Amanda

July 23, 1998—12:30 a.m.

"Whoa, whoa, hold up," Ryan said. Another thirty minutes had gone by. I was back in his lap, his hands down my pants, me rocking against his fingers. I'd reached down to unbutton his shorts, and that's when he stopped me.

"What is it?"

"I don't . . ." He sighed and leaned his forehead against mine. He withdrew his fingers, wiping them casually on the side of his shorts. I tried not to think about how he'd smell like me because of it. If other people would catch the scent and know . . . what? "I don't think this is a good idea."

"You don't want to?"

"Of course I do, but . . . there's Margaux."

I leaned back, almost tipping, then righted myself. "Margaux?"

"She's your best friend."

"So?" *She told me to have fun tonight,* I almost said, but something stopped me.

"I doubt she'd be happy with me . . . with us . . ."

"She wouldn't care. But even if she did, so what? She's your sister, not your girlfriend."

He put his hands on my waist, keeping me from falling. "I'm not . . . I'm not good for you, Amanda."

My stomach was plunging, but I tried to keep it light. "You feel very good to me."

I thought he'd laugh, but instead, he stood up and deposited me gently on my feet.

"I'm serious. You don't want to be with me."

"What if I do?"

"Well, it's a bad idea. I'm not . . . I'm not a good person, okay?"

"Come on, Ryan. I've known you for years. You're great."

"You don't know me. Trust me."

I sat on the rock. The night smelled of the lake and us, mixed together. My lips were swollen, and my body was still ready for whatever it was that Ryan wanted to do to it. His rejection felt like the cold night air. Like something that would seep into my cracks and chill me from within.

"It's me, isn't it?"

"No, Amanda. No."

"You were the one who suggested this. You were the one who wanted to."

"I know."

"And now you don't. So it must be me."

That was the only explanation I could think of. What other explanation is there when a boy says that he wants you, then changes his mind when you're in the middle of . . .

"I don't know what to say."

I was trying not to cry. I was embarrassed. Humiliated. I couldn't believe this was happening. No, I could. Of course he was rejecting me. He was *Ryan*.

I rubbed my hands on my arms, attempting to warm myself back up. The splinter in my finger caught at the fabric of my sweatshirt.

"Ouch."

"You okay?"

I held out my hand. "You never checked my splinter."

"I'm sorry."

He looked at my finger in the moonlight. He squinted, then pinched the small piece of wood with the ends of his fingers, sliding it out.

"There you go."

"Thank you."

"I'm going to go."

"Okay."

He stuffed his hands into his pockets and turned around. I stared at the row of colored bracelets on his arm. All the girls he'd been with, the things they'd done together. I'd seen the answering bracelets on other girls over the years. I'd never asked what the system meant, though I'd seen a red bracelet on Simon Vauclair's wrist after he and Margaux had sex last summer. Was there a color for the girl who wanted you to sleep with her but you stopped yourself from doing it because she was too pathetic? Puke green, maybe.

I watched him as he slid the boat into the lake, then climbed in. It was already taking on water.

"What if it sinks?" I said.

"I'll be fine."

I waited for him to ask me how I'd be, but he didn't.

"Don't tell anyone, okay?" I said as he readied his oars.

"I won't."

I tried to make eye contact, but he was already too far away, even though he hadn't moved. My bottom lip was trembling. I wanted him to go, go so he didn't see me crying. I wanted him to stay, stay and take away the pain.

He put the oars in and pushed at the rocks. The boat scraped across the bottom until it was in deeper water. He fit the oars into their slots and began to row, an uneven stroke at first, then smoother. I watched him meld into the night, and then the tears started flowing for real.

I put my head down on my knees and wrapped my arms around my legs. I was having trouble breathing; the tears were coming so fast. *Why, why, why.* I whispered it to myself over and over, waiting for an answer that never came.

I grew stiff and cold. Ryan was a speck on the lake, and then he was gone. It had taken me an hour to turn into someone who'd let Ryan do whatever he wanted to me. It'd take longer than that to turn me back into the person I was, if that was even possible.

I was about to sit up when I heard the *snap* of a branch behind me. I turned as a hand clapped over my mouth.

"Don't scream."

	Amanda	**Margaux**	**Ryan**	**Mary**	**Kate & Liddie**	**Sean**
9:00 p.m.	Lantern ceremony	Lantern ceremony	Lantern ceremony			
10:00 p.m.	On the Island	On the Island		On the Island		Crash boat
11:00 p.m.	Back Beach	Back Beach	Back Beach	On the Island		
Midnight	Back Beach		Back Beach			
6:00 a.m.	Secret Beach				Secret Beach	

CHAPTER 24

HEAD-ON

Margaux

After she'd showered and eaten some of the breakfast Amy had prepared and laid out buffet-style on the counter, Margaux decided to take things head-on and talk to Ryan. Because Mark, for all his faults, knew her better than anyone, and his advice was probably worth following. She'd voted last night to let Ryan keep the property, writing that he wasn't guilty. But did the truth matter after all these years? Yes. It mattered for Amanda. It mattered for her.

Ryan was sitting at the kitchen table in their parents' house. He'd showered and shaved and put on more appropriate clothing—chinos and a fleece rather than the suit he'd been wearing the day before. He looked rough around the edges, but so did she, she imagined. She felt that way, anyway, as if her insides had been scratched with sandpaper.

"So," she said, sitting across from him. She couldn't remember the last time she'd sat at this table. When they'd come up for the funeral in the spring, the fridge had been full of all the things that had been there when they were growing up, but they'd gone off: almost rotting milk, a brick of cheese that had started to mold, wilting lettuce that would never be used for a salad. Why hadn't her parents thrown them away before they left on their trip? One of a million things she'd never be able to ask them.

"So what?"

"I can go if you want."

"No, stop. Sorry. Sorry. Fuck. I'm already fucking this up."

"Fucking what up?"

"My plan for this morning. I want to talk to you. I want to talk to all of you."

"I want to talk to you too."

Ryan looked up. "You do?"

Margaux's heart melted. He looked so hopeful. The fact that it was something as simple as one of his sisters wanting to talk to him that brought this out was both sad and touching. This Ryan, this little boy all grown up, was what got him into trouble. You could never believe this Ryan would do anything wrong to anybody. And mostly that was true.

But not always.

"Yes."

"About Amanda?"

She reached across the table and squeezed one of his hands. "I need to know if I should be fighting for you."

"I don't understand why everyone doubts me. What did I ever do to deserve that?"

"Stacey?"

"That was an accident. That turn in the road, you know it's dangerous. And there was a horse that came out of nowhere . . . I told her to put on her seat belt." Ryan turned in his chair. He looked like he wanted to escape, but there wasn't anywhere to go.

She'd heard all this before, and he'd been exonerated. But there was more to the story, Margaux knew. The details he gave had sounded rehearsed, right from the beginning. Like something he'd learned by heart rather than something he was recalling.

"You can tell me what really happened that night."

"I *did*."

Margaux knew she wasn't going to get anything further. Maybe he didn't even remember what had actually happened, since he'd told this version so many times.

"Okay, so what about Amanda, then? You were on the Island."

"I never hid that."

"That's not true."

"I told the police."

"You didn't tell me."

He rubbed his hands across his face. "Maybe I should've, but Margaux, we were . . . Don't you remember what it was like? Everything was so crazy . . . parents everywhere pulling their kids from camp, and Mom and Dad thinking this place was going to be shut down for good. I wasn't thinking—"

"Of anyone but yourself?"

"Okay, yes, that's fair. But you didn't ask me either."

She thought back to those weeks and months after that terrible night. She'd spent a lot of time sleeping, barely eating. And then they'd returned to Montreal for school, and she felt as though she was supposed to act as if nothing had happened. As if there wasn't an Amanda-size hole in her life. Anything else would be too dangerous.

"You're right, I didn't."

"How did you know I was there, then?"

"Amanda told me you were coming to see her."

"She did?"

"Why are you so surprised? She was my best friend."

Ryan looked at his hands. His wedding ring was thick, a bit

bruised. Margaux had always liked that about him, the fact that he didn't try to hide his marriage, that he wore his wedding band where it couldn't be missed, on the ring finger on his left hand. And he was a great dad, she had to give him that. She had to give him a lot of things.

"Did you see her after I left?" Ryan asked. "Is that when she told you?"

Margaux felt her shoulders rise. What was he accusing her of?

"She told me *before* you arrived."

"Sorry."

"So you left?"

"Yes, I left."

"And . . ."

"Was she okay when I left?"

"Was she?"

"Of course she was, Margaux."

"So tell me, then. Tell me what happened."

He raised his hands over his eyes. He always used to do this when they were kids. When he'd been caught doing something and it was finally time to fess up, he'd cover his eyes as if that might make it easier to face the truth.

"We were going to hook up. I was a bit late; my cabin was being a pain in the ass. I met her on Back Beach. And we . . . well, anyway, you don't want to hear about that. We talked a bit, then, um, you know, and then, okay, I told her that she and I weren't going to work out."

"You broke up with her right after you slept with her?"

"What? No. We didn't sleep together."

"But I heard—"

"No, we fooled around a bit, but then I stopped and told her it wasn't going to work out."

"You're such a jerk."

"I did it for you."

She thought back to how excited Amanda had been that night. She was always the outgoing one, the daring one. "Come on, Margaux!" she used to say as she leaped down the trail leading through the girls' section. And Margaux would follow and do whatever it was she wanted. She missed that in her life now. That heedlessness. She probably hadn't done one spontaneous thing since that summer. Even this morning with Mark on the phone. Her realization that it was probably over—that wasn't spontaneous. It had been building inside her for years, like a slow-growth tree. If you cut her open, you could count the rings.

"How could treating my friend like crap be for me?"

"Because what about when it didn't work out? It wasn't going to work out, not long-term, and then she'd be all upset and you'd be all upset, and I liked Amanda, so . . ."

"You made her all upset."

"I guess."

"Couldn't you have figured that out before you hooked up?"

"My brain was a bit slow getting there, I guess."

"Please. She was just another colored bracelet to you."

Ryan looked at his wrist. It was bare. After Amanda, he'd cut off the rainbow of colors, the skin underneath puckered and white.

"Yeah, maybe. I kind of sucked back then, if you hadn't noticed."

"I did notice."

"But I'm different now. I am. After Stacey and becoming a dad . . . I'm trying to do right by my family here. I need the money. That's why I want to sell."

"Your business is in trouble?"

"Of course it is. John stole our working capital. I can't get new investors. I'm hanging by a thread."

"I didn't know."

"Why would you?"

The reproach in his voice stung. They lived separate lives. She didn't call as often as she should or hang out with her nieces either. She always blamed Mark—his awkwardness around her family—but the truth was that she was the one who found it easier to isolate herself from them. Not to get too involved, too entrenched. To keep her life contained, manageable.

"You're right. I should know this. I'm sorry."

"It's fine."

She could see the stress on his face. It was a stress she'd never experienced—other people counting on her, the responsibility of it. Sure, she had to show up to her job every day, but if she didn't, the school would go on. They'd pull someone from the substitute pool, and within weeks she'd be permanently replaced. She had a feeling it would be like this with Mark too. That within weeks, or at most months, she'd see him tagged in some photo on Facebook with his new girlfriend, and they'd be doing all the things she'd never wanted to do. Buying a house in the suburbs, shopping at outlet malls, having a baby.

"You need to sell," Margaux said.

"Yes. But it's moot anyway, right, because of the will."

"Is what Dad did even legal?"

"I doubt it is, to be honest."

"Why not challenge it, then?"

"And what—announce to the world that my parents thought I did that to Amanda? No, that would be the end of my career."

She watched him sip his coffee, letting the silence hang there.

"So the only way is to convince the others you're innocent."

"Looks like. Which is probably an impossible task."

"Why?"

"Come on, Margaux. Be serious. They were one vote away from convicting me last night. What's going to change by tomorrow?"

"What if you told them what you've told me?"

"Why would they believe me?"

"Because you weren't the only one who was on the Island that night."

"So?"

"Well, someone hurt Amanda. If it wasn't you, it was probably one of us."

"What about those guys from that house across the water?"

"I would've heard them. That boat they had was so loud, don't you remember? They kept buzzing the sailboats all summer. No, it was someone from camp, one of us. I've always known that."

Ryan contemplated his coffee. He looked like a man wanting to find hope. "Even if that's true, what does it matter?"

"It'll matter to whoever it is. If we threaten to expose them."

"You'd do that?"

Margaux felt her throat tighten. She loved the others as much as she loved Ryan, but the same reasoning had to apply. If Amanda deserved the truth, she deserved it no matter what it was or who it implicated. She couldn't be selective.

"It's not fair that this is happening to you if you didn't do it. So yeah. Let's get this right. Whoever's responsible for what happened to Amanda shouldn't take away your share of the property."

"But even if they vote me in, that doesn't mean the vote will be to sell."

"I know. But maybe you can borrow against the value or something. We can cross that bridge when we come to it."

Ryan stood up and came to stand next to her. He reached down and hugged her, hard. He still smelled faintly of alcohol underneath the fresh veneer of soap.

"Thank you." He let her go.

"What do we do first?" she asked.

"I'm not sure yet, but I do know one thing."

"What's that?"

"We need to be very, very careful."

CHAPTER 25

FROZEN

Kate

"That is so sick," Liddie said in reaction to the knowledge that their father had been spying on them—and cataloging it—for much of their lives.

"It's horrible," Kate said. She felt unsteady. The timeline she was looking at—her timeline—was stark, to her at least. Amy, Amy, Amy, and then a string of anonymous women even she had trouble remembering. How had her father known all this? It was one thing when they were safe and secure at camp, visible to him, easy to follow. But after she'd left? How could he know about it unless he was following her regularly or having someone do it for him? What possible purpose could doing that serve?

"Did you have any idea?" Liddie asked.

"None."

"Fuck."

Kate used the sleeve of her sweater to wipe her brow. The Craft Shop felt oppressive, like the worst days of summer, when even the night was humid. Was her father mentally ill? Is that what this was? Where did the compulsion to spy on people come from otherwise? And what did that make her twin, until now the chief spy of the family?

"Well," Kate said lightly, trying to distract herself, "at least now we know where you got it from."

"Oh, ha. Ha, ha, ha. I never did anything like this."

"Not far off though, right?"

"We both agreed to that, Kate."

Kate's mind filled with memories. Swimming silently through the black water. Seeing the man in the canoe that sat too low if there was only one person in it. Their teeth chattering as they crossed the lake again in stunned silence, trying to figure out what they'd seen, what to do.

She shook her head. They'd sworn to never speak of it, to never tell anyone. She turned to leave but was stopped by the loud ringing of the bell. Not the usual eight beats for breakfast but the emergency signal, a succession of quick pings that meant: *Come to the lodge immediately*.

"Fire drill?" Liddie asked.

"I guess we'd better go find out."

Within a minute, everyone was assembled at the lodge. Sean was standing on the balcony, the bell rope still in his hand. Ryan and Margaux arrived together, coming from the direction of the house. Amy exited from the kitchen, an apron tied around her waist, sweat on her brow. And Mary, who was in jodhpurs, leaned casually against the building.

"What's going on?" Ryan asked.

"We've got a hundred people coming tomorrow," Sean said.

"Yeah, we know."

"We've got to get ready."

"Aren't the caterers taking care of everything?" Kate asked Amy.

They made eye contact. Amy looked tired, defeated. Was that because of her? Did she wish Kate hadn't come back? But she knew she would; it was her parents' memorial weekend. Amy could've been elsewhere, asked for the weekend off. Or maybe she couldn't. Amy's finances, or lack thereof, were never something they discussed. Because at camp they were equals . . .

Even as she thought this, Kate knew it was ridiculous. They weren't equals. She was the owner's daughter and now an owner herself. Her parents had paid her a meager salary equivalent to Amy's, but it wasn't the same. She didn't have a kid, for one. Even when she'd essentially been fired, she'd dusted herself off and moved on fairly easily. She was the manager of the organic grocery store where she'd ended up. She even had a small stake in the business, and they were talking about opening another location. She didn't know struggle; it was one of the things that kept them apart.

"Under my supervision," Sean said. "Yes."

"So," Ryan said. "It's all taken care of."

"Not quite everything. We have to do a safety check on the water."

"What? Why?" Liddie said.

Sean spoke in an exasperated monotone. "Because the regulations say that there can't be a free swim unless the lifeguard staff has done one. And since camp officially closed when the campers left, we need to do it again before the guests come tomorrow. You know those guys and their cold-water challenges. Someone's gonna end up in the water."

"Will you listen to yourself?" Ryan said angrily. "What are you even talking about?"

"He means practicing sweeping the lake. You remember," Kate said. "We used to do it in precamp."

"Why do we need to do that?"

"You know why, Ryan. In case someone goes missing in the water."

Twenty minutes later, they were assembled on the beach. It was a cold, cloudy day, and Kate was already shivering in the one-piece swimsuit she usually wore to swim laps. She couldn't remember the last time she'd seen her family in so few clothes, all their flaws and differences exposed.

Ryan was wearing a long pair of shorts—he hadn't brought a bathing suit—and sporting a beer gut that his clothes hid well. His skin was the white of someone who didn't get outdoors much, and doughy. Margaux was lean and hard from years of running, her bathing suit the same two-piece she'd worn for years. Mary's rump in her one-piece navy suit was flattened out from all that riding. Liddie was wearing what looked like a sports bra and a pair of men's swim trunks. She had a disconnected set of tattoos along her ribs, some in script, some in block lettering, and a bird across her shoulders. It was odd to see her own body looking so similar and so different, though they both sported the same tattoo on the inside of their left arms.

I'll never tell, it said, a reminder to keep what they knew to themselves. They'd gotten the ink deep into the night of their eighteenth birthday after they'd completed their first pub crawl.

It had been guided by Ryan—"a brother's duty," he called it—but they'd ditched him around two in the morning and found themselves at a rooftop party, their legs dangling over the edge of a building, a beer in each of their hands. Down below, they could see a river of people and a neon sign that said simply *Tattoos*.

"Do you think Ryan thinks we're getting raped or something?" Liddie had asked, her long-necked beer rattling against her teeth.

"Why do you always say things like that?"

"Why are you always so shocked?"

"Because it's not normal. I'm allowed to be shocked by a lack of normalcy."

"You should be used to it by now. Especially with everything."

"Everything?"

Liddie looked at her. "Dude. *Amanda.* It's her birthday today too, remember?"

Kate hadn't remembered. Maybe she'd never known. She wasn't a collector of facts about people, this birthday, that anniversary. She cared more about the content of a person.

"You seriously didn't know we had the same birthday?"

Kate raised her shoulders. She'd had too many shooters at that last bar, and her head swam.

"Sometimes I think you have an erase button on your brain," Liddie said.

"I have selective memory."

"Must be nice."

"I bet we both forget this evening."

"I always remember everything," Liddie said. "It feels like a fucking curse."

Later, she'd woken up in Liddie's apartment with her head feeling as if an explosion had gone off inside it. And the inside of her arm killed. What the hell had she done to herself? She rolled over and lifted it up. It was covered with a bandage. She peeled it back and read the message in its trailing script, and then it all clicked into place.

She remembered.

A whistle blew.

"Everyone get into formation," Sean said, a yellow whistle dangling from his neck.

"Why is he in charge?" Liddie grumbled next to her.

"It was his idea."

Liddie rolled her eyes. Mary came and stood next to Kate's other shoulder; Margaux was to Liddie's left.

"You too, Ryan," Sean said.

Ryan clenched his fists but obeyed. Kate watched goose bumps rise on her arms.

"You know the drill. We're simulating looking for a missing person. Walk slowly through the shallow section with your hands spread out. When you get to where the water hits your chest, you need to dunk, take a step, and sweep with your eyes and arms."

"I can't believe we're doing this," Mary said. "The water's freezing."

It was brutal. Kate could feel the cold seep into her bones as it lapped against her toes.

"Move forward!"

Though it was the last thing she wanted to do, she obeyed Sean's command, as did the rest of her family. Each step forward was a monumental effort, the ice creeping up her legs, her teeth chattering. When it hit her stomach, it felt like a punch, knocking the wind right out of her. Was this what it used to be like, every year doing this? Was this another instance of her selective memory, deleting every unpleasant thing that had happened to her in her life?

Was she her own unreliable witness?

When the water touched her breasts, she wasn't even sure what she was doing anymore. She heard Sean yell, "Underwater!" and she obeyed, buckling her knees and dragging her head and shoulders under. The shock opened her eyes. She looked around. All she could see was a sea of blurred white legs. She rose to the surface, gasping for air. She felt panicked and dizzy. What was happening to her?

She followed Sean's instructions automatically. "Dunk," he yelled, and there she was in the freezing dark again, moving her hands in front of her, searching for something missing. She surfaced when she couldn't breathe anymore, then went down again. Usually, the longer you stayed in the water, the more used to it you got. But not this time. Each time she went under seemed to make her colder, dizzier, her breath ragged and desperate.

She broke the surface. She didn't know how long they'd been at this, but the water was up to her neck now; if she went under one more time, she wouldn't be able to surface.

Everyone bobbed down again, but she stood still, her body numb, unable to will herself to do it. She was cold, so cold. Maybe she'd be warmer if she closed her eyes. If she closed her eyes maybe she'd be able to breathe.

She felt herself fall.

Was this how Amanda felt as she took her last free breaths?

CHAPTER 26

RESCUE OPERATION

Ryan

"Kate!"

Ryan turned as he broke the surface of the water. It was Sean who'd yelled from the dock, pointing. Although the water came only to Kate's shoulders, she was drowning. Ryan reached her at the same time as Mary. They'd spread out of formation once they started dunking up and down. He reached for his sister, holding her to him. She felt like a block of ice.

"I think she's hypothermic," he yelled to Sean. "Get some towels."

He carried Kate out of the water in his arms like one of his girls. The wind whipped against his skin. His own teeth were chattering, but Kate's were clacking against one another like automatic gunfire. Her whole body was shaking and blue, and her breath was raspy and shallow. He vaguely remembered reading about hypothermia when he'd done his lifeguard training a zillion years ago, but he wasn't sure what to do about it. Get her warm, obviously, but wasn't there something about doing that too quickly? What if they did more harm than good?

"We should take her to the hospital," he said to Mary when he got to the beach. She was shivering too; they all were.

"No, no hospital," Kate murmured.

He lowered her to the towel that Sean had placed on the ground. His sisters gathered around him, hovering behind him, brushing up against his shoulder.

"We should get her out of her suit," Liddie said. "You two turn around."

Ryan thought of protesting, but why? Did he want to see his sister stripped of her clothing, cold and shaking? No. The answer was no.

He met Sean's eye, and then they both pivoted away. He picked up his towel and tried to dry himself off as quickly as he could as he listened to Liddie speaking in a soothing tone to Kate as she removed her bathing suit and wrapped her head to foot in the others' towels. He felt guilty for using his, but when he turned around, she looked like a mummy encased in a tomb; even her head was wrapped up.

"Let's get her to the lodge," Mary said.

Ryan bent down to lift her again. She was limp now, where she'd been rigid before, but he could feel the cold seeping through the towels. Her lips were still blue. He fought it, but there was no keeping the thought of another girl and her blue lips from blooming in his mind.

"Put some hot chocolate on, Amy!" Ryan yelled as they stumbled into the lodge, his sisters pushing up against him. He wished he could tell them to back off, that they weren't the only ones concerned, and he knew what he was doing. His whole life he felt as if his family never gave him credit for anything, never let him have the space to make things right on his own.

"I'll start a fire," Sean said.

"Good idea. Can you grab me that chair, Margaux?"

She went to the rocking chair in the corner and dragged it closer to the fireplace.

"What's happening?" Amy asked, coming out of the kitchen. The bridge of her nose had a streak of flour across it. "Oh my God. Kate. Katie, what's wrong?"

"She's hypothermic," Ryan said as he gently placed her into the rocking chair. Her head lolled to the side, though her eyes were open. They seemed to be focused on something no one could see. Ryan wished with all his heart that his sister didn't look quite so close to dead. "Can someone go get some blankets from upstairs?"

"I'll go," Margaux said. "Sean, you don't mind, do you?"

"Course not," he said unconvincingly.

Ryan shot him a look. He'd never thought of Sean as selfish, so why did he care about his blankets all of a sudden? Besides, they probably belonged to camp, which belonged to . . . Ah, fuck.

Amy knelt at Kate's feet and picked up her hands. "It's okay, *mon coeur*. You will be okay."

She started rubbing Kate's hands with her eyes locked on Kate's. Ryan felt something unfamiliar rise up in his chest. More than surprise—he understood at once what the meaning of this exchange was, and did it . . . disgust him? He looked away, ashamed. All those liberal pretensions, all that banging the gong in social situations about how everyone was equal, and *he* wasn't equal to a shared look of love and a term of endearment between a woman and his sister.

"Where are those blankets?" he bellowed.

"I've got them," Margaux said. "Oh, Amy."

Ryan was further ashamed by the shared surprise of his sister. Maybe that's all it was. If this were Liddie, he wouldn't think twice about it. But Kate . . . Kate had always been . . . like him, he was about to think, then quashed it.

Amy looked up defiantly. "I'll take the blankets."

Margaux held them out. Amy took them and gently removed the towels from Kate. Ryan knew he should look away like he had on the beach, but it was all done so quickly that it didn't matter. Kate seemed to come back to herself at Amy's touch. She watched Amy silently as she wrapped the worn army surplus blankets from Sean's bed around her.

"My feet are so cold," she said, barely above a whisper.

Mary walked past him, sat on the floor, and took one of Kate's feet in her hands. Amy took the other. They rubbed them gently as they turned slowly from white to pink.

Sean lit the fire. When it was crackling, he stepped back and placed the screen in front of it. Ryan approached, holding out his own frozen hands toward the flames. Kate was probably going to be okay, but this never would've happened if it weren't for Sean.

"That was a stupid idea. We all could've died."

"The regulations say that—"

"Enough with your fucking regulations. Jesus. Don't you care about Kate?"

"Of course I do."

Liddie emerged from the office. "I just called 9-1-1, and they said to keep her dry and to give her warm liquids. You've got the fire going, good. I'll go make her some tea."

No one answered her, but Ryan walked away from Sean before he punched him and followed her into the kitchen. She was busying herself looking through the cupboards, slamming them shut when she didn't find what she needed.

"I think it's in the pantry. I'll get it," Ryan said.

"No, it's fine. I'll do it."

She walked down the long galley kitchen and disappeared into the pantry. Ryan waited for her to come out, and when she didn't, he went looking for her. He rounded the corner and saw nothing. He looked left, and there she was, huddled in a corner by the milk fridge, sobbing.

"What's going on?"

She shook her head and wiped at her eyes. "I'm fine. I'm fine."

He sat down next to her. The ground near the fridge was cold, but not as cold as the lake. "Come on, this isn't like you."

"I know, right? I actively plotted Kate's death a bunch of times growing up, so . . ."

"That's not what I meant."

"I'm usually a cold, callous bitch, and the fact that I might cry over something that happened to my sister is shocking."

Ryan kept quiet.

"I know, I know, okay?"

"It's all right to cry. It was scary. I was scared."

"You were?"

"Of course." He kicked his feet against Liddie's. She pushed her shoulder against his. "I didn't do it, you know," he said. "Amanda . . ."

"Is this the right time for this?"

"Probably not. But give me a chance later, all right? When we know Kate will be fine."

"She's going to be okay, right?"

"She is." Ryan patted her knee. "Why don't we get that tea?"

"Yeah."

He stood and held out his hand to her. She took it, and he popped her up, a move he used to do when they were young. She played along, landing and throwing her hands up in the air as if she'd just pulled off a gymnastic feat.

"Still sticking the landing," Ryan said.

"At least I'm doing something right."

CHAPTER 27

FEELING SMALL

Liddie

Liddie couldn't believe she'd broken down like that, and in front of Ryan of all people. It was scary to see your sister, a carbon copy, looking so lifeless. But she knew Kate was going to be all right. Well, she probably knew. Okay, she didn't know, and the thought of that, the thought of maybe a world with no Kate in it, that's what broke her. Also, if she was being honest, the tenderness between her and Amy bothered her. She felt excluded, pushed out of Kate's world in a way she never had been before. Because even if they were with other people, even people they loved, they always came first. That was the bargain of being a twin. You didn't need to talk about it; you simply knew that sometime in the not-too-distant future, you'd be living together in some old-age home, dressed alike the way you'd been as children.

Liddie had always been okay with that, despite all the pains she'd taken to look as different as possible from Kate and even to hide her feelings from her. But she'd never asked Kate if *she* was okay with that. She'd assumed that this was how things were going to be because, well, things were usually the way she wanted them to be if she wanted it enough. Sometimes she had to wait—like with Owen—but it was okay to wait when you knew it would come out right in the end.

But looking at Kate and Amy, the way their eyes locked on to each other's, made her rethink things. There wasn't any room for Liddie in that look. There wasn't any room for anything but them.

She felt small. How selfish could one person be? How could she begrudge her sister what she had with Owen? She was as selfish as everyone had always said she was. It didn't matter what other people thought in the end, but this, this space between Kate and her? That was everything. So when she went to the pantry to look for tea, she broke. And then Ryan was there to pick her up.

She made Kate her tea and brought it to her. She was relieved to see that Kate no longer looked like death. Some color had returned to her cheeks, and her teeth weren't chattering.

"Drink this slowly, okay? I don't want to burn your frozen self."

"I won't."

Liddie hugged her, being careful not to slosh the tea all over the place. "You're not allowed to die," she whispered in her sister's ear, "before me."

"Thanks, Liddie."

She pulled back. Kate was smiling at her. A weary, worn-out smile, but enough of one for Liddie to know that there was still a place for her in her life, if she wanted it.

"You're going to say, 'Don't ever change,' right?"

Kate shook her head. "You couldn't if you wanted to."

"That's true," Liddie said lightly, but it stung. Was she so rigid? And what if she was? Was her character so bad that it needed changing?

Liddie retreated. Sean was standing by the fire with Mary and

Margaux. Ryan was by the door, looking like he didn't know where he fit.

She walked up to Ryan and asked him to follow her to the Craft Shop.

"Why?"

"Just come, okay? You'll understand when I show you."

They left the lodge. The clouds had increased, circling above. It was warmer out, but she was still chilled from the lake. She should change her clothes, but they were half-dry now, the quick-wicking fabric living up to its name. It was made for camp and all its weather. She hadn't checked the forecast in a couple of days. She hoped it wouldn't be rainy tomorrow. Whatever she felt about her parents, a rainy memorial with a hundred people swarming around in the mud wasn't her idea of a fitting send-off.

They crossed the field. The freshly mown grass perfumed the air. *It would be a shame,* she thought, to her surprise, *for all this to be replaced by condos, parking lots, too many people.* Paving paradise. Though that wasn't what this place was, not by a long shot.

She opened the door to the Craft Shop and turned on the light.

"Shit, it's gone."

"What's gone?"

"Dad's Amanda file. We found it and brought it here and tacked it up on the wall, and now someone's taken it."

Liddie walked to the wall where the physical projection of her father's labyrinthine mind had been a few hours before. The thumbtacks were still there, a few stray scraps of newsprint and paper stuck under them. But the timelines they'd discovered, the clues—if that's what they were—had disappeared. What the hell?

"Dad had an Amanda file?" Ryan asked.

"He had a Ryan file, too. One on each of us."

"What was in them?"

"Photographs, newspaper stories, Twitter feeds . . . you name it; if it was publicly available and about us, Dad had it."

Liddie stopped herself from saying some of the other things he had. Surveillance photographs. Reports that looked as if a detective had written them. Logs of where they'd been and when, and with whom. And the documents she'd thankfully hidden in her pocket, which were now hidden in her suitcase in the French Teacher's Cabin.

"That's weird."

"I'll say. Though it makes sense."

"How so?"

"It's how he came to that conclusion about you, I guess."

Ryan turned toward her. "What kind of stuff did he have about me?"

"That old collection of bracelets you used to wear, tagged to each girl, for one."

He sat on one of the small plastic chairs that were meant for someone half his size. "Ugh."

"Lots of stuff on Stacey also."

"You're enjoying this, aren't you?"

"Maybe a little."

"I know I haven't always been the nicest to you, and yesterday . . . I feel bad about that. But do you think . . . I just don't get why you think I did it."

Was her whole family affected with the same malady? Did nothing stick in anyone's brain?

"How can you say that? Do you know what that's been like for Kate and me, having to keep that night to ourselves for all these years?"

"I'm sorry."

"Yeah, you said so at the time."

"But I am. I am. And maybe I didn't get it at first, but I've spent the last ten years trying to make up for that. To Kerry, to my family, and to you, if you'd let me, but you just push me away. You don't return my calls, don't tell me anything about yourself. You and Kate both, all of you."

Liddie was stung. Did she deserve to be attacked like this? By Ryan of all people?

"We all live separate lives. It's the way it is."

"It doesn't have to be. My girls ask about you all the time. 'Where's Aunt Liddie? How come she doesn't come around anymore?' "

"They're probably confusing me for Kate."

"Not unless Kate suddenly has a body full of tattoos."

This made Liddie smile. It was true; the last time she'd seen the girls, she'd taken them swimming at the local pool. They'd been fascinated by her web of tattoos and what each one meant. But there had also been the stares of the mothers and fathers. Somehow, the tattoo revolution hadn't made it to Westmount. Liddie had covered herself up, both hating herself for doing it and Ryan for making it necessary. Neither was fair, but she couldn't help how things were. She wasn't responsible. She was a bystander.

"The girls are sweet."

"You should see them more."

"Okay, maybe I will. Only . . ."

Ryan's face was grim. "Only, you think I hurt Amanda, so . . ."

"Ryan, come on. I *know* you hurt Amanda."

"I didn't, I swear to God."

Liddie watched his expression. She wished she could tell when someone was lying. Then she could follow the expressions that were flitting across Ryan's face, and know. But she couldn't, and all she had in front of her was her brother telling her one thing and her memory telling her another.

"If you didn't, then what were you doing on Secret Beach that morning?"

CHAPTER 28

SUPPLIES

Mary

Kate's full color returned as the food truck pulled to a stop in front of the lodge, its loud gears grinding. Mary touched Amy's shoulder to get her attention. She was still sitting at Kate's feet.

"The food delivery's here. Did you want me to take care of it?"

Amy looked up gratefully. "Could you? The list is in the kitchen."

"Sure."

"I'll help you," Margaux said. "I'll go get the list; you go greet the guy."

Jean-François, Mary wanted to say. *But he goes by J-F.* But what was the point? Her family had never taken the time to get to know the help around here, except for Sean. Though, come to think of it, maybe Kate was an exception to that. She certainly seemed to have gotten to know at least one of the help quite well.

Kate and Amy. When had that happened? There were many years when Kate was the only family member at camp besides her parents.

Mary and the others came in and out, but Kate was the one running the place, despite what her parents liked to think. Was that when this—whatever it was—had taken hold? Or did it go further back? Was Amy a predator like you saw on TV, one of those teachers who slept with their students?

"Mary?"

"Yeah?"

"I thought you were going to go greet the food guy?"

"Oh, right, sorry. I spaced."

Mary hurried outside. A large white delivery truck blocked the driveway. J-F was standing on the step runner, flipping through a manifest. The *clack* of the screen door got his attention. He gave her a wide smile.

"Hey, Mary. Long time." His English was excellent, but there was a trace of French-Canadian in his accent and, sometimes, his word choices.

"Long time. I'll open the shed for you."

"Sounds good."

She walked past him to the food shed, half-hidden by the trees. She had a key for it on her key ring, a holdover from all the years when she was in charge of receiving deliveries. That was how she'd met J-F. Kate had run camp, but Mary had still come in once a week to inventory the food deliveries and make sure her parents weren't being shorted. But that had all stopped when Kate left and Sean took over running everything; though, again, her parents acted like they did it all themselves.

She wasn't quite sure why she'd never returned the key, or any of the others, for that matter. Perhaps there was some security in knowing she could still access all her old haunts, if she wanted to.

"You are receiving a lot of people tomorrow?" J-F said. "For the memorial?"

He was standing right behind her. It had been two years since she'd last seen him, but she still remembered—it was a cliché—like it was yesterday. But that's how it felt. Sometimes she'd be doing something completely benign and a flash of him would hit her. The way he looked at her. The way he loved her smell. How he inserted a finger into her in exactly the right way. How he sucked her nipples until she came.

"That's right," she said, shaking away the thoughts. "Will there be enough room in here?"

She didn't turn around. Making eye contact with J-F was always dangerous. Instead she turned the key, removed the lock, and pushed open the door to the shed. It was full of long rows of shelves containing mainly canned goods. Vats of spaghetti sauce. Enough sliced potatoes to feed a hundred. Peaches in cans.

"I will make it fit," he said.

That was the problem with J-F. Even the way he spoke was suggestive.

"Great. Margaux's coming to check the order." She blushed as she said the word *coming*. This was exactly why she'd cut off all contact. "Ghosting him," she'd heard it was called. Turning herself into a ghost in his life.

"Got it."

She felt him move away. It was nice in the shed, in the cool of the woods, without anything to fear behind her.

"I've got the list," she heard Margaux say. "Mary? Where are you?"

Mary sighed and went to join her at the truck. J-F had lowered the ramp and was starting to unload flats of bread and hamburger rolls. His arms were muscled, strong but not bulky.

"How many people are coming to this thing, anyway?" Margaux asked, handing her a piece of paper with the food order and a pen.

"Hundred, hundred and twenty."

"The lifers?"

"Yep."

"Funny, all these people who never wanted to let go of camp, and us all wanting to run away."

"Except Kate," Mary said.

"Except Kate."

"Maybe we should sell it to them. They're all rich, aren't they?"

Mary ticked a few items off the list. A giant vat of mayonnaise. Equally obscene amounts of mustard and ketchup.

"Not all of them."

"You know what I mean. I bet a bunch of them would be willing to get together and invest."

"Invest or buy us out?"

Margaux seemed annoyed at her lack of precision, but it wasn't something she'd spent much time thinking about. The lifers were a group of former campers who'd spent at least ten summers there. They ran banks and law firms and made films for a living and had a stupid club that she'd never been invited to, even though she'd spent longer at camp than any of them. They sent their kids to Macaw when they got old enough. They held on to their staff shirts as badges of honor. They loved it more than the MacAllisters. Mary was sure enough of them would love to take this place over if given the chance.

"They could buy shares or something," Mary said. "So we could still have a majority ownership and get some money out."

"Maybe."

"You think I'm being stupid?"

"I think it's a great idea," J-F said, his tanned forearms flexing under the weight of the meat order. "You want this in the fridge?"

"Yes, thanks . . ."

"Jean-François," Mary said.

"J-F," he said. "Nice to meet you."

Margaux watched him walk the meat into the rear entrance of the lodge, where the large meat fridges were located. Mary knew what was coming, and she cursed herself. She should've let Margaux handle it. Nothing good ever came from raising your hand to volunteer.

"He's cute," Margaux said when he was out of earshot.

"Yep."

"How long have you known him?"

"Ten years?"

"The world is full of surprises."

"What's that?"

"You and the grocery guy. Amy and Kate. All this time, I thought I knew everything about this family, and it turns out I know nothing."

"Everything? Come on."

"Right, okay, not everything. But . . . ah, hell, I don't know what I'm saying." Margaux sat down on the front porch step looking weary. This was what the lifers didn't understand. For them, Macaw was a repository of fun memories. But for the MacAllisters . . . For them, it sometimes felt like a matter of life and death to be away from this place.

Mary sat next to Margaux. "I stopped seeing J-F a couple of years ago."

"Okay."

"Don't be like that."

"Like what?"

"I'm trying to tell you what you wanted to know, and you're making me feel weird."

"I'm sorry. Tell me about him; I want to know."

"I like long walks on the beach, pasta, and a good soccer game. Also, I've never been on a horse," he said, coming out of the lodge's main door behind them.

Mary's stomach sank as Margaux threw her head back and laughed.

Margaux stood and turned. "You're funny. Cute and funny. Why'd you break up with my sister?"

"Oh no. That wasn't me."

And like always, things went from funny to awkward in an instant. Mary stared at the ground. She knew it was weird, her still sitting there, her back to the scene, but she couldn't make herself face it. She didn't know what the look on her face would give away. But she knew how she felt. Angry.

"I'm going to go," Margaux said.

"You don't have to," J-F said. "I'm almost done."

"No, I've stuck my foot in it. Why don't you two talk? Or not."

Margaux backed away, her hands raised to her shoulders, a forgive-me shrug. Mary recognized the move as Margaux passed her; it had accompanied many a wrong in childhood. Took your toy. Told on you to Mom and Dad. Oops. Sorry. What can you do?

J-F walked down the stairs behind her. Then he was in front of Mary and she couldn't hide anymore.

"You don't have to stay," Mary said, standing. She came up to his chin. "I know I kind of . . ."

"Disappeared?"

"Yeah."

"It's fine. We were not serious, I think. Because if we were, then that would make you not so nice a person, and I don't want to think that about you."

"You don't?"

He took a step toward her. He always smelled the same—slightly refrigerated. It was a smell Mary liked because it meant coolness to her. Not in a fashion sense but in the temperature way. He was calm, steady. And yet he made her feel wild, like Cinnamon when she'd been startled by Buster. She wanted to raise her feet off the ground and paw at the danger.

"We always had a good time, did we not?"

"We did."

"Seems to me, we could have a good time again."

"There are people around."

He smiled. "I didn't mean right this minute."

Mary stared back at her old friend the ground. She'd been kind of hoping that was what he meant. Not that they'd do it in the road, but there was always the shed.

And this was why she'd left him. Because he made her crazy. Crazy inside her head.

"You are adorable." He ran his finger down her chin and neck to her collarbone. "Meet me later?"

"Yes."

"Where?"

She said the first thing that came to mind. "The barn."

CHAPTER 29

ORIGINS

Sean

When the crisis was past, and Kate and Amy were huddled together in the rocking chair that was built for one person, Sean slipped upstairs to his room. He could feel Margaux's presence there, even though it had only been brief, long enough to retrieve the blankets from his bed. It was enough to make him uneasy. His personal space had been invaded. This tiny room, eight feet by eleven, was his, *his*. Sometimes it felt like the only thing in the world that was.

In the winter months, he'd colonize the common room at the end of the hall. Set up a table under the skylight and work on the tiny scale models of ships that he then fed into bottles. He'd started selling them online a few years ago and had quite a following. Orders that could keep him busy for years if he wanted to. Prices he could charge that would give him enough money to leave this place behind, these people, and strike out on his own.

And yet . . .

He made sure the door was shut and locked behind him, then reached under his bed to pull out a box. An old milk crate, it was the only thing on hand when he'd gone into the Craft Shop and found his life diagrammed on the wall. Not only his life but all of them, the MacAllisters, and Amy, and Owen Bowery of all people, that punk kid who became a rock star. And probably a bunch of others, but he hadn't had time to check.

He'd known what it was even before he'd looked at it carefully. Mr. MacAllister's files, the ones he'd told Sean about but never showed him. The ones he was always working on late at night, that he'd tuck away if anyone ever came into the room.

"All in good time, son," he used to say.

Mr. MacAllister said that about a lot of things. Sean getting a permanent part of camp, the deed to the Island, the certainty that he could choose to stay or leave without deference to anyone.

"All in good time."

Only that time never came, and now, despite the vote the night before, Sean knew he was going to end up the loser. He wasn't going to get what he wanted. He never did. He watched life—*her*—from the sidelines, and all he got was the leftovers. Even Amanda had been that way. Her attention was revenge on someone else.

Sean sorted the material into piles. He didn't know, exactly, what made him take the papers when he'd seen what Liddie and Kate were doing in the Craft Shop. He only knew he had to act fast.

He'd been walking up from the beach when he'd seen Buster standing outside the building, a sign that someone was inside. He'd moved quietly and looked in the side window, signaling to Buster to lay down flat. He watched them long enough to realize what they were doing and then he decided. He needed time alone with the papers to figure out what they meant. If they were dangerous or could be ignored. When they came looking for them, he'd deal with that then, if he had to.

He'd thought of the swimming drill and had rung the bell. Buster had gone bounding into the woods, and the MacAllisters had gathered at the lodge. When everyone went to change, he'd taken the papers down as carefully as he could and stuffed them into the milk crate. Then he'd climbed out the back window and skirted through the woods to get to the rear entrance of the lodge without being seen. He'd dropped the papers in his room, then hurried back to the water for the drill.

That had been a mistake; the water was too cold, and they were lucky only one person got hypothermia. But Kate was going to be okay, and in a way, this was her fault, or Liddie's at least. If she wasn't always snooping, digging into things that didn't concern her, then so many things would be different.

Mr. MacAllister had been spying on them. He knew that already. He'd even gone along with him on a couple of recognizance trips, as Mr. MacAllister called them.

"I like to know what my kids are up to," he'd say, his eyes twinkling. "Care to join me?"

"Why not just ask them?" Sean had dared to say once.

"But that wouldn't be half as fun."

Sean had gone with him without any more protest.

The truth was, he didn't mind so much when the trips involved looking into what the twins or Ryan were doing. It was when they were spying on Margaux that Sean felt his chest tighten and his hands itch. He couldn't figure out what it was that Mr. MacAllister wanted to find all those years, but now he knew. He was trying to solve what had happened to Amanda, and he thought, somehow, that information about their present would explain the past.

Was that it? Because even that, the bigness of it, the task, didn't explain the files Mr. MacAllister had on him, or Amy, or the random campers he seemed to follow. What could this possibly have to do with figuring out what had happened to Amanda? Sean had never even heard Mr. MacAllister speak about that, except once, briefly, after they'd gotten back from cleaning up the mess Ryan had made when Stacey Kensington died. Mr. MacAllister had poured himself some of that cheap wine he made and asked Sean if he thought that some people had badness in them. If they were born that way.

"Like the devil?"

"If you want to be religious about it. I'm thinking more of Macbeth. How he was cursed. Do you ever feel cursed, Sean?"

"Why would I?"

"Son of a whore, finding your mother like that."

"Don't say that about my mother."

"I apologize. It's been, as they say, a day."

Sean had wanted to hit Mr. MacAllister that night, maybe take him from behind with a frying pan. *Wham!* Sean had these violent thoughts sometimes. But then Mrs. MacAllister came in and thanked Sean for helping with Ryan—she didn't know what she'd do without him—and he'd gone back to this very room and fallen asleep to the sound of the rotating fan above his head.

The piles of paper sat on the floor. Though he was curious about all of them, he picked up his pile first and sorted it again into chronological order. Mr. MacAllister had taught him to do that. Chronology was how you found patterns, explanations, he'd told him more than once. When you had a set of data that you wanted to make sense of, this was the best first place to start.

Only, now that he'd organized it by date, it didn't make any more sense than it had before. His whole life was here. If he flipped through it, it would be like one of those do-it-yourself cartoons—a cartoon baby growing into a larger cartoon man as the pages flicked past. His birth announcement. A photo of his mother holding him at a few weeks. Receipts for a day care he didn't remember attending. His report cards, all of them, the bad grades circled. A canceled check to his mother from a name he didn't recognize. Were these all his mother's things? Had Mr. MacAllister kept them all this time, intending to give them to him someday? That didn't seem likely given the other things in the pile. Several pictures of Sean standing on the fringes of a scene with Margaux in it, looking at her. A timeline of that night on the Island. It began with the lantern ceremony on the beach. He remembered how the lanterns lit up the sky, how the night felt full of possibilities. It ended with Amanda being found on Secret Beach.

In the middle were important gaps. Things he'd tried so long to forget, to wash the shame of them away by living this monk's life.

- *9:30 p.m.—Amanda, Margaux, Mary, & campers travel to the Island (Sean takes them)*
- *10:00–11:00 p.m.—Campfire, bedtime*
- *11:30 p.m.—Ryan arrives*

Sean picked up a pencil and filled in some of the gaps.

- *12:30 a.m.—Ryan leaves*
- *1:00 a.m.—Ryan arrives at camp*
- *1:05 a.m.—Sean rows to the Island*

Amanda

July 23, 1998—1:30 a.m.

"Don't scream," he said again. "It's Sean."

Even though my heart was galloping, I felt my body go slack when he said his name. *Sean.* It was only Sean. I was okay. I wasn't going to be dragged off into the woods never to be heard from again.

He lowered his hand. "Sorry, did I scare you?"

"You did."

"I didn't want you to scream and wake everyone."

I turned around. He was wearing long pants, a Macaw sweatshirt, a baseball cap, and a headlamp. The light stung my eyes. I must've been in a far-off place not to notice him approaching.

"Can you put that out?"

"Yeah, course."

He clicked it, and it was dark again. The truth was, I didn't care about the light in my eyes. I cared about the light *on* my eyes. That it would show I'd been crying.

"What are you doing here?" I asked.

"I came to check on you guys."

Margaux, he meant. His crush on Margaux was of longer standing than mine on Ryan. Though I was over that now, I decided. I'd have to be. I wasn't going to let Ryan MacAllister ruin the rest of my summer or any other part of my life. Not for an hour of kisses.

Maybe that's all it would take for Sean? To have Margaux finally kiss him, then change her mind?

"We're fine."

"Uh-huh."

"Truly."

He looked at the lake. "Those guys were out on their boat again."

"Which guys?"

"The ones who've been buzzing around the swim dock and the water-ski beach."

He meant the group of college guys who were staying on the other side of the lake. They'd noticed Margaux a few weeks ago when she was lifeguarding in her tankini. They'd tried to beach their boat, and Sean had run them off.

"How would they even know we were here?"

"Can't risk it. Guys like that."

"They're harmless."

I sat down on the rock where I'd been with Ryan. Forever ago. "Did you . . ."

"See Ryan?"

"Yeah."

"I watched him row back. That's what made me come to this side of the Island. He was visiting you, I guess?"

"There isn't anybody else here but his sisters and a bunch of twelve-year-olds."

"Good point."

He sat next to me. He felt solid where his leg touched mine. The difference between twenty-five and seventeen. Was it as big as it felt sometimes? Would I be that solid when I was twenty-five? That firmly rooted in my life?

"Ryan's a jerk," he said.

"Yeah."

"Want to tell me what happened?"

I looked out at the water. Maybe telling Sean would help. Finally purge the thoughts and feelings from my body. It was worth a try.

"He came to meet me . . ."

I told him most of it. How I waited. How he was late. How we started to fool around and then he changed his mind and blamed it on Margaux.

"But that was crap, because Margaux gave me her blessing or whatever."

I felt a bit breathless. Telling it like that hadn't made me feel better. I was embarrassed. I wished I could take the words back, put them back inside me, where I could delete them one by one.

"You won't tell anyone?" I asked a second man that night.

"No, of course not. Only . . ."

"What?"

"I . . . Maybe it is Margaux's fault."

"How could this be Margaux's fault?"

"I didn't think much of this at the time, but a couple of weeks back, Ryan said something to Margaux about how . . . attractive you'd gotten, and she laughed. Then she got all serious with him and told him to stay far, far away from you."

"She did?"

"Yeah, sorry."

"Maybe she was joking?"

"Nah. She wasn't joking. She was looking out for you."

"Looking out for me."

"Yeah. I mean, Ryan's no good. Even Margaux knows that."

I felt rage building inside me. "What business is it of hers though?"

"What's that?"

"So what if I want to do something stupid with Ryan? I mean, did I stop her from sleeping with that idiot Simon Vauclair last summer? No, I did not."

Sean flinched next to me. Shit. He didn't know about that. Aw, well, fuck it. Fuck it. And fuck Margaux, too.

"Sorry, you didn't know."

"It's okay. I kind of did."

"She's no good for you either."

"I know."

I stretched out my legs. My foot clinked against something. I got down on my knees and moved my hands around, trying to find it.

"What are you doing?"

"Hold on."

I found it against a rock. The flask Ryan had brought, forgotten in his haste to get away from me. The cap was still on, the insides sloshing half-full. Good.

"What you got there?"

"Just what we need."

I sat on the ground with my back against the rock. I held up the flask so Sean could see it.

"You want?"

"That's probably not a good idea."

"No, it's a great idea."

I wanted to change the way I felt, and this seemed like the easiest way. I screwed off the cap, a mini tumbler.

"Turn on your headlamp, will you?"

There was a click, and then light. I poured carefully into the cap and handed the flask to Sean.

I raised the tumbler. "What should we toast to?"

"I have no idea."

"To us, then," I said, feeling silly and bold. "The MacAllister rejects."

"To us," Sean said and mock clinked the flask to the tiny cup in my hand.

And then we drank.

	Amanda	**Margaux**	**Ryan**	**Mary**	**Kate & Liddie**	**Sean**
9:00 p.m.	Lantern ceremony	Lantern ceremony	Lantern ceremony			
10:00 p.m.	On the Island	On the Island		On the Island		Crash boat
11:00 p.m.	Back Beach	Back Beach	Back Beach	On the Island		
Midnight	Back Beach		Back Beach			
1:00 a.m.	Back Beach		Camp			Back Beach
6:00 a.m.	Secret Beach				Secret Beach	

CHAPTER 30

HUDDLE UP

Margaux

When Ryan and Liddie got back from wherever they'd been, Margaux decided it was time to take charge. Kate was going to live. Mary had a boyfriend. What else didn't she know? The only way they were going to solve this thing was if they pooled their resources.

She went into the office and gathered up what she could, then dragged a whiteboard from the back of the lodge to the fireplace.

"What are you doing?" Kate asked. She still had a tinge of blue around her lips, as if she'd drawn them in with lip liner.

"We need to huddle up."

"Huddle up?" Liddie said. "Like in football?"

"Okay, so maybe that's not the right term."

"Are we voting again?" Mary asked, eyeing the markers in Margaux's hand.

"What?" Ryan said. "No, please . . ."

"Not yet," Margaux said. "I think we need to do something else first."

"What's that?" Sean asked, coming down the stairs. He gave Margaux a guilty look, then broke eye contact. Margaux felt nervous. What if one of them *had* hurt Amanda? Even if she'd made assumptions about Ryan for all these years, they were only assumptions. Feelings weren't proof of something she didn't know if she could accept. It wasn't evidence of something that might throw her world into chaos. But she'd promised Ryan, and she owed it to Amanda.

Margaux set up the whiteboard, wiping off the leftover Pictionary sketches and staff meeting reminders.

July 22–23, 1998, she wrote across the top.

She made six columns and headed them with their names: *Amanda, Margaux, Ryan, Mary, Kate & Liddie, Sean.*

"You're missing someone," Ryan said. "Two people, in fact."

"Who?"

"Mom and Dad."

"Ryan!" Kate said. "That's disgusting."

"Why is it more disgusting than any of the rest of us having done it?"

Ryan stared at Kate as they all watched her struggle to come up with an answer. "I don't know. But if they'd done it, why would Dad put that condition in his will? That doesn't make any sense. Besides, what reason could they possibly have to do that to Amanda?"

"But I have a reason to? That's what you think, isn't it?"

"Ryan," Margaux said. "Please."

He backed off. "Sorry."

"It's okay. Look," Margaux said. "This whole situation is nuts, but Mom and Dad weren't on the Island that night. They weren't even at camp, remember? They were at that Camping Association meeting and only got back the next morning. Sean was in charge. So they're out of it. It's only us. We owe it to Ryan to figure out whether he did it. Or whether it was someone else."

Liddie came and stood in front of the whiteboard. "So what's this?"

"A way to figure it out."

Margaux picked up another marker and drew horizontal lines this time, making a series of boxes. Then, in the left-hand boxes she wrote the time.

9:00 p.m.

10:00 p.m.

11:00 p.m.

All the way down to *6:00 a.m.*

"I thought we could all put in where we were that night."

"Your big giant plan for helping Ryan is to figure out which one of the rest of us did it?" Liddie said.

Her stomach churned. "It's only fair, isn't it?"

"What if this proves Ryan did it?"

"I didn't," Ryan said.

"If you say so."

"Come on, guys. Let's try and see how it goes." Margaux looked around at her family. She saw a variety of emotions, from mild curiosity to . . . was that fear? No, that was Liddie looking angry, and Kate looking concerned, and Mary inscrutable as always. Sean was frowning, and Amy looked mildly curious. Only Ryan looked eager, almost happy to see what this might bring. Somehow, this solidified things for Margaux. If Ryan had no fear, then this must be the right path to take.

"Sure," Mary said. "I'll play along." She picked up one of the pens from the table and filled in her box at *10:00 p.m.* with the words *On the Island.* Then she drew an arrow down each of her boxes to indicate she was in the same place the whole night. She stood back to admire her work. "That was easy. Here, I'll fill you in too."

She did the same in Margaux's column.

"Wait," Margaux said. "That's not right."

Mary looked puzzled. They'd always been each other's alibi, but

Mary was forgetting that Margaux had gone to find Amanda. "It's not what you think." She walked to the whiteboard and erased the line in the *11:00 p.m.* square. She replaced it with the words *Back Beach*. Then she crouched down and wrote at *5:00 a.m.*: *Searching for A.*

She stood back and looked at what she'd written. As she reread the words *Searching for A.*, she shuddered. The memory was so vivid: the odd panic she'd felt when she'd opened her eyes as the sun crept up and Amanda wasn't sleeping next to her. She didn't believe in premonitions, but it was hard to think what else it was. She was the first one awake, she realized as she sat up. The campers, who'd finally worn themselves out talking around one in the morning, were breathing heavily, their arms flung up over their eyes to block out the rising sun.

She'd untangled herself from her sleeping bag and looked around. Mary was also missing. Somehow this relieved her, but then her heart started sprinting when Mary emerged from the woods with a roll of toilet paper and a camp towel.

She walked over to Mary. "Where's Amanda?" she whispered.

"How should I know?"

"Did she come back last night?"

"I fell asleep."

That was true. Mary had been asleep when Margaux returned from Back Beach. She'd been annoyed, worried the kids would take advantage, but they hadn't even noticed.

"Amanda didn't come back?"

"I don't know. Stay with the kids, okay? I'm going to go looking for her."

Margaux had rushed off through the woods toward Back Beach. Halfway there, she'd tripped on a root and landed on the forest floor with her hands out in front of her. She stood, her legs shaking, her hands stinging from the scrapes she'd gotten on the rocks. But she moved on anyway, a fear like she'd never known pushing her. Maybe it was the odd dreams she'd had all night, her brain tossing out images from the ghost stories the girls had been telling around the fire. Suddenly, Margaux stopped up short with a memory. Had that been a scream she'd heard? Or was that a dream?

She continued. When she was close enough, she started calling for Amanda. Maybe she and Ryan had fallen asleep? She didn't want to walk in on anything she didn't want to see.

"Amanda!"

Her voice echoed off the water as she arrived at Back Beach. She was alone. She turned around in a full circle.

"Amanda?"

Her heart was racing. Where could she be? Had Ryan ever shown up? She should've gone looking for her when she hadn't come back by midnight. But it had been warm in her sleeping bag, and she didn't want to disturb her with Ryan and . . . There was no excuse. None at all. Where could she have gone? Their canoe was on the other side of the Island. The only way back was to swim.

She'd stood still and listened. She wasn't sure what it was she wanted to hear, but there was something tugging at her. There, that was it. The sound of something clunking against the rocks, a dull wooden *thud*. She took off her shoes and walked into the water. Something caught her attention to the left of the small bay. She pushed through the cool water, ignoring the fact that her pants were getting wet. She could see what it was now. A paddle, caught among the rocks. She picked it up. It had the marking all the Macaw paddles had, an intertwining C and M. It felt like spiders were crawling down Margaux's spine. She turned the paddle over and stifled a scream. It was smeared with blood.

"What were you talking to Amanda about?" Liddie asked.

"What?"

Margaux shook herself back to the present. The memory of that awful discovery was clinging to her like the sap from a pine tree.

"Me," Ryan said.

"Oh?"

"Yeah, here." Ryan picked up a red pen, then looked like he thought better of it and reached for the black one. He filled in the squares below his name: *Lantern ceremony*; *Back Beach*; *Back Beach*; *Camp*, and then drew a line down to *6:00 a.m.*

"What time did you get to the Island?" Kate asked.

"Around eleven thirty."

"And then?" Liddie asked.

"And then we, you know, fooled around for a bit."

"And you left at one?"

"More like twelve thirty. I was back in my cabin by one. Ty was covering for me, and we talked for a few minutes when I got back."

"Do they know what time Amanda . . . ?" Mary asked.

"I don't know," Liddie said, looking at Ryan. "Do we?"

"She was fine when I left her."

"Fine?" Margaux said. "I doubt she was fine."

"Okay," Ryan said. "She was upset. I wasn't . . . Things weren't working out between us. But I didn't do that. I swear to God. When I left, she was sitting on the beach, looking out at the water, watching me row away."

"What happened to her then?" Amy asked.

"I don't know."

"This is such horseshit," Liddie said.

"Liddie," Kate warned. "Shhh."

"No, Kate. I'm tired of keeping this to myself. If he wants us to give him the benefit of the doubt, then he has to stop lying. He has to stop lying right now."

"Lying about what?" Margaux asked. "What do you know?"

"Are you going to tell them, Ryan, or should I?"

Ryan stood there, looking lost.

"Fine, then. Fine." She walked to the whiteboard. She used her hand to rub out the line in Ryan's *6:00 a.m.* column. Then she crouched and wrote: *Secret Beach.*

CHAPTER 31

THE HEART WANTS WHAT THE HEART WANTS

Ryan

Ryan felt as if someone had reached into his chest and squeezed his heart. This wasn't how this was supposed to go. This wasn't how any of this was supposed to go. He should've known that Liddie had had enough. He should've known that when Margaux laid out her plan—not even a plan, a stupid suggestion to become amateur detectives—it wouldn't work. People cling to secrets. Ryan knew that better than anyone. If you went looking, if you started trying to peel away and expose them, even the innocent felt threatened.

"Ryan?"

"What?"

Margaux was standing in front of him with that look on her face. He'd seen it before, not only from her but from every woman in his life who he'd ever disappointed. His mother. His wife. Stacey Kensington in the minutes before it had all gone wrong.

"Is what Liddie said true? Were you on Secret Beach that morning?"

"Yes."

"Oh my God."

"It doesn't change anything."

"How can you say that?" Margaux said. "It changes everything."

"I didn't do anything to her."

"Then why were you there?"

Ryan felt that pressure in his chest again. Like his heart was being cold-pressed. How could he explain? No one wanted his explanations. No one believed them.

It had been like that with Stacey too. Even though he'd accepted responsibility, that wasn't enough. He'd had to do more.

Because the real mistake he'd made, the thing he was entirely responsible for, was talking to Stacey at all. He and Kerry had been dating for years. Things were serious, and Kerry wanted them to be more serious. He wasn't sure he was ready for all of it. Marriage. Fatherhood. He needed a bit of time to figure it out, but Kerry wasn't having it, because his doubts felt personal. If she was who he was meant to be with, then he should know. He shouldn't wonder. He was waiting for someone else to come along. Someone better. That's what she said. Try as he might, he couldn't explain to her that *he* was the one he wasn't sure about. He'd never seen himself as a father. He hadn't thought he'd settle down. Kerry had come as a surprise. She'd challenged his perceptions of himself. He wanted things he didn't understand, that he would've scoffed at only a few years earlier. Maybe he was growing up. Or maybe he was still as fucked up as he'd been from fifteen on, when girls were interchangeable to him. He didn't want to let Kerry down. If he was being honest, he didn't understand why she loved him.

Meeting Stacey had been like a redo on his meeting with Kerry. Her younger brother was a camper. She was there for the family weekend. He'd come up to camp after a fight with Kerry to try to figure out, once and for all, what he was going to do. Break up or commit. That was the choice he had.

And there was Stacey, twenty-two, beautiful, interested in him the way girls were always interested. He knew what it meant. He was the right prescription for someone looking for a weekend of fun. That's what family weekend was about. She laughed a lot, that he remembered. But in the intervening years, what she had actually looked like faded. In fact, she looked similar enough to Kerry that sometimes, when he tried to remember the details, it was Kerry laughing next to him on the dock, Kerry tugging at his hand under the dinner table, Kerry who he pulled into the woods and kissed against the staff cabin the way he'd kissed so many girls before.

She'd wanted cigarettes. That's what she said, her hands on her hips, her hair wild from the humidity. "Take me for some cigarettes," she'd said. Ryan wasn't sure if that was some kind of euphemism for having hot sex in his car or she simply cared that much about smoking. He didn't think that much about it. She laughed as they made their way through the trees to the parking lot, and again when he fumbled for his keys. He'd only had one beer that night, *one*, so he knew he was okay to drive. But he was nervous, scared of what he was thinking of doing.

They'd gone into town, her hands in between his legs. He'd pulled over at one point so he could touch her. He still remembered the *zip* of the seat belt as it flew away from his chest. She'd climbed into the back seat, and he'd followed her. The sex was raw, and Kerry was in his mind the whole time, and even before he came, he felt bad. What the fuck was he doing? He'd had this. He'd always had this. It wasn't what he wanted anymore. He could see that clearly now. But he'd screwed up things with Kerry. Because when she said he should take a couple of days to figure things out, she most definitely did not mean to go fuck some stranger in the back of his car on the side of the road.

Stacey had been unaware of his turmoil. Why should she care? He was a guy who was willing to have sex with a girl in a car a few hours after they'd met. She'd judged him accurately.

"I still want those cigarettes though," she'd said when they'd rearranged their clothes. He'd taken her to town and bought her two packs of cigarettes, and when he went for the driver's side, she'd rushed ahead of him and said she wanted to drive.

"How much have you had to drink?"

She pouted. "Don't be like that."

"Concerned for your safety?"

"A spoilsport."

"You had those two drinks I brought you," Ryan said. "Anything else?"

"No, sir."

Ryan's shoulders tensed. "Sir" was what people called his dad. He looked at Stacey. She didn't seem drunk. There was something about her though. She was keyed up. Was she on something? Ryan hadn't ever been into drugs, not serious ones anyway. Pot didn't count, and he knew she wasn't high.

"Why do you care about driving so much?"

She raised her arms above her head. She was wearing a tank top, and her limbs looked too thin extended that way. "I want to have fun! Not be analyzed about it."

He held out the keys. "Fine, sure. Take them."

She leaned in and kissed him, her tongue in his mouth, her teeth against his lips. He thought she might drag him back into the rear of the car, but instead, after a moment, she broke the kiss and slipped behind the wheel.

He barely had time to buckle up before she backed out of the parking space. He told her to put on her seat belt, feeling like a dad, *his dad*, but she stuck out her tongue and rolled down the windows.

She lit up a cigarette and drove like they do in the movies, her head half out the window, yelling at the night. Ryan tried to squelch the urge to tell her to slow down. He was distracted by thoughts of Kerry. Did he have to tell her what happened? No. What good would that do? Besides, they were on a break of sorts. If this stupid night had crystalized things for him, if he now knew what he wanted, *her*, wasn't that enough? Did she have to know the details?

They came around a curve. He saw it too late. A horse on the road, a blonde braid flashing in the headlights. He tried to reach over to the wheel, but Stacey had already hit the brakes. The car fishtailed, and then it got hazy. There was a scream and the sound of a horse panicking. Maybe they were the same noise. He might've been screaming. He never blacked out, but the world was tumbling, askew. He was upside down. The car had turned over in the ditch, and Stacey wasn't next to him anymore. He unclipped his seat belt, trying to brace himself as best he could from falling on his head. The car was dinging because the keys were in the ignition, that awful *ding, ding, ding* that always drove Ryan nuts. He managed, somehow, to get out of the car. The air smelled of burned tires and gasoline. Where was Stacey? Where was the horse? Who'd been on it?

He knew with a sickening certainty. *Mary*. He ran up the embankment. One of the camp horses named Miranda was in the ditch on the other side, pawing at the ground. Mary was on the tarmac, an awful shade of white. And then, in the distance, somehow, a siren. He'd learn later that someone had heard the accident and called 9-1-1—the ambulance was nearby on a false alarm—but that night he couldn't understand it. They were ten miles from town. How were they coming so fast?

He made himself concentrate. Stacey was missing. His sister was lying crumpled on the road. He had to do something. Mary sat up.

"Stay still," he said, rushing to her side.

"What happened?"

"There was a car accident."

"I was riding."

She was confused, drunk, he realized. She smelled like alcohol. Although she was twenty-six then, she'd always seemed younger to Ryan. Naive. Still living at home and riding horses. Ryan didn't have enough time to think properly; thoughts were racing through his mind. Mary had been riding her horse on a dark road drunk. She'd caused a car accident. Stacey might be . . . Whatever she was, Mary was going to be in trouble. Lots of trouble.

"Can you stand?"

"Why?"

"Do you think you could lead Miranda into the woods over there and go home the back way?"

She stood, swaying slightly. There was a trickle of blood on her forehead, and her eyes seemed unfocused. "Yes, but why?"

"I'll explain later. Just do it, okay? And quickly. I don't want the police to know you were here." The sirens grew louder. "Go, Mary."

She scrambled down the hill, wobbly but in control. Ryan crossed the road back to the car, standing at a safe distance as the ambulance turned the corner and slowed. A police car arrived a minute later. Mary was out of view, a retreating speck in the woods that you wouldn't look for if you didn't know to.

The EMTs checked him out, but he was, amazingly, all right. They found Stacey a few minutes later. They wouldn't tell Ryan how she was, but he knew by their faces. He wasn't entirely sure what he was thinking other than that he needed to protect Mary, but when the officer asked him what had happened, who was driving, Ryan had looked at the car and the seat belt that he hadn't forced Stacey to wear, and he thought of his sister hiding in the woods, of the whole fucking mess, and said, "It was me."

—

"Ryan?"

"What?"

Margaux was still standing in front of him. She seemed out of focus, but that couldn't be right. "You . . . Are you okay?"

"I'm having trouble breathing."

"Why is he holding his arm like that . . . Oh, shit. Liddie, call 9-1-1. Call 9-1-1 now!"

CHAPTER 32

PAST DUE

Kate

As Kate watched Ryan being taken out of the lodge on a stretcher and loaded into an ambulance, she made a decision.

"Where are you going?" Amy asked.

"I need to make a call. Margaux, will you wait for me before going to the hospital?"

"Of course, but hurry up."

Kate went into the office. She sat at the desk and stared at the old rotary-dial phone. She had to do this, but she hesitated. Right now, they were in a bubble. Even though bad things had happened, they seemed self-contained. Once she made this phone call, it felt like all the worry and problems and suffering from this weekend and all the time before that would seep out.

So she hesitated, then dialed the number she knew by heart, because she might forget some things but never numbers. It rang once, twice, and then the voice of a small girl said, "MacAllister residence. How can I help you?"

When she got off the phone, Kate hesitated again. Now she had to go confront something else. All because of Liddie. Stupid Liddie. Years and years of silence and tattoos about never telling, and all it took was one pissy afternoon and she was blabbing all over the place. Well, it couldn't be helped now. She'd have to explain herself to Margaux, once and for all.

Margaux was standing on the porch with Amy. They were making small talk, which was ridiculous because they'd known each other forever, but there was a new reality now. Amy and Kate together. She could tell that this was what Margaux was adjusting to. Only it wasn't reality; it was the past. Margaux might be catching up on past episodes, but Kate knew the end, the date they were canceled. There wasn't going to be some groundswell of fan support to bring the show back for one more season on Netflix. They'd always been a cult hit, and nothing had changed in the intervening years except they were both older now and knew better.

"We should get to the hospital," Kate said.

"You want to take my car?"

"I don't have one, so yeah."

"Right," Margaux said. "Forgot, sorry."

"It doesn't matter. Where's Liddie?"

"She went with Sean and Mary."

Kate felt her anger at Liddie growing. She always acted as if she was so brave, and yet here she was avoiding her. Was she feeling guilty? If Ryan died tonight, if his heart gave out, would she blame herself? Kate's own heart constricted. Ryan couldn't die, no, not Ryan. Whatever he did, he couldn't do that.

"You want to come, Amy?" Margaux asked.

"I've got to meet with the caterers in an hour."

"That's still happening tomorrow, isn't it?"

"Too late to cancel, probably."

"Yeah," Kate agreed. "Too late." She reached out and touched Amy just below the elbow. "I'll see you later?"

"Sure."

Margaux coughed, a sign of discomfort. She wondered what Margaux would do if she saw them kissing. And then she realized that she didn't have to imagine it; she could find out. She leaned over and kissed Amy full on the mouth, wrapping her arms around her. Amy resisted briefly, then reciprocated the hug, if not the kiss.

"He's going to be okay," Amy said.

"I hope so."

Margaux's car bumped over the rough road. It was old and comfortable, kind of like Margaux. Not that Margaux was old; she only seemed that way a lot of the time, older than their mother had in many ways.

Of everyone in their family, the person she'd understood the least had been her mother. When Kate thought of her, she always seemed diaphanous. Like one of those Instagram filters had been applied to her, washing her out, smoothing away the lines. Nothing ever seemed to stick to her, not criticism or her children, not even her husband. She simply floated around, photographing it all, removed. What must it have been like in her mind? Living inside those thoughts? Did she have any clue what impact her behavior had on those around her? Kate could only hope that she'd had no idea, because the alternative was too terrible to think of. That she knew but continued on anyway.

"Are we going to talk at all?" Margaux asked as they pulled off the camp road and onto the highway. "Or just sit here stewing in our own thoughts?"

"I guess you want to talk about what Liddie said."

"Well, yeah."

Kate looked out the window. It was still light out, coming up on dinnertime. She felt a rush of hunger, then felt guilty. Ryan could be dying, and here she was craving a cheeseburger.

"What do you want to know?"

"Is it true that Ryan was on Secret Beach that morning?"

"Yes."

"And you knew? This whole time you've been lying for him?"

Kate turned away from the window. "No, we've been lying for you."

The car swerved, cutting into the gravel on the side of the road before it righted itself.

"Do you need me to drive?"

"I'm all right. Only, what do you mean? Lying for me?"

"That's what Ryan told us, that we had to keep it secret for you."

Margaux's hands gripped the wheel tightly. Kate watched her. She was focused on the way ahead, the turns in the road. Kate knew that none of what she was saying made sense, but then it had never made sense. Not that frantic swim in the night. Or later, as they picked their way along the path to Secret Beach in the early morning, blisters forming on her feet where she'd shoved them, wet, into her boat shoes. They hadn't known what they were going to find when they got to the beach, or what they'd seen on the lake, but they were expecting something.

What they didn't expect was Ryan.

They'd almost run into him as they turned the last corner to Secret Beach. He looked terrified.

"What are you doing here?" he'd asked. "Turn around. Go back."

"We saw . . ." Liddie said. "What's going on? Who's on the beach?"

"What do you mean, you saw?"

Ryan seemed wild, undone.

"We saw someone swimming, pushing a boat. And someone was in the boat . . . Was that you?"

Ryan covered his face with his hands. His knuckles were grazed. "Oh my God. Oh my God."

"What's happening?" Kate had asked. "Are you in trouble?"

His breath was ragged. "Something . . . something happened to Amanda."

"Amanda?" Liddie said. "What?"

"She . . . I don't know, okay, I don't know what happened to her, but I think . . . I think she's dead."

Kate fell to the ground, not fainting, just exhausted. It was hard and full of roots, and what was happening? Amanda was dead? She'd been alive at dinner the night before, stopping to ask Kate a question about how her skit was coming for talent night. *Let me know if you need some help,* she'd said. *Anytime.* And Kate had blushed because she had a crush on Amanda, a crush that no one knew anything about, not even Liddie.

"Whaddaya mean?" Liddie said. "There's a dead body back there?"

"Keep your voice down."

"We need to get an ambulance. Or Mom and Dad," Kate said.

"No! Not Mom and Dad . . . They're not here." Ryan crouched down to Kate. "You okay, Katie?"

She started to cry. "I don't want Amanda to be dead."

"Me neither. I'm not sure . . . I don't know what to do. I don't know what to do."

"Why can't we get the grown-ups?" Kate asked.

"Yes, maybe . . . Maybe you can do it."

"Why can't you do it?"

"Because I . . . People might think I did it."

"You hurt Amanda?"

"I didn't. But they might think so, do you see?"

"No."

"I don't know how to explain it, Katie. But listen. How about this? Can you and Liddie be brave? Really, really brave?"

"Maybe?" Kate said as Liddie said, "Of course!"

"Okay, okay, maybe this will work. I'm going to leave now and go back to my cabin. You count to a hundred, and then you run back to camp, and you find whoever you can and tell them you found Amanda in a boat on Secret Beach, and you're not sure if she's okay. Tell them to call an ambulance. Don't tell them I was here, okay?"

"But what are we doing out here? We're going to get in trouble."

"You were . . . you were looking for flowers or something, for a project. I don't know, make up a story."

"I'm not good at that."

"I am," Liddie said proudly.

"Listen to Liddie, okay? Just say whatever she tells you to." Ryan stood, helping Kate up. "I'm going to go now, all right? I'm going to leave, and you count and then you do as I said."

Liddie stood in front of him, her hands on her hips.

"Why should we? What's in it for us?"

"I'm not enough, huh?"

Liddie gave him a look, an are-you-kidding-me smirk.

"Do it for Margaux, then."

"Margaux?"

"Yeah," he said. "You're doing this for Margaux."

CHAPTER 33

FLATLINE

Liddie

Liddie had a horror of hospitals. This wasn't a rational reaction. How could it be? Somehow she'd managed to survive an entire reckless childhood without ever needing a cast or stitches. The same with Kate. She couldn't put her finger on what it was, exactly, that made her feel this way. Why she was full of dread. It wasn't only Ryan's condition or the fact that she was a large part of the reason he was in the ambulance whose lights were rotating in front of them. She shouldn't have pushed him like that. What had she hoped to achieve?

Sean was driving, and Mary was in the back seat. She kept waiting for them to say something. To blame her or ask her what she meant in the lodge. But they said nothing. Why had she chosen that moment, of all of them, to finally out her brother? Was it because of the lifetime of guilt she'd felt about how she and her sister had acted that night? No. It was the way *she'd* acted that night, that morning, all of it.

The car hit a bump, and Liddie's head cracked against the glass.

"That sounded like it stung," Sean said, glancing at her. "You okay?"

"I'm fine."

She rubbed at the lump forming on her forehead.

"Ryan's going to be all right," Mary said.

Liddie turned around in her seat. Mary looked calm, her hands lying loosely in her lap. "How do you know?"

"Forty-year-olds don't die of heart attacks. If that's what it was. Probably more like a panic attack."

She was suddenly furious. "Shut up, Mary."

"Hey, now," Sean said. "That's not necessary."

"She doesn't know what she's talking about."

"She's trying to make you feel better."

"I don't need her help."

"Fine, then," Mary said. "Fine."

Liddie turned around, and they lapsed into silence. She thought back to that morning, all those years ago. The shock of what they'd seen out there on the water. But what had they seen? A figure, a boat, a flash of long hair. Then, finding Ryan in the woods. Ryan, who knew what was on the beach they were going to investigate. Who told them Amanda was probably dead. Who wasn't sure if they should tell anyone. Then his plan. Counting to a hundred like they were playing hide-and-seek, then going and getting the help Amanda needed, if she wasn't beyond help already.

"This is stupid," Liddie had said to Kate after Ryan was out of earshot. Kate had reached twenty in a low voice, counting like she was in a time-out.

"What?"

"We should go see Amanda."

"Ugh, no. I don't want to."

"Come on, let's go."

She grabbed Kate's hand, but Kate resisted. "I told you, I don't want to. Remember *Stand by Me*? That dead body they saw. That was horrible."

"That was a movie."

"Right, this will be worse."

"I'm going. You coming?"

Liddie turned her back on Kate and started running down the path. She knew Kate would follow. There was no way she would go off on her own. She never had. As Liddie pushed through the bushes, she wasn't sure why she wanted to see Amanda so badly. Part of her was hoping that what Ryan had said was a joke, that they'd find nothing and they could tell him his trick hadn't worked. Another part of her was excited.

Then the last branch snapped aside, and there was the boat, Amanda laid out in it like when Anne of Green Gables had played the Lady of Shalott. Her skin was white. Blood oozed from a gash on her head. Liddie swayed on her feet.

Kate arrived. "Omigod, omigod."

"Shhh."

"Stop saying that."

They'd stopped talking then, and Liddie didn't have a clear memory of what had happened next. The shock, the fog of time, she didn't want to remember. They'd looked at the body. Touched it, even. Fingers searching for a pulse? A hand laid over her mouth to see if they could feel breath? Had they made things worse? They'd lost time, that was for sure. Then they were running back through the woods, tumbling up the stairs to the lodge, yelling for someone to wake up.

And much later, after a day of drama, when they were in their bunks, she'd heard Kate's small voice whispering in the dark.

"Did Margaux do that?"

They spent the next hour and a half waiting on uncomfortable chairs for an update about Ryan. Before they knew anything, Kerry arrived, her three daughters in tow: Maisy, Claire, and Sasha. Kerry's flats clacked against the old tile floor, while the kids swirled around her, looking wild-eyed.

"Where's Ryan?" she asked. She was wearing old jeans and her hair was in an untidy bun. Liddie had never seen her look so disheveled.

"They took him back there," Mary said, pointing over her shoulder to where Ryan had been wheeled through a set of swinging doors. "We haven't gotten an update."

"Have you asked?"

Her voice was grating, high-pitched. Liddie couldn't blame her; she'd spent an hour and a half in a car with three children wondering if her husband was dead.

"I'll go," Liddie said.

Kerry looked at her to protest, then nodded and collapsed into a chair. The girls surrounded her, and Sasha, the youngest, climbed into her lap.

Liddie went to the triage area. A nurse in printed scrubs was pecking away at a computer.

"Hi, um, I'm looking for an update about my brother?"

"Name?"

"Ryan MacAllister. He came in the ambulance . . ."

She pecked at a few keys. "There's nothing here. Hold on."

The nurse left and went through the door at the back of her cubicle. Liddie half listened to the conversation behind her. Her nieces talking to Mary and Sean, asking what happened. Mary doing her best to tell a less scary version of the story, leaving out how Ryan keeled over, the way he was sweating, the hard grasp he had on his arm. No one mentioned the whiteboard, still sitting there in the lodge, half filled in, explaining nothing.

The nurse came back. "The doctor's with him now. The family should be able to go back shortly."

"So he's going to be all right?"

"I'll let the doctor tell you."

The nurse smiled at her. She was redheaded and freckled, and Liddie knew that her smile meant it was going to be okay, Ryan was going to be okay, even if she couldn't say that now.

"Thank you."

They were called back twenty minutes later.

They all stood in the doorway of Ryan's room. He looked large in the bed, too large almost, with leads attached to machines taped to his chest, something beeping incessantly. There wasn't space for the whole family in there, so Liddie hung back. She wouldn't be wanted anyway. Not by Ryan. He was going to be okay. It was a mild infarction. He'd be put on medication and monitored, and he'd have to change his diet. For now, no surgery. He could go home soon.

Kerry started to cry, and Sasha wanted to climb into bed with him. Liddie found herself backing out of the doorway, feeling claustrophobic. She tried to go to the waiting room but took a wrong turn somewhere and ended up at the entrance of another wing of the hospital. Long-term care. She pushed through the doors automatically. She didn't know where she was heading until she got there: a row of rooms where the push and pull of respirators was the predominant sound. Liddie marveled at how all the doors were open, how anyone could walk in without being asked what they were doing or who they were going to see. Whether they had the right to be there at all.

She stopped at the third door. Had she been here before? Or had she simply heard it described enough times back when Margaux used to visit regularly?

She stepped into the room. There was a picture from camp on the wall, a beautiful sunset captured in a style she recognized as her mother's. Beneath it, Amanda lay on the bed, not quite frozen in time. She was thin, so thin, and her hair had faded. Her chest rose and fell with regularity. The monitor next to her showed an even line of brain activity. Or no brain activity. No, not quite. Minimal, yes, that was the word she'd heard all those years ago. Amanda was alive but only minimally. A persistent vegetative state that couldn't be undone, until one day, sometime in the unpredictable future, when even the machines could no longer keep her alive.

Either way, whatever she knew would stay inside her, evidenced only by that small heartbeat of movement on the screen.

AMANDA

There's so much about that night I remember. The taste of Ryan's mouth.

The salt in my tears.

The whiffling sound right before the blow.

Then darkness. The muffled cry of the person who discovered me. The lilting of the boat.

Have I told you this before?

It's hard for me to know. Time stopped for me that morning with the twins. I remember shouting, the wail of a siren. Needles and tubes and people crying.

That's how it's been since then.

The same bed.

The same room.

Needles and tubes and people crying.

I'm not awake. I'm not asleep either.

Not alive but not dead.

I'm left with only these memories. That last night of my life playing over and over like a loop.

Is this hell?

Is this heaven?

I'll never tell.

	Amanda	**Margaux**	**Ryan**	**Mary**	**Kate & Liddie**	**Sean**
9:00 p.m.	Lantern ceremony	Lantern ceremony	Lantern ceremony			
10:00 p.m.	On the Island	On the Island		On the Island		Crash boat
11:00 p.m.	Back Beach	Back Beach	Back Beach	On the Island		
Midnight	Back Beach		Back Beach			
1:00 a.m.	Back Beach		Camp			Back Beach
5:00 a.m.		Searches for A.		On the Island		
6:00 a.m.	Secret Beach		Secret Beach		Secret Beach	

SUNDAY

CHAPTER 34

OTHER VOICES, OTHER ROOMS

Margaux

"Come on, Margaux!"

They were eight and running through the woods up to the playing field. Then they were ten, eleven, twelve. Amanda the fearless, running ahead of her, her chasing along. Even that last summer when they were seventeen. Margaux wasn't going to go to camp; she was going to talk to her parents, convince them to let her get some other job, something that had nothing to do with her family. For the summer, at least, she wasn't going to be a MacAllister anymore, only Margaux. Margaux MacAllister . . . She wasn't sure who she wanted to be, but it wasn't that. She'd pick some new last name—not that her last name was famous or anything, but so many kids had gone through Macaw that she was bound to run into one of them somewhere along the way. But that summer, if that happened, she was going to pull the twin trick, pretend she was someone else. "You must be talking about that other girl who looks like me . . . Did you want one scoop or two?"

That was the plan.

When she'd told Amanda about it, she'd looked so disappointed. "What am I going to do without you?" she'd asked. "What about our plans?"

Margaux didn't remember making any plans. She only remembered Amanda talking about being back in camp that summer and her nodding and not saying anything. And now, even as her hopes were being dashed, she knew that she'd follow along again. All Amanda would need to say was, "Come on, Margaux."

And she'd go.

She did. Those first four weeks, she was thinking, *This isn't so bad. Amanda was right to push me to come back.*

And then Amanda was, for all intents and purposes, gone.

Margaux woke in that hour between night and light with a jolt. Where the hell was she and what had she done to her neck?

Hospital. Hospital. She was in the hospital because: Ryan.

She sat up, blinking against the light. She was sitting in a waiting room chair that was not meant for comfort. Earlier, after everyone had left and she'd insisted on staying, she'd drifted off to . . . it wasn't quite sleep. The "gloaming." That's what she and Amanda used to call it. That minute before you fell asleep, like the minute before the sun disappears. Magic time, it always seemed like, before life rushed away.

God, she felt maudlin. The crappy sleep and being in the hospital, *this* hospital, with the certain knowledge that Amanda was somewhere in the building. She'd been brought here twenty years ago after she was found, barely breathing but still alive. Margaux had arrived back at camp after a frantic row across the lake in time to see her loaded into the ambulance. A crew of counselors had helped the EMTs bring the stretcher through the woods from Secret Beach. One of the EMTs was straddling Amanda, pumping his arms up and down, keeping her heart going, while another held an oxygen mask in place.

Even though the wake-up bell hadn't been rung, camp was chaos. Kids were streaming out of the girls' and boys' sections, their eyes wide in fear. Most of the girls were crying. Margaux's knees were trembling as she tried to reach Amanda, but someone held her back. Sean. He wrapped his arms around her, and she buried her face in his neck, so overcome she couldn't speak. She didn't know how long she stayed like that. She heard the doors to the ambulance shut and the vehicle drive away. Then there was another car, its doors slamming, and her mother was peeling her away from Sean asking, "What happened? What happened?"

Later, at the hospital where they'd all gone to wait, Swift arrived. He'd huddled with her parents in the corner, and then he talked to Ryan. Amanda's parents were there by then, and she didn't give his presence much thought. It was only after, when the police began questioning everyone, that Margaux understood. Ryan was a suspect. Ryan, who wouldn't look her in the eye.

Now here she was, back in the hospital with Ryan again, and Amanda was still here. All these years, Amanda's parents had chosen to leave her in this place. It was one of the things that made it so hard to come back to camp—knowing Amanda was in a hospital twenty minutes away. How could she be having fun, moving on, *living* when Amanda was in stasis? She couldn't do it.

Neither could Amanda's parents, it seemed, because how else could they simply abandon her so far from their home? As if Amanda wasn't something worth keeping close, now that she'd moved beyond their help.

Maybe that wasn't fair. It was an excellent facility, away from the hustle and bustle of Montreal, surrounded by massive trees and sweet-smelling grass in the summer. But it was also far enough to create the excuse not to be there every day, or even every month. That went for all of them, but Margaux made herself feel better by making it about Amanda's parents. Their neglect made hers okay. They'd all moved on. Stopped going for regular visits, stopped checking in with one another on whether anything could be done. Amanda had faded, first from view and then even from her thoughts.

That was screwed up, she knew. She should get up right now and find the right hallway to Amanda. She should stand in her room and listen to the hum of the machines, hold her frail hand. Amanda was her best friend. Her best friend who she'd never replaced because she wasn't dead, she just wasn't available.

That was what she should do. But instead, she went to find Ryan.

Margaux stopped in the doorway to his room. He was lying on a bed that wasn't quite big enough for him, surrounded by his family. Sasha and Maisy were in the bed with him. Kerry was sleeping in a chair they'd brought in for her with Claire tucked in next to her. They looked so perfect, despite the circumstances. Margaux's heart hurt. Perhaps she did want these things, this life that she'd pushed away. Mark wasn't so bad; maybe they could . . . Good lord. What was she thinking? If this was her biological clock waking up at last, she had a bone to pick with it. Her neck was stiff. She smelled funky. She wanted to go home.

"Margaux?"

Ryan was awake.

"Hey, Ry."

"My heart hurts."

"Mine too."

He was whispering. She moved in closer. Maisy was snoring gently. Sasha's back was curled against him, and Margaux couldn't understand how she was even staying in the bed.

"Some family reunion, huh?" Ryan said.

"Right?"

"We should talk about it."

"*You* want to talk?"

"Right?" Ryan mimicked her. He patted the small piece of bed that was free.

She approached and knelt down but didn't sit. "Is this the time or the place?"

"If not now, then when?"

"Don't say that. You're fine. You're going to be fine."

"Am I though?" He looked at the window. Margaux turned to see what he was looking at. All she could see was green and dappled sunlight.

"It's pretty here."

"It is."

"Do you think she likes it?"

"I hope so."

"I think she does."

"Okay."

"I didn't put her in here."

"You said."

"But I also didn't tell you about being on Secret Beach."

"You did not."

Kerry coughed and turned over. Margaux watched her for a moment, how she curled herself around Claire. She wondered if Kerry was listening to their conversation, only feigning sleep. Why would she do that? She was probably as exhausted as they all were, even more so. Ryan was her husband, the father of her children. She had to hear that he might be dying and then drive in a car with their children without knowing whether he'd be there to greet her. She couldn't image how awful that must've been. She wished she could be more sympathetic, but it eluded her. Why did she feel like this about Kerry? Why had she always? Jealousy? Anger on behalf of Amanda?

"I didn't hurt her on Secret Beach either," Ryan said.

"Then what were you doing there?"

"You don't know?"

"How could I?"

"I thought I was saving you."

She almost laughed. "What would you be saving me from?"

"I thought . . . I thought you were the one who . . ."

"I . . . What?"

"Hush, you'll wake the girls."

Margaux stood up. She felt dizzy. She picked up the visitor's chair and put it down in the place where she'd been crouching. Ryan's eyes were closed, as if the words he'd said had drained whatever energy was left in him.

"We shouldn't talk about this here."

He opened his eyes. "No, let's do this."

"I don't understand. You never said anything before. Not even earlier, when I was basically accusing you of doing it."

"I . . . I've tried to forget. I didn't want to believe that you had anything to do with it."

She felt sick to her stomach. "But why would you think I did in the first place?"

Ryan's hands were shaking against the thin covers. "Because who else could it be? I knew it wasn't me, so who did that leave?"

"But why would I do that to her?"

"I thought you might . . . I thought you might have had a fight."

"About what?"

"Me."

"My God, Ryan. You're so full of yourself."

"I know, okay? I know. But back then . . . I told Amanda I couldn't be with her because of you, and so I don't know . . . I was out of my mind that night . . . and I thought, I thought that she was so mad at me that she'd taken it out on you, and . . ."

"I picked up a paddle and clocked her on the head?"

"Now that you say it out loud, it sounds crazy, but . . ."

A loud buzzing filled her ears. She remembered the weight of that paddle, the way the water had colored red when she'd washed it off. How some of the blood had clung to her hands as she plunged them into the water, rubbing them like she had when she'd auditioned to play Lady Macbeth.

". . . Back then, it seemed like the only explanation."

"You're going to need to give me more than this. Rewind, please."

"Where should I start?"

"How about with how you knew where to find Amanda?"

Maisy stirred. Ryan brushed the hair off her forehead and gazed down at her. "It's true, you know."

"What's true?"

"You never know what love's like until a piece of you is walking around inside another person."

"Ouch."

"I didn't mean it that way."

"Didn't you?"

They stared at each other.

"So," Margaux prompted. "That night, after you left Amanda . . ."

"I got back to camp around one, like I said. I talked with Ty for a bit and then I went to bed. I fell asleep for a few hours, but not real sleep, you know? I woke up around five. I couldn't go back to sleep. I felt bad for what I'd done . . . walking away from her like that. So

I got up and went down to the lake at about five thirty. I thought I'd go back to the Island and apologize before we had to see each other in the lodge, in front of everyone at breakfast, but when I got to Boat Beach, I saw . . . There was a canoe about halfway between shore and the Island, and I could see that someone was in it but not who. I ran up to the lodge to get the binoculars out of the office. When I got back to the lake I climbed the lifeguard tower so I could see who it was, and . . . it was her, just . . . floating near Secret Beach. Her arms, my God, her arms . . . I wasn't thinking; I took off running through the woods, and when I got to Secret Beach, she was there in the canoe. She was so pale, and the blood had stopped flowing from the gash on her temple, and all I could think was that I'd read somewhere that when the blood stops, that means . . . Well, you know. I got it into my head that you must've been the one who did it, because, like I said, who else could it be—"

"You thought that. All this time . . ."

"Mostly, I tried not to think about it."

"Think about what, Daddy? Who's Amanda?"

CHAPTER 35

HAY BALES

Mary

Coming back to Macaw in the dead of night from the hospital with the twins, Mary wondered why she'd gone in the first place. What was she hoping for? That she and Ryan and her sisters would have some big kumbaya moment and rectify a lifetime worth of injuries? That wasn't likely. Movies thrived on the idea that a brush with death changed a person, but she was realistic. People didn't change. They might become more of what they were before—better or worse—but the core remained the same. And even if there was a change, something on the surface, if it was brought about by something as selfish, as narcissistic as realizing *you* wouldn't be around anymore, what good was that? It was still all about you.

Where did Mary fit in this family? The twins had each other, and Ryan and Margaux had always had a connection. Where was she? Stuck in the middle.

The radio was half static, and Margaux's car had a slight musty smell to it. The back seat was filled with music folders and instrument cases. She'd pushed it all onto the middle seat, the seat in the family van she'd spent her childhood sitting on.

Ironically, she'd always liked that song "Stuck in the Middle With You." It was up-tempo, and it made her feel happy because it was a good thing to be stuck with the right person.

Margaux had sung it that night on the Island, around the campfire. "For Mary," she'd said, as she struck the first chord. She'd been feeling superfluous until that moment. She was only a counselor-in-training, and the kids didn't listen to her. Why had she even come? But then Margaux had started singing, and Mary blended her voice to hers in a way that always made her feel part of a bigger whole, and the night was looking up. She hadn't even minded when Amanda joined in, slightly off-key. She'd felt content, watching the fire. Happy.

Happy. When was the last time she'd felt happy?

They turned onto the camp road. There was no moon, and the trees loomed large.

"Drop me off here," she said to Liddie.

"At the barn?"

"I never fed Cinnamon. She'll be starving."

Liddie stopped the car. Mary climbed out and didn't look back. Her heart was racing, though she wasn't quite sure why. Leftover adrenaline, probably.

Buster was standing sentry in front of the door. Mary reached down and patted him on the head. She laughed at her fear the day before. You could really drive yourself nuts if you tried hard enough.

She lifted the wooden bolt on the barn's heavy side door and entered. She felt calmer. This was where she belonged. Surrounded by dried hay and animals that had no animosity in them. Mary walked down the long row of empty stalls. An old oil lamp hung from each beam, the backup system for power failures. Cinnamon was standing in her stall, her eyes half dozy from sleep and lack of water. Her trough was empty, the hay net without its usual fill. Mary hummed to herself while she watered and fed Cinnamon, reassuring her that it was going to be all right. Cinnamon couldn't talk, not in the way most people thought, but she moved her rump against Mary, a friendly gesture that made her feel less like the unnecessary member of her family.

"There you are."

She dropped her grooming brush, her heart squeezing like Ryan's must've yesterday. *It's J-F,* she told herself, *only J-F.* Her hands started to sweat.

"You frightened me," she said, giving herself a minute before she faced him.

"And you stood me up."

She turned around. He was wearing jeans and a white long-sleeved shirt. He looked like a cowboy. He even had a few blades of hay stuck in his hair. All that was missing were the boots and the hat.

"Not on purpose."

"So you forgot about me?"

Mary looked at the ground. This feeling again. Half panic, half want. She wished she had more control of herself around him.

"My brother had a heart attack. Or something like that. I was at the hospital."

"I am so sorry."

She raised her head. "He's going to be all right."

He took a step toward her. "That's good."

Mary didn't answer.

"I fell asleep," he said, "in the hayloft."

"That explains it, then."

"What?"

She reached up and removed a blade of hay from his hair. "This."

"Oh. Not so cool."

He reached into his shirt pocket and took out a pack of cigarettes. Mary knocked it out of his hand instinctively.

"Why did you do that?"

"You can't smoke in a barn!"

"Okay, *chérie*, calm down."

"Look up," Mary said. He did. Above them was a winter's worth of hay, as dry as kindling. "This whole place is one big bonfire, waiting for a match."

"It did not occur to me."

"It's okay."

"Have you been in a fire?"

"No . . . but I've seen other barns that have gone up."

There'd been a barn fire at her neighbor's a couple of years ago. A lightning strike had started that one, but it didn't make it any less terrible. The horrible stench of burned horseflesh. The stricken look of the children. It was something she never wanted to experience again.

"Sorry, I wasn't thinking."

He stepped closer. She could smell the tobacco on him and shuddered at the thought of how many cigarettes he might've smoked waiting for her.

"Where did you put your butts?"

"What?"

"Your cigarette butts? From earlier?"

"In one of the rainwater barrels."

"There was water in it?"

"Of course."

Mary let out a long breath. "That's all right, then."

He took his thumb and ran it along her jawline. "Should I go?"

"You must be tired."

"I am not tired. Are you?"

"I am a bit."

"I'll go, then."

He leaned in and brushed her lips with his. That was all it took. Like the barn, she was a batch of kindling waiting to be lit.

Afterward, they lay in the stall next to Cinnamon's, their clothes scattered around them. Mary's head was foggy; J-F was breathing heavily. Every nerve ending in her body felt alive. Why had she given this up? Yes, he made her feel confused sometimes. But this, this was worth it.

"How did we end up in here?" she asked.

He chuckled. "I will take this as a compliment."

"You should."

They turned toward each other and kissed. Mary could taste herself on him.

"What are you thinking?" she asked, feeling silly and girlish.

"I was trying not to wonder what Cinnamon was thinking."

"That's . . . weird."

"Is it?"

"Yes."

He pulled her closer. "So . . ."

"So."

"I forgot about that."

"Forgot about what?"

"How you repeat what I say after we fuck."

Mary flinched. She hated that word. It was so cold. That was a feeling that came with J-F too.

"I guess we both forgot some things."

She sat up and pulled her shirt over her head. She wished her clothes would go back on as magically as they'd come off.

"You are leaving?"

"There are a hundred people coming here for a memorial in a couple of hours. I've got to get ready."

They dressed silently. Mary avoided making eye contact, feeling ashamed for the way she'd acted, the thoughts she'd had. Each piece of clothing brought her back to the person who'd pushed him out of her life. Pushed everyone.

She pulled her sweater over her head and shivered.

She felt colder with her clothes on than off.

Amanda

July 23, 1998—2:00 a.m.

Alcohol blurred the lines.

Time. Who I was with. What I thought the night would be.

It's not that I forgot I was with Sean and not Ryan. I knew it was him the whole time. It was more that I cared less about the differences and focused more on how they were the same. Same height, approximately. Hair that had an unruly curl to it as the day wore on. And because everything took on a certain musky scent at camp, they even smelled similar. Woods, campfires, the oil that went into the crash boat. All these things mixed together were part of Ryan's appeal, and part of Sean's, too, by the time half the flask was gone.

When I kissed him—*I* kissed *him*—his lips didn't feel that different from Ryan's. His mouth tasted like mine, booze and our long-forgotten dinner. I kept my eyes closed and imagined it was Ryan, before he'd betrayed me and run away. Ryan before we'd ever kissed or he'd done something to give me hope. The Ryan I wanted him to be.

Sean's kisses were different, older, more experienced. Enough Ryan to pretend, but not too much to remember.

Sean went along with all of it. He let me place his hands on my breasts, first over then under my shirt. He didn't back away when I took off his shirt. He asked, "Are you sure?"

"Yes," I said. "Yes."

I was. I was sure I wanted to erase this terrible night with something that felt good. And it did. Sean/Ryan: I didn't care whose hands were on my skin, rubbing my nipples with his thumb, fingers tracing the edge of my underwear and then underneath and then inside, oh my God. Yes, this. This. It felt like everything it was supposed to feel like. And more, more. I wanted more. His mouth replacing his fingers. The ground was hard beneath me, but I didn't care right up to the moment when he was inside me. Then there was a sharp pain, and my body pushed against it. He hesitated and asked again.

"Are you sure?"

"Yes," I said. "Yes."

I kissed him and he was inside me and my hands were on his back, my legs up around his waist. It didn't feel the same as what had come before, both better and worse at the same time. I still wanted more, but then he groaned and shivered and it was over, his breath tickling the edge of my neck.

Then it all changed. Though his body covered me, I felt exposed. My eyes were still closed, but I knew it was the wrong man who was still inside me. That wasn't his fault. I'd asked for this; I'd wanted it.

But now, I wanted him to go away.

	Amanda	**Margaux**	**Ryan**	**Mary**	**Kate & Liddie**	**Sean**
9:00 p.m.	Lantern ceremony	Lantern ceremony	Lantern ceremony			
10:00 p.m.	On the Island	On the Island		On the Island		Crash boat
11:00 p.m.	Back Beach	Back Beach	Back Beach	On the Island		
Midnight	Back Beach		Back Beach			
1:00 a.m.	Back Beach		Camp			Back Beach
2:00 a.m.	Back Beach		Camp			Back Beach
5:00 a.m.		Searches for A.	Camp/ Boat Beach	On the Island		
6:00 a.m.	Secret Beach		Secret Beach		Secret Beach	

CHAPTER 36

THANKS FOR THE MEMORIES

Ryan

Ryan had made so many mistakes. Mostly, they were about other people. Assumptions he'd made about how they'd feel, what they'd want. He'd done it with all the women in his life. Margaux. Mary. The twins. Kerry. Amanda. Stacey. He'd projected something he was feeling onto them and assumed they felt the same.

Take Stacey. He was feeling trapped and willing to take a risk to dislodge himself from his life, and he'd assumed she was like him. That she wasn't fully reckless, just looking for a good time. If he'd been paying attention, if he'd looked *at* her instead of who he wanted her to be, he would've seen she was unstable. That she wasn't to be trusted, certainly not with a car, not with his life, not even with her own. Instead, he assumed because he wasn't dangerous, neither was she. But that was wrong, wasn't it? He was dangerous. Look at all the chaos he'd been a part of. His family would be better off without him. It would've been better if he'd died.

"Don't die on me, okay?"

"What?"

Kerry was standing next to the bed. He felt cold. The girls were no longer snuggled up against him. Where had they gone? He must've drifted off after Margaux left, and these deep thoughts were a dream he was having, one where he took responsibility for his faults and did something about them. Not like life, then.

"Don't die," Kerry said again. "If that's what you're thinking. We're not better off without you."

Ryan didn't know what to say. It wasn't the first time Kerry had done this, read his mind, but it always freaked him out. He never knew what she was thinking, even after all these years. He'd been sure, for instance, when she learned about Stacey that she'd leave him without so much as a second thought. Instead, she'd set about planning their wedding, accepted his apology and his proposal, and said they never needed to talk about it again.

"I wasn't—"

"Before you go thinking I'm some kind of witch, you were talking in your sleep."

"I was?"

"You do it all the time." Kerry tucked a loose strand of hair behind her ear. She looked beautiful and tired.

"I do?"

"You do."

"So that's . . . that's how you've known . . ."

She smiled. It was a sad smile, but it was enough for now. "Yes."

"And all this time . . ."

"You thought I had magical powers? Damn, I should've kept this to myself. Anyway, the point remains. Don't die. Don't leave us. We need you."

"Did you hear what Margaux said?"

"Yes."

"And still?"

"I've known about that for a long time."

Ryan pulled the sheet up to his shoulders. Why was it so damn cold in here? "Because of the sleep talking?"

"Partly. Also things I've pieced together. A few things your father said."

"My dad? He told you . . . ?"

"No, I asked him."

"What?"

Kerry twisted her engagement ring around her finger. That solitary diamond she'd picked out after she'd agreed to marry him because he'd proposed without a ring, which was also typical.

"After everything with Stacey, I thought . . . He said something . . . something about how women weren't safe around you, and I asked him what he meant. I thought I was pregnant—"

"What?"

Ryan's heart was racing. That couldn't be good. He glanced at the machine next to the bed, the one monitoring his vitals, expecting his panic to register, but the lines moved up and down with the same frequency.

"I'd missed my period, and then all that stuff with Stacey happened, and I was trying to decide what to do. Leave you or stay. Was I going to keep it? If I left, could I be a single mother? Would I even tell you about the baby? Then you apologized and asked me to marry you, and I said yes, but I needed to be sure."

"So you spoke to my dad?"

"Not about all of it. But I wanted to know what he was talking about, so I asked him."

"What did he say?"

"He said he thought you might be responsible for what happened to Amanda, and then he showed me all these documents he had, this timeline he was working on."

"That's crazy."

"It was a bit crazy, Ryan, to be honest."

"You knew this whole time that my dad thought that about me, and you never said anything?"

"You have to understand. It seemed like a stupid project, something even he knew didn't work."

"I don't follow."

"Anyone could see from his timeline that it didn't add up. For instance, why would you go back to the Island and bring Amanda to Secret Beach? Why not leave her for the others to find in the morning? It didn't make any sense, and I told him so."

"You did?"

"Yeah. And he laughed and agreed, but I'm not sure he actually got it."

"And then?"

"I got my period. I wasn't pregnant. We got married. You know the rest."

"But my dad?"

"We never spoke about it again."

Ryan tried to let it all sink in. The pregnancy that wasn't. The reason Kerry had agreed to marry him. Her knowing this whole time that his dad blamed him. That he was crazier than any of them thought.

"Why didn't you tell me?"

Kerry stretched her hands out in front of her, interlacing her fingers. "You'd begged me for a fresh start, a 'clean slate,' you called it, and I was still in love with you, and I thought, okay, I'm going to do this. But if I do, then I need to be fair and give you another chance. If I wasn't able to do that, then I thought it was better for both of us if

I let you go. I kind of put it out of my mind. That seems weird to say now, but that's what I did."

She lowered her arms so they rested lightly on his chest. She looked vulnerable, as if she were uncertain about their future. Not because she was thinking of leaving, but because she wasn't sure what Ryan might do with this information.

He knew what he needed to say.

"I'm glad you didn't leave me, but you really should've told me this. Maybe some of this could've been avoided."

"Some of what?"

"You're not going to like it."

"Try me." Kerry sat on the edge of the bed.

"Where are the girls?"

"I sent them for breakfast with one of the nurses."

"Okay, well . . ." Ryan took a deep breath. It hurt, but not as much as what he was about to say. He told her everything that had happened in the last two days. The will, and the vote, and that stupid whiteboard. Kerry listened, shocked into silence.

"He really was crazy, then," she said eventually.

"More than I ever thought possible."

"You should've let me come down here."

"What would that have changed?"

"Maybe your sisters would've listened to me."

Ryan picked up Kerry's hand and kissed it. "Sweetheart, I love you, but you know my sisters aren't big on listening to others."

"Margaux would've."

"Margaux's already on my side."

"What do we do now?"

"Not sure. Soldier on, I guess. If you'll have me."

"You mean, give up?"

"What other choice do we have?"

"Up and awake, I see," a woman in a white coat said as she came into the room.

Kerry stood up. "Ryan, this is Dr. Townsend."

"Nice to meet you."

"You gave your family a scare."

"Apparently."

"Well, the good news is that it wasn't serious."

"That is good news."

"But you're going to have to manage your diet and stress levels going forward."

"I can do that, I think."

Dr. Townsend smiled. "Good. Now I heard you have a pretty special event to attend today."

"Who told you that?"

"We did!" The girls came running into the room, smelling like cafeteria food. "We can still go to the memorial, right, Dr. Townsend?" Sasha asked.

"I think so."

"Oh, goody," Ryan said.

"Don't you want to go, Daddy?"

"Of course I do, honey. Daddy was just being silly." He met Kerry's eyes over the girls' heads. "You sure you want to do this?"

"We're worth fighting for."

Ryan hugged Maisy to him. "We are."

CHAPTER 37

IN A FLATBED FORD

Kate

When Liddie parked the car in the parking lot next to the rusted-out truck that had been there forever, Kate was glad for the stop in movement. She felt queasy, like she did on the ride home from the airport after a flight, one too many moving pieces sending her over the edge.

They sat in silence, the early morning sounds of the world waking up, floating in through the cracked windows. There was a touch of frost in the air, and Kate thought she heard the distant cry of a Canada goose, wheeling overhead, already in search of a warmer clime.

"Crazy night, huh?" Liddie said.

Liddie had a way of boiling things down to their essence; you had to give her that.

"I'll say."

"I can't believe there are a hundred people coming."

"It'll be fine."

"We should cancel."

"No," Kate said. "We can't do that."

"I know."

"So why suggest it?"

"You know me," Liddie said. "Any excuse to get out of an obligation."

She felt the laugh bubble up within her. "Oh God, Liddie. Things are so messed up."

Liddie unbuckled her seat belt, reached over, and hugged her. "It'll be okay."

Kate hid her eyes in the crick of Liddie's neck, like she used to do with her mother when something scared her as a child. See, there. Their mother hadn't been that bad. What was wrong with them that they thought she was?

"How can it be?"

"Don't know. I just feel it. Shall we go?"

"Sure."

Liddie let her go, and they got out of the car. She pretended not to see the streak of tears across Kate's cheek, and Kate pretended she couldn't feel it. She didn't like crying. But then again, did anyone?

It was still more dark than light. Liddie took her phone out of her pocket and enabled the flashlight function. Kate wished she'd turn it off. Standing in the dark under the domed sky, listening to the forest talk—she'd missed this.

"You go ahead," Kate said. "I'll be along in a bit."

Liddie's eyes rested on hers. "Waiting for someone?"

"Maybe."

"Fair enough."

Kate thought she'd receive more resistance, but instead, Liddie turned and aimed her light at the trees. Kate watched her disappear. Then Kate turned around and tapped on the side of the truck.

"Your sister's loud," Amy said, sitting up as Kate climbed over the side of the flatbed.

"She is."

"Makes it hard to be a sneak."

Amy was wearing a dark puffy jacket and a knit hat. She was sitting on a Hudson's Bay blanket, its distinctive white stripe like a strip of neon. Kate remembered this blanket well. How many nights had they hid under it in this very spot, trying to keep the world at bay?

"Don't call her that."

"You have enough times."

"That's different," Kate said. "I'm allowed to call her whatever I want."

"You're right. I'm sorry."

Kate sat down next to Amy, then lay on her back. Amy lay down next to her, probably out of reflex, maybe thinking back, like Kate was, to when they'd come to watch the stars and get lost in each other.

"Thanks for meeting me," Kate said when Amy was settled next to her.

"Your text said it was important."

"I want . . . I want to tell you what happened that night."

"With Amanda?"

"Yes."

"Why?"

"Because the only person I've ever shared it with is Liddie, and I didn't even choose to do that."

She could feel Amy's eyes on her. She turned her head so they could look at each other. The sky was lightening by inches, so Amy wasn't clear, even though she was close. But Kate could tell Amy didn't want to hear what she had to say.

"It's not going to change anything between us," Amy said. "Whatever it is."

"We weren't the ones who did that to her."

"No?"

"You think we did?"

"You tell me, Kate. If you want to, I'll listen."

She turned away and settled onto her back. She couldn't see any stars anymore; it was too light out.

"It was Liddie's idea," Kate said.

"Of course it was."

"Hush," Kate said. "Listen."

Kate told Amy what she remembered, telling it like a story, a recovered memory, something she'd rehearsed, even though she hadn't. As she spoke, she felt transported back, drawn by her own voice, which sounded, in the rough of the morning, so much like Liddie's.

She remembered how Liddie had forced her from bed in the middle of the night with promises of fun and surprising the other kids from their cabin on the Island. They'd wanted to go on the overnight, but they were grounded because they'd been caught in the boys' section a few days earlier (Liddie's fault again). By the time Liddie had convinced her and they got changed into their swimsuits, it was four a.m. Camp was silent as they walked down to Boat Beach; every twig they walked on made a sound so loud she was sure everyone could hear.

The lake was cold at first. She was shivering hard until they got their rhythm going. It took about an hour to swim to the Island normally, but they never made it there. Instead, when they were about halfway, Liddie grabbed her arm.

"Look there," she'd said.

Liddie pointed in the direction of the Island. Kate blinked the water from her eyes. It was hard to tell what she was looking at, exactly. A canoe. A man—a *boy*?—was sitting in it, paddling. Who was it? He looked familiar, but it was hard to tell from his outline against the dark night. Maybe it was Ryan. All these years, whenever she let herself think about it, she convinced herself it was him, then dismissed it. She thought that if it was Ryan, she'd know for sure. But instead, she had doubts.

They treaded water silently. Somehow, they knew not to talk, even in a whisper. They watched whoever it was paddle the boat. His head was down as he leaned in to what he was doing. He wasn't heading directly toward them. *Secret Beach,* she thought. *That's where he's going.* When he was about ten minutes out from Secret Beach, he stood, then dove into the water, the splash surprising both of them. Kate wanted to ask what he was doing, but it became clear soon enough. He was pushing the canoe toward shore.

"Let's go," Liddie whispered in her ear.

"Why?"

"There's someone in that canoe."

"How do you know?"

"I saw an arm in the water."

That was enough for Kate. They turned and swam as fast as they could toward Boat Beach without drawing attention to themselves. When they reached it, they could barely move their arms. They lay on their backs, the rocks pushing against their skin, trying to catch their breath. Kate was exhausted and terrified. She started counting stars out loud to try to calm herself.

"Stop that," Liddie said.

"I can't help it. What are we going to do?"

"We should get off the beach."

Kate had agreed, and they'd pushed themselves up, wrapped their towels around their waists, and shivered their way to their cabin, getting there at a quarter after five.

"I was shivering so hard," Kate said, "that I could barely change into dry clothes. Like yesterday with that safety check on the beach—"

"But you went to Secret Beach," Amy said next to her in the truck, impatient.

"We did."

"Why?"

"We fought about that. What was the right thing to do? I said we'd get in trouble, and we didn't know for sure what had happened. Maybe Liddie was wrong, and it was nothing."

"But it wasn't."

"I know that now. I'm just telling you what I thought at the time."

"If you'd gone to find an adult right away, then maybe Amanda would be okay. Maybe they would know who did this to her." Amy's accent crept back when she was upset.

"You think I don't know that? I've felt guilty about that for twenty years. But we were twelve and exhausted and scared and—"

"Have you felt guilty?" Amy sat up.

"Where are you going?"

"I can't do this."

"We weren't doing anything."

"Come on. That's why you called me here, right? Because you wanted to confess and start over. You thought if you told me about this, then, what? We'd have something between us again, something private, like we used to?"

Kate didn't know what to say. What could you say when your base motivations were exposed so clearly?

"Okay, yes, I was probably hoping that would happen."

"God, Kate."

"I miss you, okay? I love you."

Amy stood. She loomed large above Kate. "You say you love me, and yet you thought that confessing to being an accessory to what happened to Amanda would bring us back together?"

"Please lower your voice."

"Who's going to hear us?"

"I don't know. That's the problem."

Amy threw her arms out wide. The old truck creaked beneath her. "I'm here with Kate!"

"What are you doing?"

"I'm telling anyone who cares to listen that we're here together. And you're . . . you're embarrassed, aren't you?"

Kate stood up. "I'm not embarrassed," she said quietly.

"Please. You're thirty-two years old, and until today, no one in your family even knew you were gay."

"That's not true."

"If they know, it's not because you've told them. You never told them about me. It was always hiding. Everything had to be hidden."

"I thought you wanted things that way?"

"No, Kate. That was you."

She felt frozen. Was this possible? All these years, had Amy simply been waiting for her to make the first move? To proclaim her love to the world?

"Amy, I . . ."

"You don't know what to say."

"Yes."

"You never did," she said, then climbed down from the truck and walked away.

CHAPTER 38

FAMILY TIES

Liddie

It wasn't often that Liddie felt as if she were totally alone, but today was one of those times. They'd all felt helpless at the hospital, but this was something different. Mary had her horses, and Kate had Amy, and Liddie had . . . Well, she had things, she had someone, but still, in this moment, it was nothing. It felt like nothing.

She was grimy from the hospital, but the shower in the French Teacher's Cabin wouldn't warm up, so she went to the lodge because it was closer than her parents' house and showered upstairs. Sean's shower, she always thought of it, because it smelled like him: simple soap and the woods.

She peeled the clothes from her body and stood under the spray. She wanted to scrub the hospital smell out of her hair, her nostrils. That mix of disinfectant and sadness that was impossible to forget. God, she hated hospitals. And camp. She hated camp, too.

That thought stopped her. Was it true? Yes, in many ways, she did hate it. It was a family member she'd never chosen to have and wouldn't choose if she could. But here she was fighting over its survival, taking part in who would get a share of it—Ryan or Sean. Why? Did she think Ryan had hit Amanda? All the evidence pointed toward him. Out there, in the water, twenty years ago, she'd been certain that's who was in the canoe, paddling away from the Island with whoever was on the other end of that trailing arm. Finding Ryan at Secret Beach later had confirmed it. And all the times he'd insisted they keep his secret . . . he'd said it was to protect Margaux. But Liddie knew in her bones Margaux hadn't done it. So who did that leave? Could Ryan have been innocent all this time?

Liddie shivered in the scalding water. If he was innocent, then one of them did it. Not her. Not Kate. They were each other's alibi. She'd never believed that it could've been those college boys living on the other side of the lake. What possible motive could they have? So that left someone she knew and was probably related to. Someone she cared about. And if that was true, then that person was a stranger to her, and she didn't know what that meant. Her mind turned to the documents she'd swiped the day before. Her family had so many secrets. In all the chaos, she hadn't had time to puzzle out what the documents meant. She should do that before the vote this afternoon.

She turned off the water. She could hear Sean snoring when she got out and wrapped her towel around herself tightly. She wondered about him. What was his role in all this? Because when you cleared away the obvious, the Ryans of the world, you were left with the Seans.

She went downstairs. The whiteboard was where they'd left it. All those boxes with that half-filled in information, none of it new. Not to Liddie. But the crucial hours, the hours before they'd set out on their swim and the hours that encompassed it, they were blank. They were where the puzzle would be solved.

Liddie returned to the cabin and pulled on some clothes she'd filched from Owen. She fetched the documents she'd hidden from Kate and read them carefully. She felt weary with the weight of them. She lay down to try to sleep. She surprised herself by drifting off quickly, but then woke every half hour as if she had a plane to catch. When the bell rang at eight thirty, the Sunday time for bell ringing—did Sean ever miss the chance to ring that thing?—Liddie gave up and rose. She looked out the window at the lake. It was choppy, the clouds low and threatening. It would rain later, in all likelihood. A perfect day for a funeral, perhaps, but not for a hundred people to be tramping around.

What would they do, for instance, with all the mud?

Liddie found Sean at Boat Beach. The door to the boat hut was open, and he was carrying paddles down to the beach.

"What are you doing?"

"Getting some canoes out. What's it look like I'm doing?"

"Planning your escape."

Sean looked up at her from the water's edge. A patch of sun broke through and hit the back of his head, creating a halo effect. That orange-red hair. He used to wear it longer, until kids started calling him "Clowney." Then he shaved it close, an act that made it look darker except for when he stood in the sun.

"Escape?" Sean said. "What for?"

"To get away from us."

"I should've done that a long time ago."

"Probably."

"What'd you come down here for, Liddie?"

She still wasn't sure. Back in the cabin, she'd thought she needed to face him. But looking at him now, standing there with a paddle in his hand, the legs of his pants rolled up, almost in shadow, gave her the shivers.

She put her hand into her pocket and felt the rough edges of the pieces of paper she'd taken. "I found something."

"What?"

"Shouldn't you ask where?"

"Okay, where, then?"

"My dad had it."

Sean didn't react. Liddie thought he might have an idea of what was coming. But it seemed as if he didn't. Or he was a fantastic actor.

"What is it?"

"It's about you."

Sean walked toward her. He was swinging the paddle, his thumb and forefinger making a *U* around it.

"Why would Mr. MacAllister have a paper about me?"

"He had papers on all of us."

"He did?"

"You don't sound that surprised . . . Wait. Did you take the papers?"

"What papers?"

"From the Craft Shop. The ones Kate and I hung up yesterday. You did, didn't you?"

"What if I did?"

The paddle swung again, higher this time so that it whiffled by Liddie's face, a few inches from touching her.

"Watch it."

"Sorry."

Sean swung the paddle down and buried its tip into the sand.

"Why would you take them?"

"Like you said, they were about me. I wanted a chance to look at them in private."

"But you took all of them."

"I didn't have much time."

A light went off. "You . . . you made up that shit about the water search, didn't you? It was a distraction so you could get the papers out. Kate nearly died!"

"I didn't know that would happen."

"Jesus."

Sean took a step closer. He was breathing hard, like he'd been running. Liddie's pulse quickened in response.

"What do you have that's mine?"

"Nothing."

"You said you did."

He was standing over her now. Liddie felt small. Scared. Somehow, she'd never noticed before how much bigger than her Sean was. The powerful arc of his muscles under his shirt.

"I said I found something about you. Not that it was yours."

"If it's about me, then it's mine."

Liddie wished she hadn't come down here, but it was too late for that. She made a quick calculation about which of the papers in her pocket was the least dangerous for her, figuring out which was which by feel. When she touched the edges of the seal, she knew. She pulled out the thick vellum paper and unfolded it.

"This is what I found."

"What is it?"

"Your birth certificate. Why would Dad have that, you think?"

When she left Sean ten minutes later without any answers, she went to go and find Kate. They needed to talk this through and come up with a plan. But instead, she ran into Margaux in the road, holding a large parking sign. She was wearing a black cocktail dress with a gray sweater and tights. Her hair was blown out, and she even had some makeup on. Liddie had seen her sister dressed up before, but it felt off in this setting.

"What's that for?" Liddie asked.

"What do you think?"

"Are you mad at me?"

"Honestly, Liddie?"

"What?"

"You and Kate hid the fact that Ryan was on Secret Beach for twenty years, and you're asking me that?"

"And you knew he was on the Island, and you didn't tell anyone that either."

"That's different."

"How? Because it was your secret and not ours? Typical."

"What's that supposed to mean?"

Liddie knew she was in the wrong. Especially after what she'd talked to Sean about on the beach, but she persisted. Her anger felt righteous somehow. "It's the way things are, right? Perfect Margaux never makes a mistake. Whether it's in school or cleaning up after her brother's attempted murder—"

"I didn't clean up after anything." But the color had drained from Margaux's face.

Liddie grabbed the parking sign. "What is it, Margaux? What did you do?"

"Nothing . . . I didn't do anything."

"You are so full of shit."

"Let go."

Liddie released it. "Fine. But if I find out that you've been keeping other things from me . . ."

"Are you threatening me?"

A car door slammed, startling both of them.

"Who's that?" Margaux asked.

"Someone way too early. God, these fucking lifers."

"We'd better go greet them."

They walked up the road and turned in to the parking lot. Liddie had trouble understanding what she was seeing at first, like looking at one of those dot paintings where there's supposed to be an image inside, but it takes you a moment to focus on it.

Because standing there in a group, looking only slightly less puzzled than Liddie and Margaux, were Owen, Mark, and Swift.

CHAPTER 39

I ACHE TO REMEMBER

Sean

Damn it, Sean thought as he smashed the paddle into the beach over and over. The sand flew, and still he swung. Swung for himself. Swung for his mother. How dare they? How dare they try to control his life like this, deciding what he could know and what he couldn't? Like he wasn't someone who was worthy of knowing the most basic details of his life.

He felt pure rage. Rage and shame, because here he was reacting the way everyone would expect him to react.

He stopped swinging. His arms ached. He threw the paddle to the ground and sat on the dry dock, which acted as a sort of platform on the beach. Usually, it was a nice place to sit. Shaded by an old conifer, you could see the whole bay. The clouds were low this morning, and the lake was rough. It was going to rain later; he could smell it in the wind.

He tried to calm himself, taking in a deep breath and letting it out slowly. He didn't know where this rage had come from. It wasn't something he usually felt. But when Liddie had shown up, Sean thought he was done for, found out. That wasn't what he was worried about now. His secret was still intact. No one knew he'd been on the Island that night after dropping off the campers. No one knew what had happened between him and Amanda.

He closed his eyes and remembered. The taste of her. The feel of her skin. What it felt like to be inside her. He was ashamed that he'd slept with her. She was only seventeen and not the girl he was in love with. When he was kissing her, he knew she didn't want him. He was a replacement, a distraction. He'd thought that was okay, because that's what she was to him too.

That night, with his eyes closed, Amanda had become Margaux. Her lips, her slippery hair. It was exactly like he'd imagined. He knew it was wrong. He was so much older, and Margaux was like a sister to him.

He'd been watching Margaux. She was fifteen at the time, and even as he was looking at her, he was thinking it was wrong. He was trying to make himself turn away.

Then Mrs. MacAllister had spoken behind him. "The heart wants what it wants," she said. He turned around. She had her camera around her neck, as she often did, and she snapped a picture of him.

"What does that mean?" he'd asked.

She'd stared at him for a moment and told him that it meant we didn't always choose who we love. "But," she said, "you can choose what to do about it."

He'd understood. He could look, but he couldn't touch. And he hadn't, not ever.

Until that night with Amanda.

She'd started it, if that was any excuse, though he knew it wasn't.

When it was over, and he could feel their mutual regret hanging over them, she'd sat up and dressed and said the words he knew she would.

"That was a mistake."

And even though he'd agreed, he'd felt so, so *angry*.

CHAPTER 40

WE GATHER HERE TODAY

Margaux

Margaux spent the next hour and a half placating Mark when all she wanted to do was throttle him. It had taken all she had not to break up with him right there in the parking lot. It was so typical of him, showing up when she'd expressly told him not to. Instead, she slapped a smile on her face and told him how happy she was to see him.

So he was happy. He followed her around as she checked in on the kitchen and the extra catering staff. Then they went to the Drama Tent, an open-air structure where they were going to hold the memorial. She filled him in on what he'd missed since the last update she'd given him Saturday morning—had it only been a day ago?—while they unloaded more than a hundred folding chairs from the storage locker and set them up in rows.

"This would be a nice place to get married," Mark said when they were halfway done.

"What?"

"You must've had weddings here before?"

She was afraid to turn around. What if Mark was down on one knee? She breathed a sigh of relief when she found that all he was doing was looking pensive. He'd put on a jacket and tie for the occasion, his teacher clothes. Gray wool blazer, white shirt, conservative tie, and dark-wash jeans. She'd always liked him in this outfit. He was still as trim as when they'd met, his blue eyes peering out from under the lock of dark hair that wouldn't stay put.

"Maybe? A long time ago though."

"You've never thought about it?"

"I wasn't the kind of girl who dreamed of weddings."

But that wasn't true. She and Mary and the twins used to have mock weddings in the Drama Tent all the time when they were little, wearing toilet-paper veils and getting scolded by their mother for stealing all the candles. Sometimes they'd make Ryan participate, with Sean officiating. He'd say the vows in this silly deep voice, and the girls would fall to the ground laughing so hard their sides hurt.

"And what about now?"

Margaux knew this whole conversation was a land mine, and she treated it that way.

"I haven't . . . Mark, my parents' memorial service is in an hour."

"Yeah, sorry, not the time."

She felt a beat of tenderness for him. He was still the man she'd been with for the last five years. He hadn't changed. She had. She didn't know why.

"Not the time. Let's finish setting up these chairs, okay?"

"Sure."

They finished with the chairs, then went to the lodge to make sure everything was ready for the meal that would happen after. It would be a late lunch; they'd decided they weren't serving two meals. At sunset, they'd all gather on the beach for a last lantern ceremony.

The invitations they'd sent out had asked everyone to bring their own lanterns if they wanted to participate. Margaux could imagine them, all these somber adults who she'd known since she was a kid, driving to camp, their paper houses sitting on the back seat, telling their spouses and kids about their memories. That time on the lake, or that campfire, that skit night.

Margaux hadn't followed instructions. She hadn't taken the time before she came to Macaw to build a memorial for her parents, even if it was out of paper. Her parents deserved better.

"I'm going to get some supplies," she said to Mark. "Wait here?"

"Will do."

She went into the office and rummaged around until she found what she was looking for—tissue paper and glue. There were Popsicle sticks in the pantry. She glanced at her watch. Ten thirty. She had enough time.

She left the room. Mark was standing at the whiteboard.

"What's this?" he asked.

"We were trying to figure out what happened to Amanda, but then Ryan had his almost heart attack. Why?"

Mark turned around. He looked at her as if she were a stranger. "It looks like you did it."

"What?"

She pushed past him and looked over the board. It wasn't as they'd left it the night before. Someone had filled in some of the empty time slots. Her eyes landed on Sean's column. He'd been on the Island in the middle of the night. On Back Beach with Amanda. What? *What?*

"What is this?"

Mark's finger was pointing at the 4:00 a.m. row. It was blank across the board, except that in her spot, someone had written in her name and circled it in red. Over and over until half of it was blotted out.

"Why would someone do that?" Mark asked again ten minutes later.

"I have no idea."

But that was a lie. Margaux would recognize the handwriting on the whiteboard anywhere, as familiar as her own. She knew who'd pointed to her; she pushed away the why. There had to be an explanation. She'd figure it out when she had a moment to think.

They were upstairs in the lodge, hiding the whiteboard away before anyone else could see it. Already, Margaux could hear voices coming down the road. Laughter. Excitement. This might be a solemn occasion, but it was also a reunion.

"This is dangerous," Mark said.

"What is?"

"This." He waved at the board. "Figuring this out."

"You're the one who told me to do it."

"I wasn't thinking. Whoever did that to Amanda . . . they're dangerous."

"That's what Ryan said."

"He's right."

"Nothing's going to happen . . . not with everyone here."

"And what about after?"

"We'll vote again."

"But before the vote? You complete this, and then you know who did it?"

"That was the idea."

"And now?"

"I don't know, okay, Mark? I wasn't planning on doing any of this. People are coming, and I have to go speak to them about my parents, and . . ."

She was in his arms. They felt good around her. Solid. She turned in to them, buried her face in the familiar smell of his chest. She wanted this weekend to be over. She couldn't think straight here. She'd never been able to.

"It's okay. You're going to be okay."

"I'm scared."

"Me too."

She pulled away. "You thought I was guilty."

"No."

"Come on, not even for a minute?"

"No," he said, but he hesitated. She was surprised but not upset. More like she didn't know he had it in him to think that badly of her.

"Is my face a mess?"

"Wait, here." He took a piece of cloth out of his pocket, one of those old-fashioned handkerchiefs. He tilted her face up and wiped away her tears. "That's better."

"Thanks."

He folded it up and put it in his pocket. "I know, you know."

"Know what?"

"That you're unhappy. That you're thinking of leaving me."

She looked down at the floor. The boards were old and cracked, the spaces between them wide enough to lose things down. It was funny the things a person thought about when their life was coming apart. She was thinking about *The Borrowers*, those little creatures she'd read about when she was small who lived in the hidden spaces in everyday life.

"Why are you saying this?"

"Because it's true. Isn't it?"

She looked up at him. She'd wanted to do this on her own terms, but he was forcing the issue, like he forced everything else. But maybe this was okay. He was allowed, after all, to be with someone who wanted to be with him. He deserved that.

"Yes. I'm sorry."

"That's all you have to say?"

"What do you want me to say?"

He sighed. "I wanted you to say I was wrong."

"I'm sorry."

"You said."

She looked at the floor again. It was easier than looking at the tears in his eyes.

"What happens now?" she asked.

"Do you want me to leave?"

"No, you can stay."

"I meant . . . the apartment."

"I'll move out. I'll stay with one of my sisters until I find a place."

"Okay."

Margaux heard a sound, a cough, and there was Sean coming out of his room. He'd been in there the whole time. He shrugged at her. *What are you going to do?*

"Hey, Mark," he said, holding out his hand.

Mark batted it away. "She's all yours, man."

"Mark!"

"What?" he said, looking back at her over his shoulder as he walked down the hall. "You know it's true."

She didn't know what to do. She knew she was supposed to be running after Mark, asking him to stay and work things out. Convincing him that she didn't care about Sean that way—this at least was true. She'd never felt anything like that for him. Right now, with all that was happening, she felt even less.

"Are you all right?" Sean asked. He'd put on the suit he'd worn at the funeral. A dark blue, almost black, like a bruise.

"Yeah, I'm fine."

"What did Mark mean?"

"Nothing, ignore him."

"Hey, come on, talk to me." He put his hand on her shoulder.

She ducked away. "Don't."

"I'm sorry, I didn't mean . . ."

She drew in a ragged breath. She'd never understood less about her life than at that very moment.

"What were you doing on the Island that night, Sean? Did you hurt Amanda?"

She looked him squarely in the eye. She expected him to deny it, like her brother had.

But he didn't.

Amanda

July 23, 1998—3:00 a.m.

I never knew what shame was until that night. I'd been embarrassed. My parents told stories about me in diapers to their friends or asked me to perform some sketch I'd done when I was eight, years later. My grandmother wore a hearing aid that didn't have the volume right so she yelled in public and everyone could hear her when she said that she "had to tinkle."

Embarrassing, not shameful.

But what Sean and I did, me using him like that to get over Ryan, him using me to get over—to get back at—Margaux, that was shameful. You could feel it around us from the moment it was done and he was resting above me. It made me feel sick and cold and like this was the last place I wanted to be on earth. This was what my first time was. This was what I was going to remember forever.

We lay there in silence for a while, then he rolled off me, and I got dressed with my back turned to him. My mother's voice was in my head, all those lessons she'd given me about how I wanted my first time to mean something. I didn't have to be in love, but I shouldn't regret what happened. I already did. Added to it was the fact that I knew I'd have to keep this to myself. I couldn't tell Margaux; I couldn't tell anyone. What we'd done wasn't illegal, but still. He was a member of the senior staff, much older. He could get fired, and I could get sent home, and we'd both become one of those stories everyone told when they were gossiping about camp.

"I won't tell anyone," Sean said. "Don't worry."

"I know."

"And you won't either, right? Not even Margaux?"

I slipped my sweater over my head and turned around. "As if Margaux would care."

I knew it was cruel as I said it, but I didn't expect his reaction. I'd never seen rage flood through a person like that before, like a switch had been flicked. He was on fire, and I was certain I was going to get burned.

	Amanda	**Margaux**	**Ryan**	**Mary**	**Kate & Liddie**	**Sean**
9:00 p.m.	Lantern ceremony	Lantern ceremony	Lantern ceremony			
10:00 p.m.	On the Island	On the Island		On the Island		Crash boat
11:00 p.m.	Back Beach	Back Beach	Back Beach	On the Island		
Midnight	Back Beach		Back Beach			
1:00 a.m.	Back Beach		Camp			Back Beach
2:00 a.m.	Back Beach		Camp			Back Beach
3:00 a.m.	Back Beach					Back Beach
4:00 a.m.					Swimming	
5:00 a.m.		Searches for A.	Camp/ Boat Beach	On the Island	Camp	
6:00 a.m.	Secret Beach		Secret Beach		Secret Beach	

CHAPTER 41

REMEMBRANCE DAY

Mary

The bell rang once again to call them to the ceremony. Mary pressed down invisible wrinkles in her unfamiliar dress and joined the somber crowd walking to the Drama Tent. She half listened to the gurgle of French and English voices surrounding her, the background noise of camp. She greeted the people she knew and received a few hugs. Sandra Peoples from her riding group and Simon Vauclair, the guy who'd broken Margaux's heart so many years ago. Mostly, everyone looked the same, only washed out around the edges. But there were also those she simply didn't recognize until they said their name. What happened in a life that made the difference between being recognizable or a stranger at forty to your childhood companions?

They arrived at the Drama Tent, a perfect place for her parents' memorial. There was always drama when the MacAllisters were around.

The tent sat in a circle of pines. It was the place at Macaw with which Mary felt the least familiar. She'd never taken drama and had avoided attending the staff productions that took place there. Sometimes she forgot it even existed.

She found a place in the front row next to Swift. She didn't want to sit up where everyone could see her, but it was expected. The front was for family, for show. She knew about shows, had ridden in them all her life, so she knew how to arrange her face and to smile at the right moments. She could do this. She could.

They'd decided weeks ago, in a series of emails she'd barely read, that Sean would lead the service. It ought to have been Ryan's job, but when Sean offered, Ryan had simply said he thought it was a great idea. That was before anyone knew about the will and Sean's place in it. Ryan might not let himself be so easily replaced today if that were public knowledge.

Or who knows? Ryan wasn't big on duty, obligations. Not the Ryan Mary knew. Was he so different now that he had a family? She should've taken the time to find out, but she hadn't. He was sitting at the other end of the row in the middle of his daughters. He'd been discharged from the hospital in time to make it to the ceremony, and they'd crossed each other in the house. Mary had been genuinely happy to see Kerry and the girls; it had been too long. She should make more of an effort there. At least she wasn't any different from her sisters in this regard; they all neglected their nieces equally.

Ryan turned his head, and they exchanged a glance. They held it for a moment, then looked away. Mary wished she knew what he was thinking. Was he feeling guilty that he wasn't the one nervously clearing his throat and smoothing out a piece of paper? Or was that relief she saw? There was something to putting down your burdens, Mary knew. Giving up the struggle of it. She'd been thinking about that, off and on, since before her parents died, and now she was right in the middle of it. But could she do it? Could she finally put the past behind her?

Sean cleared his throat again, but no one heard him above the din. He raised his hand. One by one, like Mary's family had done earlier in the weekend, everyone stopped talking and raised their own hands in response. A silent salute, a moment of attention. She felt a lump form in her throat. There were two easels set up on either side of the podium, each holding a blown-up photo of her parents. Them on their wedding day in flowing hippie clothes, and then together in front of the Camp Macaw sign in what must've been the first year they ran the place. Her mother was heavily pregnant, and her father's hand sat proudly on her belly. Mary wished she'd known this version of her parents. What would they think if they were here, if they knew everything that had happened? Would they approve? Was this what her father had wanted?

Sean let the silence hang in the air as the hands slowly fell.

"Hi, everyone," he said into the microphone. His voice sounded deep and sonorous, like a radio announcer's.

"Hi, Sean!" the crowd said back.

Mary smiled. These people were so predictable. "Hi, Sean," was a thing that started so many years ago she couldn't place it. It was a joke, making fun of him but also including him in the joke. It was how campers greeted one another everywhere—an elongated *Hiiii, Seee-aaan*. She was never sure what Sean thought of it, but he was smiling now, and he'd done it on purpose. It was a good beginning.

"It's great to see so many of you today. I know the MacAllisters would be happy to have all the members of their extended family here for this. Camp Macaw is a special place."

"Macaw!" someone yelled, and then the echo of *mac-caw, caw, caw* went around the tent, a call-and-response that flooded Mary's brain with memories. Ryan showing her how to do it properly when she was four. When she taught it to the twins. How she and Margaux used to say it as they ran after each other in the barn.

Sean continued when the calls fell away. "I've been lucky enough to spend a lot of my life here. Most of you know that the MacAllisters took me in after my mother died. They brought me into their family, gave me a home and later a job and so many opportunities I never would've had if I hadn't met them."

Liddie coughed loudly twice. Sean colored in response and looked down at his paper.

"That's the easy version of my story. But I wanted to take a moment to tell you what it was like for me so you can understand. My mother had a difficult life. We moved a lot, never staying in one place long enough to make friends or put down roots. I never met my grandparents, never knew who my father was. My mother was the only constant, and while she did her best, it wasn't any way for a kid to live.

"The MacAllisters changed all that after she died. They found me a local foster family that was okay with housing me during the school year and giving me up for the summers so I could spend them here. For the first time, I had a place that would always be there for me.

"The MacAllisters didn't have much money, and they already had five children, but they helped me financially where they could. And when I asked to come work here full time, they said yes.

"I'm not good at talking about my feelings. But I can say that because they did that for me, I was able to do things I never would've been able to. And that's how I like to think about this place. It's a place where anything is possible. Whoever you are, you can be your best self here. That was their gift, not just to me but to all of you."

He paused and looked around. Mary could hear someone sniffling behind her, and she felt on the verge of tears. She was looking at Sean in a way she never had. What must it have been like for him? His mother had died when he was eight, right before she was born, so he was like Margaux or Ryan—something that was always there, something that would never change.

"Mr. MacAllister used to tell me that the true magic of camp was that you could let your imagination go. You could dream and become what you want. What you are outside of here, it doesn't matter. Being here is what's important.

"If you remember one thing from what I say today, one thing about this place, it should be that we learned and grew and tested and failed and succeeded and loved and moved on, touched by what we experienced here in ways we can't even begin to explain. We have been shaped by it, and that shape is permanent.

"Camp Macaw has always been my safe place, and I know it's yours. We don't know what the future holds for us yet, but whatever happens, this place will go on in our hearts and in our memories."

He turned to the photograph of Mary's parents. "Thank you," he said simply.

He stopped speaking. The applause started at the back and rolled through the tent like thunder. Mary was swept up in it. All of them, clapping and crying, and Sean looking down with a beatific look on his face, a man at peace.

A man who'd set down his burdens.

CHAPTER 42

ANOTHER MARK ON THE BOARD

Kate

Kate felt as if she'd lost track of things during the service. Sitting in the Drama Tent, listening to Sean speak, she felt caught in a mobile of her life. The images bobbed up and down in front of her: this production of a silly TV spoof they used to do when she was small, the Sunday nondenominational services her father led ("inspired by nature and Shakespeare," he called them), she and Liddie staging their own made-up plays.

She knew she should be thinking of her parents. When was the last time she'd spoken to them before they died? She couldn't remember. She'd spent an entire day trying to after Margaux had called with the news, but each time she pulled out a memory, it felt false. She'd seen them since they'd betrayed her over camp; she was certain she had. But when?

Then the service was over, and her hand was in Margaux's—she didn't even remember Margaux sitting next to her—and Margaux was whispering in her ear that they needed to talk privately, *STAT*.

"But it's lunch. Everyone will notice if we aren't there."

Margaux bit her bottom lip, working away at a small piece of loose skin. "They'll be too busy reminiscing."

"But we ought to be there, participating in—"

"Participating in what? Acting like everything is fine when you know what we have to decide today?"

Kate felt puzzled, which must've shown on her face, because Margaux let out an exasperated sigh.

"The vote? About Ryan? Did you forget?"

"I didn't forget. I know what today is."

But that wasn't entirely true. Kate *had* sort of forgotten in the turmoil of, well, *today*. This morning with Amy. This whole weekend was something she'd rather forget. Based on past experience, she would.

"So why are you resisting my request, then?"

"I'm not. Where should we go?"

They were surrounded by ex-campers and their families. A sea of navy and black, which no little kid should have to wear. Everyone else was laughing now, smiling. It was like watching people behind glass.

"We should go to the house," Margaux said.

"Go to the house for what?" Liddie asked, materializing out of nowhere as only Liddie could do.

In the end, they all ended up at the house.

Ryan and Kerry and their girls were already there when Kate, Margaux, Liddie, and Owen arrived, because Sunday lunch wasn't gluten-free and nut-free and whatever other food-free things their kids needed. Mary had been jostled in the crowd leaving the ceremony and had fallen and scraped her knee. Swift had helped her back to the house, fussing over her in a way no one ever did. When Sean saw them all walking to the house, he joined in, naturally.

Based on the vote on Friday, there was a good chance they were going to own this place with Sean. She hadn't thought about that till now, that the consequence of voting against Ryan would be that they'd end up with Sean. It was obvious, but even so, it was hard to absorb. It was like pitting the devil you know against the angel you didn't. Only, neither of those was right—Ryan wasn't the devil, and Sean wasn't an angel.

They gathered as they had two days before in the living room. Was it only two days? She thought of all that had happened since then, the fractured sleep, the visit to the hospital, the final break with Amy. It seemed like enough to fill a year, not a weekend.

Kerry was in the kitchen with the girls, preparing their food, but except for that amendment and the fact that Owen was there, sitting on the other side of Liddie, they were all seated in the same places. Swift was standing near the windows, waiting for them to silence.

"Are you going to tell us, Margaux?" Liddie asked. "Why did you want to talk?"

"I didn't want to talk to you. I wanted to talk to Kate."

Ouch, Kate thought, feeling Liddie flinch next to her.

"Come on, I think we're past all that now, aren't we?" Ryan said. He looked surprisingly calm given everything. Maybe he didn't care anymore. Kate could understand that. Holding on to things—this place, Amy—hadn't gotten her anything she wanted in life. Perhaps letting go was a better approach.

Margaux twisted back and forth in her seat. Kate wondered what had happened to Mark.

"What is it, Margaux?" Liddie said. "Just tell us."

"It's not my story to tell."

"Whose, then?"

"It's mine," Sean said. "She wants to tell you about me. But it's better if I do it."

"You don't have to," Margaux said.

"No, I do." Sean loosened the tie he was wearing. He was standing behind the chair Ryan was sitting in, and something about the way their shoulders rolled forward, the tilt of their heads, reminded Kate of something.

Then the truth clicked into place, as clear as day. And before Kate could help herself, she blurted, "He's our brother."

CHAPTER 43

RUMINATION

Liddie

Liddie was thinking those very words when Kate said them.

Owen had his arm around the back of the sofa, touching her shoulders, and that made it better, but still. She'd been feeling left out. Seeing Margaux whispering into Kate's ear like that, like a conspiracy. Having to ask to be included. Knowing that they'd agreed reluctantly to let her in on the secret.

She was sitting in the middle of her family, but she was on the outside.

Was this how Mary felt?

"Wait, what?" Ryan had stood up so quickly that he'd knocked over the wing chair. He wheeled on Sean, looking like he wanted to punch him.

"Don't hit him!" Margaux said.

"I wasn't going to hit him."

"You might want to lower your fist, then."

He slowly lowered his hand. "What's going on?" he asked Kate, but it was Liddie who answered.

"I found his birth certificate in Dad's things."

"And it said Dad was his father?"

"No, the father was blank, but it makes sense, doesn't it?"

She was looking back and forth between Sean and Ryan. How had she never noticed the resemblance between them before? They were the same height and build. Neither of them looked like her father, but then again, none of the MacAllisters did. The girls all took after their mother—in looks, anyway—but Ryan looked like their grandfather, Macaw's original founder, a man they'd never met. There were pictures of him on the mantelpiece though, taken when he was around forty-five. Liddie used to spend hours looking at those pictures when she was a kid, wondering what her life might've been like if he hadn't died.

"Is it true?" Margaux asked Sean. "Are you our brother?"

"I . . . I don't know. My mother never told me."

"And Dad, did he say anything?"

Sean waved a hand in front of his eyes. "He never said it. He implied it sometimes. I think."

"You've always wanted to be one of us."

"Ryan!"

"What, Margaux? It's true."

Liddie wasn't so sure about that though. Sean didn't want to be Margaux's brother, that was for sure. Thank God she'd never returned his feelings. Would her father have said something if she had? She shuddered.

Owen was looking at her quizzically. She shook her head, stood, and walked to the mantel. She picked up a picture of her grandparents, standing in front of the Camp Macaw sign, like the one of her own parents taken a few years later. Her whole family was one big feedback loop.

"He looks like Grandpa," Liddie said.

She passed the picture to Kate, who looked from it to Sean and back again. "He does."

"How did you guess, Kate?" Margaux asked. "Did you know about the birth certificate?"

"No, Liddie didn't tell me. I just . . . realized it all at once."

"Figures," Mary said, her voice shaking. "That she'd keep it from you."

"Yeah," Liddie said. "It does. Kate's terrible at keeping secrets."

"Not so terrible," Margaux said, giving Kate a look.

Liddie felt that queasy feeling again, like she was at sea in her own life. Owen touched her elbow. "You okay, babe?"

"I'll be all right."

They stood there, the photograph passing from person to person.

"Swift's been awfully silent, haven't you, Swift?" Ryan said.

"I'm not sure what you're implying," Swift answered, his voice rising.

"You know, don't you? Is Sean our brother?"

"Half brother," Mary said through gritted teeth.

"Yes, thank you, Mary, for that precision," Margaux said. "Very helpful."

Mary turned her back on them, looking out the window at the lake.

"So is he?" Ryan insisted.

Swift gave a nervous cough. "That would be protected by attorney-client privilege."

"Excuse me?" Sean said. "I'm not allowed to know who my own father is?"

"I'm sorry, Sean, but if Mr. MacAllister told me something in confidence, I'm bound to keep it."

"But he's dead."

"He was the only one who could waive the privilege, and that right died with him."

Sean's face grew redder as Swift spoke, making him look more like Ryan than ever. That identical seething look. Liddie was convinced now. Come what may, he was family.

"It makes sense though, doesn't it?" Margaux said.

"What," Ryan replied, "his legal mumbo jumbo?"

"No, that Sean's our brother. It explains why Dad took him in, his role in the will, all of it."

"Not *all* of it," Kate said. "I mean, if he's our brother, half brother, whatever, then he should inherit equally with us."

"That would've been hard to explain," Margaux said. "We'd want to know why."

"I'd want to know," Liddie said.

"You would," Ryan said.

"We'd all want to know," Margaux said. "But why hide it for so long?"

"Mom," Mary said from the window. "That's why. He didn't want Mom to know."

Liddie thought it over. When had her parents started dating? What was that story they used to tell? They'd met during a semester abroad in Australia. Two Canadians meeting on the underside of the world. But what year was that? Sometime in the seventies, but when?

"Did Dad cheat on Mom with . . . with your mother?" Kate asked Sean. "Is that the timeline?" Her lip was trembling.

"That's what's making you upset, Kate?" Liddie said, exasperated. "That Dad might've gone to a prostitute?"

"It's all of it, okay? Everything. What the hell is wrong with this family?"

No one had an answer for that, and Kate's rhetorical question seemed to suck the air out of the room. They all looked at one another, waiting for someone to come up with an explanation, feeling like the solution had to be somewhere in this room, if only someone would talk.

"Well," Ryan said finally. "There's one way to resolve the Sean question, at least."

"What's that?" Margaux said.

"A DNA test."

"Oh," Liddie said, her hand flying to her mouth.

"What is it, babe?" Owen asked.

She wasn't sure why her courage was failing her all of a sudden. She used to be so sure. Something about this weekend was eroding her sense of self. She felt as if she were turning into Kate—unsure, forgetful, wanting everyone to get along.

"Maybe we don't need a DNA test," she said.

"Why not?" Ryan said. "Do you know something?"

She reached into her pocket and touched the piece of paper there. She'd thought it was evidence against Ryan, but now it was all clicking into place.

"It depends . . . Sean, were you on the Island that night?"

Sean's eyes darted toward Margaux. "Yes."

"He took the kids over in the crash boat, remember?" Kate said.

"I didn't mean then. I meant later. Did you go back to the Island?"

Another look at Margaux. "Yes."

"What?" Ryan said. "You did what?"

"Quiet, Ryan!" Margaux said. "Let Liddie do this."

Was that what she'd wanted to tell Kate? That Sean had been on the Island? Had she known that this whole time? But if so, why was she protecting him, even now?

"When did you go over there?"

"I got there about one thirty."

"Did you see Ryan there?"

"No, he'd left. I saw him come back to camp. I left right after."

"I *told* you," Ryan said.

"Hush, Ryan. Why did you go?"

"I heard those guys out on their boat—they woke me up, you know how sound carries across the water at night. I wanted to make sure that . . . I wanted to make sure everyone was okay."

"But you didn't come to our side of the Island," Mary said, still not turning around. "We didn't see you."

"No, I went to Back Beach."

"Why? Were you trying to sneak around?"

"I saw Ryan coming from there. I was . . . I thought I'd go see what he'd been up to."

"So it wasn't because of the guys on the boat."

"Not only, no."

"What happened when you got there? Did you see Amanda?"

"Yes."

Liddie tried to imagine the scene. Amanda sitting on the beach, probably crying because of Ryan treating her like shit. Then Sean arriving, like . . . what? Liddie's imagination couldn't take her far enough.

"Did you . . . did you sleep with her that night?"

Sean paled.

"Why would you think that?" Kate asked.

Liddie removed the second piece of paper she'd taken from the Amanda file from her pocket and unfolded it. "Dad had this. It's a DNA test from Amanda's . . . rape kit, I guess."

"She was raped?"

"No," Swift said. "There was no sign of forced sexual contact."

"Did everyone know that?" Liddie asked, searching the faces of her family. "Margaux?"

"I didn't know," Margaux said. "No one was talking about that at all."

"It was kept quiet at the behest of her family," Swift said.

"But Dad had the test results?" Kate said. "How?"

"I don't know how he got it from the police file . . . but anyway, they tried to match her, um, sample to Ryan—I guess you gave them your DNA?"

Ryan's eyes were wide, his breathing shallow. *I should stop this now,* Liddie thought, *before he has a real heart attack;* but she couldn't.

"Yes," Ryan said. "I could've refused, but Swift said it was the best way to exonerate myself if I was innocent."

"I did," Swift said. "Ryan had admitted in his interview that he'd been on the Island that night to see Amanda and that they'd had a disagreement, and once the police heard that, they basically disregarded any other possible suspects."

"I told them the truth, but they didn't believe me. So I did it, I gave them a sample. And then a few weeks later they closed the case. They never told me why they wanted the sample though. I always assumed it was because they'd found some blood on her, or skin under her fingernails or something. They never told me that she slept with someone that night. But you knew, Swift?"

Swift looked embarrassed, perhaps for Amanda. "Yes. I had a . . . contact on the force. It was the reason I recommended that you take the test. You were so adamant that you hadn't been intimate with her. It was the only way to prove it."

"And the results confirmed I wasn't."

"Ah, well, the results were inconclusive, actually," Swift said. "They found your DNA on her—a hair sample, I believe—but as for the, ah, semen, there was only a partial match." Swift looked around at their confused faces. "You have to remember that DNA testing then was not like it is now. There weren't kits you could order on the internet; the techniques were not as refined. And since your father was away from camp that night, and there were no other male relatives on-site,

I convinced the police that there must've been contamination in the lab. When that was put together with Ryan's alibi—he'd spoken with another counselor, Ty, when he got back to camp—they dropped the case."

Ryan wheeled on Sean. "You slept with Amanda."

"Yes."

No one stopped Ryan from punching Sean that time.

CHAPTER 44

RAGE AGAINST THE DYING OF THE LIGHT

Ryan

Ryan knew he should stop himself, that violence didn't solve anything, but God did his fist hitting Sean's face feel good. So he did it again, and then again, though he could hear the shouts of his sisters and felt hands on his back, trying to pull him away, off, to get him to stop.

"Ryan! You're scaring the girls," Amy said.

He dropped his arms and let Sean go. He turned around slowly. His daughters were huddled around Kerry. They looked frightened, a look he'd promised himself he'd never produce on any woman's face again. He'd failed in that already this weekend. He might be innocent of what his father accused him of, but that didn't mean he wasn't guilty of other things.

"I need help," Ryan said, looking at Kerry. "Will you help me?" He crossed the room to her. She wrapped her arms around him. She smelled warm and like the honey-lemon scent of her shampoo. If he could hold on to this feeling, to her, he knew he could make it through.

"Why were you hitting Uncle Sean?" Maisy asked through her hiccuping tears.

He let Kerry go to drop down and look his daughters in the eye. "I found out something that upset me. But it wasn't okay what I did. It is never okay to hit another person, even if they hit you."

"We know, Daddy," Sasha said.

"Yeah," Claire added. "Mommy always says, 'Violence doesn't solve anything.' "

Ryan chuckled at this dead-on impersonation of Kerry. "She does say that, doesn't she?"

"Whenever we start fighting. Which is pretty much all the time."

Ryan felt as if his heart were breaking again, like the night before in the lodge, but he'd survive without a trip to the hospital this time.

He knew he needed to stand up and take stock of what he'd left on the other side of the room, but he wanted one more moment of this. The innocence of his daughters' faces. A fresh moment where his family knew and finally believed that he was innocent, but before they'd have to push through to the awful conclusion that if it wasn't him, it was Sean.

Sean. He'd always hated him in a way. Was jealous of his connection to their father. Wondered what he could do to be given the responsibility Sean seemed to have. Allowed to drive the boat, allowed to drive the camp van—whatever stupid thing Ryan was using as a measure of how his father had failed him.

But he'd gotten that wrong; they both had. Ryan *had* failed his father, and his father had put his trust in the wrong person.

"Ryan?" Margaux asked.

"Yeah."

"What's going on?"

He looked up at Kerry. She was looking down at him with concern. "Are you going to be okay? Should we call an ambulance?"

He kissed Claire's forehead and stood up. "I'm all right. But maybe Sean . . ."

He turned around. Sean was sitting on the ground, his head hanging between his knees. His nose was bleeding. It was dripping on the carpet. Everyone else seemed frozen in the place he'd left them. Mary still at the window, though she'd turned around. Liddie and Kate huddled on the couch with Owen. Margaux standing by Swift's side. They were all looking at him. For what? Was he supposed to solve this?

"Kerry, can you take the girls down to the lodge?"

"Honey?"

"We'll be okay. I'll explain it to you as soon as I can." He turned around and faced her. "They shouldn't be here for this."

"Yes, okay. You'll join us soon?"

"As soon as I can. Be good for Mommy, girls."

"Uncle Sean is bleeding on the rug," Maisy said. "Grandma wouldn't like that."

"You're right, bug. She wouldn't. Margaux, can you get him a towel?"

Margaux passed him, heading to the kitchen. He felt a strange sense of power as Kerry led his daughters out of the house. Was this how his father had felt? In charge? Was it because they'd just witnessed his violence? Were they simply frightened of him?

Margaux returned with a wet towel. She knelt down by Sean, who seemed to be dazed, and pressed it to his face. He started at her touch and stood, pushing her away.

Ryan had a million questions for him—or was it just the one?—but he felt the need to delay the inevitable. Or maybe he was savoring it. He deserved that, didn't he? After everything?

"What I don't get, Swift, is why, knowing all of this, my father would still think I did it."

Swift blinked a few times, getting his bearings. "He didn't know."

"How is that possible?"

"I didn't tell him the details. I simply told him that the DNA evidence had backed up your story and that the investigation was closed. I had to protect my source, you see. We could've both gotten in hot water if it had come out."

Ryan felt a measure of relief. His father hadn't chosen a guilty Sean over an innocent Ryan. "How did you convince the police to drop the investigation? Why wasn't partial DNA enough?"

"Like I said before, DNA wasn't what it is now. It was only a few years after the O.J. Simpson trial. And the police lab out here had its own screwup in a rape case a few months before. When the results came back inconclusive, I knew there was an opening. They didn't want another embarrassment on their hands. We'd been successful, you see, up until then, in keeping it out of the press."

"How did you do that?"

"Yes, well, I, um, convinced the local press not to run with innuendo. Camp Macaw was—is—a respected institution in the Townships. Nobody wanted to see it ruined. It ran as a small story that made it seem as if it was an accident. The newspapers in Montreal never picked it up."

"Amanda's parents went along with this?"

"That posed a problem. But they saw reason eventually."

"You bought them off."

"Yes."

"With what money?"

"Your parents' retirement fund. They were quite diligent savers, and your father had made a few well-timed investments. They liquidated their portfolio and set up a trust for Amanda's care so she could have a private room in the facility here and extra nurses when she needed them."

"So that's why," Kate said. "That's why they wouldn't let me take over."

"Perhaps. We never discussed it."

"I would've understood if they told me," Kate said. "I wish they'd told me."

It was almost too much for Ryan to take in. His parents *had* paid someone off to make this all go away. And yet . . .

"What changed his mind?" Ryan said. "I mean, if he did all this back then, he must've thought I was innocent."

"I believe he did."

"Then why? Why set up the will like that?"

"He found the DNA test somehow," Liddie said. "It was in his files."

"What files?"

"The files he had on all of us. Kate and I found them in the house. He'd been following all of us around forever. Investigating us."

That must have been the explanation, but still, it stung. Faced with a DNA test that could point in two directions, he'd chosen to believe Ryan had done it. And even though he understood why—he'd admitted being with Amanda, being on the Island, he had a temper, Stacey—he wished his father was still there to ask: Had he even considered Sean, or had it never even entered his mind as a possibility?

He couldn't ask his father. But he could ask Sean. It was time.

Ryan walked over to the fallen wing chair and righted it. "Sit here, Sean."

Sean was backing away from him, pressed up against the glass patio doors.

"I'm not going to hurt you . . . again. I promise."

"I understand why you hit me."

"Yeah, well, I shouldn't have. Will you sit?"

"Oh, let him stand where he wants," Margaux said, her voice high-pitched. "Who cares if he's sitting?"

And like that, the spell was broken. Ryan could feel the power shift away from him, like a receding tide.

"Fine. Do what you want. Tell us how it happened."

"How what happened?"

"What you did to Amanda."

"I didn't do anything."

"Please."

"It's true. I did . . . I did sleep with her that night. That was very wrong of me. I shouldn't have taken advantage of her like that, when she was vulnerable because of . . ."

"You're not blaming me for this, are you?"

"I'm trying to explain."

"You're doing a bad job."

Sean dropped the wet cloth to the floor. His nose was broken, crooked, and there was already a bruise forming under his eye. Ryan felt an answering twinge of pain in his hand. His knuckles were scraped and red.

"I hurt Amanda," Sean said. "I did, but I didn't hit her in the head with a paddle. When I left, after . . . she was okay. I don't know what happened next."

"Why should we believe you?"

"I've never given you any reason to doubt me."

"You never told anyone that you were there . . . what you did together."

"I was protecting her." His eyes moved to where Margaux was standing, a few feet away. "You understand, don't you, Margaux?"

She shook her head. "I told you before that I didn't."

"Before? What?" Liddie said.

"Sean told me about this before the memorial. It's what I wanted to talk to Kate about."

The anger was leaving Ryan's body, like a slow leak. All that was left was exhaustion. "You wanted to know if you should tell everyone before the vote?" he asked Margaux.

"I'm sorry."

"We *should* vote," Liddie said.

"What? You still think Sean should get the property?"

"I didn't mean about that. I meant if we should call the police."

"The police," Margaux said, her voice trembling. "Why?"

"You heard Swift. They only closed the investigation because of the DNA evidence and Ryan's alibi. But Sean doesn't have an alibi. Do you, Sean?"

Sean's eyes were moving back and forth rapidly between Margaux and Liddie. "No."

"I didn't think so." She turned to Kate. "We saw him. It was *Sean* we saw, not Ryan."

Kate looked stunned. "Sean?"

"Yes."

"You saw Sean when?" Mary asked.

"That night," Liddie said. "We . . . we were swimming that night, and we saw a man pulling the boat Amanda was in away from the Island."

"And you thought it was me," Ryan said.

"We didn't know who it was."

Ryan felt the weight of it. All the secrets. The burden he'd placed on his sisters. How much easier this all might've been if they'd talked to one another twenty years ago. But they were kids. Kids. Even he was a kid then.

"I say we vote," Liddie said.

"Liddie, babe," Owen said. "Maybe this isn't—"

"Stay out of this, Owen," Ryan said. "What are you even doing here?"

"I'm here for Liddie."

"Well, you can be here for Liddie by shutting it, okay? This is a family matter."

"Owen is my family," Liddie said.

"It was your idea to vote."

"Fine. Forget the vote." She stood and walked toward the phone. "I'll call the police myself."

"Hey!" Ryan said. "Come back here."

Sean was moving, running, on his way out of the house before anyone could react.

"Goddamn it," Ryan said. "Why didn't you stop him?" he asked Mary, who Sean had bolted past.

"How do you expect me to do that?"

"I'll get him," Margaux said. "Just hold off calling the police, okay, Liddie?"

"How do you know where he'll be?"

She looked resigned. "He's going to the Island."

CHAPTER 45

THE ISLAND—PART TWO

Sean

Sean rowed like a starter had gone off in his head. When he'd gotten to Boat Beach, he'd grabbed the first boat he came to, the old leaky rowboat that they should've thrown away years ago. He didn't bother with a life jacket, and he was grateful that everyone was still at lunch so he didn't have to try to explain where he was going. He kicked off his shoes, rolled up his pants, and pushed the boat into the cold water. He climbed in, positioned the oars, then counted off the strokes as the wind whipped around him and the waves crashed into the prow.

A hundred feet from shore, it was taking on water. But Sean knew if he rowed fast enough, hard enough, he could make it to the Island before it sank.

His muscles warmed as words and images banged around in his head. Mr. MacAllister, calling him "son." He never called Ryan that. Mrs. MacAllister warning him away from Margaux—did she know? She must've guessed something, even if she never asked outright. The way she'd notice when his pants weren't fitting right. Or how she'd recommend a book to him. "A good sailing adventure," she'd say, and then give him a wink. The way he felt as if he'd been at camp already when they took him there that first night. How he knew where the light switch was in the bathroom, though it wasn't obvious. How the living room had smelled familiar.

Had he been there before? Had his mother brought him to visit when Mrs. MacAllister was away? What had happened between Mr. MacAllister and his mother? Was it a onetime thing? Or was he a regular, one of those men whose car was parked outside the Twilight night after night after night?

Mr. MacAllister must've sent his mother away when she'd told him she was pregnant. But the seed had been planted, oh, the seed had been planted, and when they found him on the side of the road that morning, cold and frightened and wailing for his mother, maybe Mr. MacAllister didn't want to take a chance. He wanted to keep him close, just in case he was his son.

Sean's muscles burned as Macaw receded. What was the use in thinking about any of this? He was never going to get an answer to his questions. Even if he did, would it make him feel any better? Was the truth a more acceptable explanation? This was his family, and they hated him. This was his family, and they were going to turn him in. This was his family, and it included Margaux.

Margaux, Margaux, Margaux.

He rowed on, his boat beating against the current until, suddenly, it stopped.

Margaux found him not much later. He was sitting on Back Beach, staring at the low gray sky over the uneven lake, a rock in his hand.

Next to him was the cairn he'd started twenty years ago, the memorial to Amanda. The girl he didn't want but could never forget. The girl he'd let down, though she hadn't been counting on him.

"Sean."

"Go away, Margaux."

"You know I can't do that."

She was still in the black dress she'd worn to the memorial. Her hair was tumbling around her shoulders. Even on this dark day it was a bright light, golden, unmistakable.

He couldn't help loving her, even now.

"Do you think she knew?" Sean asked.

"Who? Amanda?"

"No, your mother. Did she know who I was?"

Margaux sat next to him. He could smell the lake on her skin. He didn't know how to adjust his thoughts about her. "That might explain a few things."

"Like?"

"She asked me once if I liked you. *Liked* you, liked you. She never did that usually, ask me about personal things."

"Was it a warning?"

"I'm not sure. I told her I didn't, and she said something about looking outside camp for my happiness. I didn't think it meant anything at the time."

Margaux didn't like him. Not *like* him, like him. He knew that, but it wasn't fun hearing it just the same. Why hadn't he been good enough for her? Why hadn't he been good enough for any of them?

"She warned me away from you," Sean said. "I thought then that it was because she thought I wasn't good enough for you, but now . . ."

Margaux picked up a rock and threw it at the waves. "I'm so mad at him."

"Who?"

"My dad. All of us, actually, but him most of all. It was so dangerous, what he did. Keeping all this to himself. And this business with the will, with Ryan. All of us torturing him this weekend. He could have died."

"It feels like it's my fault."

"Is it, Sean?"

"Everyone thinks I did it."

"You need to tell me everything."

"I did."

She looked down at her feet, her impractical sandals. She'd broken a toenail on the paddle over, and blood was seeping out.

"No, you didn't. What about the boat? Kate and Liddie saw you. It *was* you, wasn't it?"

Sean thought back to that horrible night. He'd tried to bury the memories, which was easier than it should've been. Amanda deserved to have all of her remembered, even the bad parts.

"It was me."

"Tell me."

He squeezed the rock in his hands; it wouldn't give.

"It won't change anything."

"Maybe it will."

He hated her right then. For pushing him. For putting him in this position in the first place. He wasn't blind to her faults. Margaux had always been self-involved. He might as well give her what she wanted. Why stop now?

"After we . . . you know, after it was over, Amanda wanted me to leave. I couldn't blame her. We both knew it was a mistake. I was . . . angry."

"Why?"

"I'm not sure."

"With yourself?"

No. He'd been angry with Margaux. As if his bad choices were her fault, but there was no use in telling her that.

"Yeah. We said some things that were not so nice, maybe. Eventually, I got in my canoe and I started to paddle away. The moon was gone by then, so it was dark. I got maybe a hundred, a hundred and fifty yards from shore and I just stopped paddling. I felt frozen. I didn't know what to do—go back to Amanda and try to make things right or go back to camp and try to forget. I don't know how long I sat there, but it must've been a while because when I checked my watch it was already four a.m. I was about to start paddling again when I heard something, voices, then a scream. I turned around and saw Amanda fall to the ground. I paddled as hard as I could, but when I got back to the beach, Amanda was unconscious. She had this awful gash in her head. I couldn't find a pulse."

Sean pushed the scent memory away. That awful metallic smell of blood. It had felt like it was everywhere as he checked her frantically, cursing himself that he'd never done more than the basic lifeguard training. He was scared of breaking her ribs if he tried a chest compression. He'd put his head to her torso and heard nothing. He'd held his hand above her nose and mouth and felt nothing.

"Was she breathing?"

"I didn't think so. I tried CPR. I tried and tried, but then . . ." Sean's throat started to close. He wasn't sure he could go on, but after a moment, somehow, he did. "I was wrong, obviously, so wrong. But I thought she was dead, and I wasn't thinking straight. I felt like if I got her off the Island, then everything would be okay. I put her in my canoe, and I paddled it out into the lake. When I got close enough to Secret Beach, I jumped out and pushed it so it would get there with the tide. So she'd be found. Then I swam back to camp and snuck into the lodge. I got changed, then took all the clothes I was wearing and hid them in the lost-and-found barrel. An hour later, Kate and Liddie came running from Secret Beach, saying we had to call an ambulance. You know the rest."

"Why didn't you tell anyone what had happened?"

"How could I?"

Margaux leaped to her feet. "You might've saved her. If you'd brought her back to camp and called 9-1-1, she might be okay today. Living a life. Married, kids. Not hooked up to some machine that breathes for her."

"Don't you think I know that? I've tortured myself with this for twenty years. Could I have saved her? But I tried to save her and I thought she was dead, and . . ."

"And what? You knew you'd get blamed for what happened to her if you told the truth, and so you did everything you could to save yourself. You might as well have hit her."

Sean rose. The rock dropped to the ground, cracking against the shore. Yes, he'd made terrible mistakes that night. They all had. But this, this was too much.

"I did it for you."

"What does that mean?" She twisted away from him and winced as her toe scraped against the sand. "You said that before at the house. How could this possibly have been for me?"

Sean felt incredulous. He was trying to protect her, still, even as she was rejecting him, even as she was blaming him for everything that happened. He couldn't stand it anymore.

"Because you hit her, Margaux. I saw you."

CHAPTER 46

PAPER HOUSES

Margaux

Margaux felt like someone had taken a paddle to her own head. How else to explain the dull thud in her mind, the addled thoughts? All that was missing was the wound. The blood.

This could not be happening. She wouldn't let it.

"What?"

"I saw you, Margaux. You were the one who hit Amanda."

"That's ridiculous! I'd never do that. You said it was dark. You couldn't see who it was."

"I could see enough. I could see this." He reached out and touched her hair. She recoiled. He looked like she'd slapped him. "And later, at camp, when you came back, and the ambulance was there—you had blood on your hands. On your hands and on your shirt."

Margaux thought of how she'd washed off the paddle when she'd found it in the water. She'd cleaned her hands so carefully, she believed. The next thing she knew, she was falling into Sean's arms when she saw the ambulance. Then later, her mother had taken her into the house, had forced her into the shower, and had taken her clothes away.

"I wouldn't do that! Ever."

"You can stop pretending with me."

"You really think I could do that to her?"

"I didn't want to, but . . . Don't worry, okay? You should know by now I won't tell."

Margaux stared at Sean. He was so convinced; it made her feel as if she were going crazy. Like talking to someone who calmly explains how aliens have been visiting earth for thousands of years.

"You won't tell," Margaux found herself repeating, like a mantra, like a wish.

"I won't. But what I've never understood was why. You didn't care if I slept with her."

Sean waited for her to reply. She could hear the words he was saying but only as a bass note to her heartbeat.

"I would've cared, if I knew."

"Don't lie to me. I deserve better than that." He was pacing on the beach now. She felt like running, but where did she have to go? "I told myself and told myself that it was okay that you didn't say anything when it looked like Ryan was on the hook for it, because if they were going to charge him, it would've happened, and if they did, you'd come forward, and then they didn't, and . . ."

"You don't care about Ryan."

"Okay, okay, you're right. I don't. But this weekend, when you voted, and there was one vote for Ryan, that was you, wasn't it?"

"Yes."

"I thought it was your way of apologizing for the fact that you let him twist in the wind like that."

"I voted for Ryan because he didn't do it."

Sean stopped pacing. "What's going to happen now?"

"I think you should go."

"Go? Go where?"

"Somewhere not here. I need to think."

"You need to plan."

She looked at him. What was there to say? Sean thought he was going to be a part of all this. But he wasn't. He couldn't.

"I need to plan," she agreed.

"Where should we meet?"

"Meet?"

"When you figure out what to do. I can't go to jail, Margaux. I can't."

"You won't."

"Do you promise?"

"I promise."

She forced herself to meet his eyes. Was he going to believe her? He had to believe her, because she needed to be alone. She needed to think.

She needed to remember.

Sean rowed away a few minutes later. She'd told him to go to the other side of the lake, and she'd meet him in Magog later that night. She didn't know what she was saying; she needed him to leave.

When he was around the Island and out of sight, she sat down on the ground, her legs giving out from under her. She still had that muddled feeling, like she'd received a blow to the head. No, a paddle, a paddle, that was right. But it wasn't right, was it? Something was wrong with her. She couldn't get her brain to work properly anymore. She couldn't think. She couldn't remember.

Sean had seen her, he said. Had seen her hit Amanda, then walk away, leaving her for dead. She didn't remember doing this. Was it possible she'd blocked it out? That happened in movies, but did it happen in real life? Was that why she'd avoided seeing Amanda all these years, had stayed away from camp, hadn't put down roots or had a family? Because she knew, deep down, that she was dangerous?

Was her whole life a lie, even to herself?

She stood on wobbly legs, trying to remember. Why had she washed off the paddle? Why hadn't she told anyone about it? She knew now, with the benefit of hindsight and the information that had been kept from all of them, that her questioning by the police had been perfunctory. It made sense, when all the facts were assembled. She'd been with twenty girls and Mary all night. Amanda was her best friend, and they weren't fighting. She'd been found in a canoe that had been at camp earlier. She'd had semen in her. They knew who did it, even if they couldn't prove it in court. They'd had no reason to look at her closely—no one had.

Even her mother hadn't asked too many questions. Margaux had mumbled something about blood being on the rocks to explain the blood on her, the reason she'd panicked and paddled back without the kids. Her mother had nodded and told her not to think about it. To take a shower and forget. And she had.

But the act itself. The blow. The anger that must've preceded it. That wasn't her. She loved Amanda. If she'd walked in on Amanda and Sean, would she have cared? Would she have been angry? Would she have wanted to punish Amanda? Or maybe they had fought. Maybe she'd called Amanda out for what she was doing, trying to get back at Margaux because Ryan had rejected her. That's what Sean thought. And Ryan. Even Sean thought she'd done it.

Even Sean.

Was he right?

She had to make herself remember. Either that, or forget.

Time passed without any answers. When she finally climbed back into the canoe she'd paddled over in, the sun was starting to set. It was hard to tell beneath the cloud cover, but Margaux could feel it in her bones.

She was exhausted when she got close enough to camp to focus on the beach. It was full of people, probably a hundred. Of course. The memorial. The lantern ceremony.

Mary was standing on the dock, waving at her.

"Margaux! Paddle over here."

She obeyed. Mary bent down and caught the prow, holding it steady while Margaux climbed out. She attached the bowline to the dock with neat efficiency.

"I was about to come over and get you. We've been waiting on the photo."

"The photo?"

"The camp photo," Mary said. "All of us with the lifers. You know, like we used to do every summer?"

This was what they had instead of family photos. Her mother would climb onto a ladder and use a special camera before everyone's iPhone had a panoramic setting. All of them would be in it, even her, because she'd put it on a timer and rush in.

Mary had her mother's camera slung around her neck. No iPhones for her.

"Are you okay?" Mary asked.

"What? Yes. I guess."

"Where's Sean?"

"He left."

"You let him leave?"

"What was I supposed to do?"

Their eyes locked. Mary looked tired. This weekend had worn all of them down.

"Did Liddie call the police?"

"No, they decided to wait for you."

"Do you think we should?"

"Mary! Margaux! Everyone's waiting! *Allons-y.*"

She looked over Mary's shoulder. Simon Vauclair of all people was standing with Mark, calling to them to get the picture done.

"We should go," Mary said.

Margaux didn't know what to say, so she followed Mary off the dock to where everyone was crowding together on the beach for the photograph.

"Where were you?" Mark asked, appearing at her shoulder. "Everyone was asking."

"I had to take care of something."

"On the Island?"

"Just leave it, Mark, okay?"

He took a step back. She felt badly—this wasn't his fault—but she couldn't handle him right now. Why was he still here? They'd broken up. That had happened before the memorial, she was almost certain of it.

She walked into the crowd, deflecting the questions of the curious. She found Kate and Liddie. She felt safe with them. Amy and Owen were there too but hanging back.

"Where's Sean?" Liddie asked.

"Gone," Margaux said.

"I guess he did it," Kate said.

"Course he did, dummy," Liddie said.

"Don't call me that."

"Keep your voices down," Margaux hissed. "Both of you."

Mary climbed onto the ladder. Ryan was in the front row with Kerry and the girls. Their eyes met briefly and he mouthed, *Where's Sean?* Margaux shook her head.

"Get closer, everyone! Closer!" Mary yelled as the wind whipped her braid of hair around. They obeyed, and Mary set the timer. She left the camera on the ladder and scurried down, finding a place in the shot.

"Okay, now everyone say, 'Camp Macaw'!"

"Camp Macaw!" they bellowed as one.

Then the repeating began, *mac-caw, caw, caw.*

After the picture was taken, it was time for the lantern ceremony. Even though it wasn't dark yet, it would still be effective. Mary took the position Ryan had so many years ago on the dock, a lighter in her hand as everyone lined up with their lanterns.

"I brought this for you," Kate said, handing her one.

"I didn't get time to make mine."

"I figured."

"Thanks, Kate."

Kate was holding her own lantern. Margaux could see her wish, a simple word: *Amy*. Kate saw her looking, then lifted her chin. "I'm not hiding anymore."

"Good."

Owen was standing off to the side of the line, his guitar strapped across his shoulder, gently strumming a tune. Margaux recognized it after a moment. "Amazing Grace." Tears sprang to her eyes. That was her mother's favorite around the campfire. Had Liddie told him that, or did he remember on his own?

"That's a pretty good guy you got yourself there," she said to Liddie as they stepped onto the dock.

"I know." Liddie's eyes turned serious. "What are we going to do?"

"Let's do this first. We'll talk after, okay?"

"Okay."

Margaux held the lantern between her hands. The wind was stronger now, blowing the lanterns around as they were released. They rose anyway, the combination of heat and physics working as it always had. Margaux watched them, overcome by a web of memories. Not the ones she was trying to recover on the Island but the real moments before that. Amanda and her on the dock. How Ryan was holding his lighter. How Amanda was hiding her wish from him. Margaux could see it all now—*Ryan* had been her wish. How he'd winked at them, she'd thought then, but it must've been at Amanda.

Oh, Amanda.

The line moved quickly, Mary efficient. She lit Kate's lantern, then Liddie's. Now it was Margaux's turn. She held hers out.

"There's no wish," Mary said.

"I forgot."

"Here, I've got a pen. Step out of line."

She did as she was told. Mary passed the lighter to Liddie and instructed her to keep the line going. Liddie mock saluted her but was clearly pleased at the responsibility. So silly. They were all so silly, these rituals they clung to.

Mary dug a pencil out of her pocket and handed it to Margaux.

"Can you hold it while I write on it?" Margaux said.

"Sure."

Mary held it sideways as Margaux bent over it. Her hair fell forward, obscuring the space. She brushed it back, wishing she'd braided it like Mary.

Like Mary.

"Hurry up," Mary said. "You're going to miss it."

Margaux's hand was shaking as she wrote: *I want to remember.* She watched the words form, her handwriting acting like open sesame. The memories tumbled out. The handwriting on the whiteboard. The person who'd written that Sean was on the Island that night and wrote in her name.

It was Mary.

She looked up. Mary's mouth was open slightly, a round *O* of surprise at her wish. Could she tell what Margaux was thinking, what she was puzzling out?

"Are you going to let me light that or what?" Liddie asked.

"Here, I'll do it," Mary said, plucking the lighter out of Liddie's hand. She flicked it, and Margaux's lantern was ablaze.

"Let go, or you'll get burned."

She let go.

CHAPTER 47

THE SECRET GARDEN

Mary

Margaux was staring at Mary with a strange look on her face.

They'd left the docks and were on the beach, watching the lanterns float up into the sky. Owen was still strumming his guitar, shifting through a range of tunes. Mary could smell the rain in the air. They didn't have long now before it would strike.

"What is it, Margaux?"

"You did it," she said. "You hit Amanda."

Mary turned away. She felt almost nothing at this accusation. Only a small measure of relief. "That's ridiculous. Sean did it."

"He said he didn't, and I believe him."

"Why?"

"Because he thinks *I* did it."

"You'd never hurt Amanda."

"You're right. But if Sean thinks I did, then he obviously didn't do it. Which leaves only one person."

Mary's eyes were fixed on her own lantern, the last one released. She'd never believed in wishes, and yet, she'd written a name on hers like she had every year. His name.

"Why are you so convinced all of a sudden? It could've been anyone . . . those boys on the other side of the lake."

"It wasn't them."

Owen started playing "Fire's Burning." One of the lifers began singing, then Kate and Liddie joined in. Mary expected Margaux to do so as well, but instead she kept looking at Mary in that same accusatory way.

Ryan walked up to them. "It's going to rain. We should probably get everyone back to the lodge." He leaned closer so he couldn't be heard. "Then we should reconvene at the house and decide what to do."

Now Mary felt a measure of fear. "Decide what to do about what?"

"Sean."

"You're not actually going to call the police, are you?" Margaux asked.

"I think we should, and Liddie agrees."

"Don't do that," Mary said.

"You think we should just let him go?" Ryan said. "Let him get away with it?"

"He's not going to get your share of camp. Isn't that enough?"

"No," Margaux said quietly. "I don't think so."

Margaux was on the verge of tears. Mary understood what that meant. Margaux was sad because she was going to do something she didn't want to do, but that wasn't going to keep her from doing it.

"Please, Margaux. It won't solve anything."

"We shouldn't talk about this here. Let's get everyone to the lodge, and we'll meet at the house and decide, okay?"

Mary nodded, but she had no intention of complying.

The rain came earlier than expected. It was easy to slip away in the chaos that followed. Shrieking kids acting as though getting water on their Sunday best was going to melt them away. Concerned parents trying to make sure all their belongings were coming with them. Her family acting as shepherds. And what was she? One lone figure in a rain jacket she'd pulled from the lost-and-found barrel in the lodge, rushing up the road.

Lightning cracked overhead. Mary counted automatically. One, and two, and . . . It was five seconds away, five miles. The rain was falling in thick sheets, a curtain that wet her to the bone despite the yellow slicker. It wasn't a warm summer rain but that cold, wet rain of fall, one that will leave you shivering and running for the indoors.

Mary reached the barn. She felt as if she'd run for miles instead of minutes, her mouth full of spit, her muscles screaming. She hung her raincoat on a peg and flipped on the lights. The long row of stalls was empty save for Cinnamon. Thinking about this calmed her. She only had to make it to tomorrow, maybe even tonight, and she could return to her home, her solitude. She'd ride outside all fall until the snow fell, and then she'd go somewhere warm for the winter. She'd struggled these last few years, under the cold graying sky. Seasonal affective disorder, she read online after she'd typed in her symptoms. A form of depression related to the weather.

Seasonal defective disorder, as Mary had read it the first time. It was how she thought of it still. A fitting diagnosis for her, the defective member of the family.

Cinnamon was staring at her, probably wondering why she hadn't come over to rub her nose. Horses were so attuned to the people who cared for them, any slight change in routine. They were much better than people that way. Mary remembered how her mother had fretted over Margaux after Amanda was found. Why didn't anyone notice her, comfort her? Sean had held Margaux as if she were a prize he'd won at the fair, his face lit up, happy. After he'd let Margaux go, and it was only her, he hadn't offered the same solace.

Sean. It was best not to think too much about him. Mary had lots of practice at that, and if he was their brother—their half brother, though the thought of this made her almost physically sick—then all the more reason to tuck him away for good into the place where she kept all the things she wasn't supposed to think about.

Like that night on the road when Ryan had been with that girl. Stacey Kensington. It was family weekend, and Mary had been in the staff cabin with some of the lifers. She never used to go there, but that night, she was feeling restless. She didn't usually drink much either or smoke what was passed around, but she did both. There she was, twenty-six, still living with her parents. Kate was too, but she was younger, and it was what Kate wanted. Mary wanted to leave. She wanted to be free. For a few minutes, she'd felt that way.

Then she'd kissed Simon Vauclair on the path to the bathroom. He told her she looked like Margaux, who hadn't come, as usual. That's when she did it. He tasted like liquor, and his mouth was aggressive. When he'd reached for the zipper on her jeans, she'd broken free and run away from him. Run right to the barn. She'd gotten on a horse, Miranda, who had a dark coat, and raced up the road. Then lights, that awful scrape of metal. Miranda reared, and she'd fallen into the ditch. Then Ryan had been there, making sure she was okay, telling her to go and hide in the woods. She learned about Stacey later. She'd felt a bit guilty about that. It was her fault, that accident. She shouldn't have been riding drunk at night.

But Stacey was also a stupid, reckless girl who'd had cocaine in her system. That and the fact that she wasn't wearing her seat belt, and Ryan's tests had been clean, had saved him. Ryan told her he would keep her involvement to himself, and Swift had appeared, as Swift always did when there was something threatening camp. Mary wondered at his loyalty sometimes, but he'd been the family lawyer for forty years. Swift took care of things; Stacey's parents said they were going to sue, but when her tox screen came back, that was the end of that. Another crisis averted.

I probably never thanked Ryan properly, she thought as she scratched Cinnamon's muzzle. But that was okay. She'd thank him tonight and encourage him to call the police on Sean. It would be okay to do that. He probably wouldn't go to jail. Not after twenty years. Sean wouldn't confess to something he didn't do. He wasn't stupid enough to take the fall for Margaux, not now.

The barn door opened, and there was Margaux, as if Mary's thoughts had conjured her. Her hair was matted to her head.

"Planning your escape?" she asked.

Mary tried to keep her tone light, but her voice came out rough. "Should I be?"

"This isn't funny."

"I didn't say it was."

"You have to admit what you did. If you don't, the others are going to call the police and blame Sean."

There was that twinge of guilt again. But Mary could deal with it. She must.

"Innocent people don't go to jail," she said.

"That's ridiculous. Sure they do."

"Not . . ."

"People like us?" Margaux completed her thought. "But Sean's not like us, is he? He's the camp caretaker who slept with a seventeen-year-old girl when he was in his midtwenties. And he moved her body and hid both those facts all these years . . . That doesn't sound too innocent to me."

"Maybe he did do it, then."

"No."

"How can you be so sure?"

"I told you. He thought I did it."

"So what?"

"You should be asking me why. Why he thought that."

"Okay, why, then?"

"Because he thought he saw me. He was out on the lake, and he saw who hit her."

"It was dark. He was mistaken. And that doesn't make it me."

Margaux took a step toward her. She tugged at the end of Mary's braid.

"What are you doing?"

"Hold still for a second."

She felt Margaux's fingers in her hair, undoing it. Then she shook out her own wet hair. It was shorter than Mary's, falling only to her shoulders. But Mary got her point. With their hair down, even in the light of the barn, they looked similar. Not the twins she'd always wished they'd been, but close enough.

"He saw a blonde girl hit Amanda in the head with a paddle," Margaux said. "It could only be me or you, and it wasn't me."

Mary felt trapped. By Margaux standing so close, by the words she was saying. She was having trouble breathing.

"He thought he saw you," she gasped. "Maybe he was right."

"He wasn't. I can prove it."

"How?"

"You made a mistake, writing on the whiteboard like that. Pointing a finger at me and at Sean. No one knew Sean was on the Island that night."

They stared at each other. Mary could smell sweat. Her own. That had been a stupid, stupid mistake. She wasn't quite sure why she'd done it. Only, when she'd looked at the whiteboard early that morning after she returned from the barn and J-F, her guilt screamed out at her. Everyone's actions seemed accounted for but hers and Margaux's. Someone was going to notice that soon. When they did, if they started asking questions, someone might figure it out. She'd picked up the pen and written that Sean was on the Island, and then, for good measure, she'd written in and circled Margaux's name at the time it happened.

Then she'd gone to the bathroom and scrubbed the marker off her hands.

"You don't know I wrote that."

"I recognized your handwriting."

"I knew Sean was on the Island that night. So what?"

"It means you were up. It means you saw him with Amanda."

She looked past Margaux to the door. She wasn't going to get out of here easily, not without hurting Margaux. And Margaux was strong, stronger than her.

She took a step back, opening Cinnamon's stall and slipping inside. She shut the gate quickly behind her.

"What are you doing?"

"You're frightening Cinnamon." Margaux would let her leave if she asked. She'd let her ride out of here.

"You have to confess."

"No."

"You can't let Sean go to jail for something you did. Besides, isn't that why you did it in the first place? Because of Sean?"

Mary recoiled. She felt like a bug that'd been hiding under a rock that had been flipped over. Exposed. She was against the back of the stall now, its wooden slats rubbing at her back.

"Stop it," she said.

"Tell me. Tell me what made you do it. Was it because you saw him with Amanda? Was that it?"

"I said, stop it!"

Mary bent and grabbed a bucket from the corner of the stall. She pushed it up against the back wall, stood on it, and grabbed at the sill. She hoisted herself up and onto one of the beams in the ceiling below the hayloft, straddling it.

"What are you doing? Come back here!"

Margaux's voice receded as Mary pushed herself up into a standing position, holding on to the wall. She tried to steady her breathing. The next step was tricky. There was another beam above her, but she'd have to jump to get to it, then use it to swing into the hayloft. She'd done it before, she and Margaux both had, but it had been years. More than twenty.

"Mary!"

The thunder cracked again, closer this time. Mary controlled her panic as she sighted the beam. She could do this. It was only a matter of timing.

"Mary, don't. You'll kill yourself."

Mary blocked her out and counted. *One, two* . . . on three, she was springing through the air, her hands in position to catch the beam. She did it, and held, then swung her legs back and forth, gaining momentum for the second move. Her hands felt slick, but she couldn't slip, she couldn't, *and one, and two, and* . . . She released and flew through the air. Her feet hit the hayloft floor, and she shifted her body weight forward, landing on her knees on a pile of scratchy hay.

She laughed. She'd done it!

"Mary, come on, get down from there."

"No!"

"You can't stay up there forever. You're going to have to come down eventually. Or . . ."

"Or what, Margaux?"

The thunder crashed again, so close it was deafening. She heard a large crack.

"I think it hit the tree outside," Margaux yelled up.

Mary ran to the other side of the hayloft. There was a window that looked out at the paddocks. The large maple that had stood there for a hundred years was split down the middle, its insides smoking. One side had taken out one of the fences. The other had flattened a hayrack.

Good thing about the rain, Mary thought, *or the barn could've caught on fire.*

"Mary? Where did you go?"

She came back to where she could see Margaux, who was standing below, looking up at her.

"Here I am."

"Are you going to come down?"

"For what? So you can call the police and I can be hauled away to jail for the rest of my life? That doesn't sound very appealing."

"But you'd let Sean go in your place? I thought you loved him."

Mary hugged herself. Sean, Sean. She did love Sean. She always had. But it had started so many years ago, only the echo remained. The scar.

"You'd choose him over me?" Mary asked.

"I'm not choosing anyone. You chose. When you hit Amanda. When you lied about it all these years."

Mary felt the rightness of those words. Margaux always did know how to hit the nail on the head. She'd chosen. To get up when she was sure Margaux was asleep. To go looking for Amanda, because Liddie didn't have to be the only sneak in the family. She'd always hated Amanda. Before Amanda, Mary had been Margaux's best friend. Then Amanda had waltzed in her first summer at camp and stolen Margaux away. Mary didn't make friends easily. She'd been so alone. But now Amanda was running around at night, probably meeting up with someone. If they got caught—if Mary caught them—Amanda might have to go home. Then things could go back to the way they were. Margaux and Mary. Sisters. Irish twins.

She wasn't sure why she'd taken the paddle with her. She'd seen it lying against a rock and picked it up. And then, when she'd gotten to Back Beach, Sean was there and . . . Mary shuddered. She didn't like to think about that part. She didn't think she'd meant to do that to Amanda. Nothing so permanent, anyway. Not a forever kind of hurt.

"Mary?"

"I chose," Mary said, looking down at Margaux. "It was my fault."

"Maybe Swift can work his magic and . . ."

But even Margaux didn't believe that. Mary could see what would happen if she came down to the ground. The tight cuffs that would chafe her wrists. The small interrogation room with the bad coffee and the stern faces. She'd crack quickly—what resistance did she have to professionals? Sean would come forward, and the timeline would make it all clear. Her or Margaux. But she was the one who'd written on the whiteboard; they'd be able to prove that. She'd chosen that, too.

The rain stopped as suddenly as it began. She could smell the charring wood in the air. She thought of the lanterns that had probably been wiped out by the rain, her wish—his name, *Sean*—and the lighter that was still in her pocket. If she could do it, if she could be brave for a minute, she could choose a different path.

"Margaux," she said into the silence.

"What?"

"Take Cinnamon out of the barn, okay?"

"Why?"

"Just do it."

Margaux got ahead of her again. "Oh no. No, Mary, don't."

"Please, Margaux."

Margaux was crying, and so was Mary. She wasn't sure she was strong enough to do this, but it was the only way.

"Tell them what I did, okay? Tell them I'm sorry."

"No, Mary, please. Don't."

Margaux made for the ladder that lay against the wall.

"Stop!"

Mary pulled the lighter out of her pocket and spun the wheel with her thumb. A flame appeared. "You don't want to be here for this. Get Cinnamon. Get her out of here."

"Please, Mary. Please."

Margaux was so stubborn. She was going to have to give her an inducement. She picked up a piece of hay. She held the lighter to it. "Get out of here, Margaux."

"No, Mary. No! I'm not leaving. I'm not leaving you."

Was that true? Mary doubted it, as much as Margaux might believe it in this instant. So be it. Now Margaux was choosing.

"Please save Cinnamon, Margaux. She's innocent."

"Mary!"

But Mary wasn't listening to Margaux anymore. She worked her thumb on the lighter again. The hay caught instantly, singeing her fingers. She dropped it into the larger pile at her feet. There was a second where Mary could have stamped it out, taken off her wet sweater and smothered it. But she didn't do that. Instead, she counted like she was counting thunder.

One and two and . . . three.

Amanda

July 23, 1998—4:00 a.m.

I was glad to see the back of Sean. He'd been mean on the way out, maybe I had too. But he'd gone when I finally asked him to. Now I was alone, sitting on the same rock I'd sat on before, watching him paddle away, trying to work up the courage to go back to the kids and Margaux. How was I going to tell her about everything that had happened tonight? I couldn't even process it myself. Sean's boat stopped moving. Maybe he was as stuck out there in the water as I was. It was late, so late. The kids would be up in a few hours and I was exhausted. I closed my eyes, maybe I fell asleep for a minute, and then:

"You had to take it all, didn't you?"

I started, my heart jumping as I leapt to my feet and turned around. Mary was standing there, a large flashlight in one hand, a canoe paddle in the other.

"Mary. What are you doing here?"

"I saw you."

I felt sick. "You . . ."

"I saw you with him. You're disgusting. It was disgusting."

I stood up. I felt wobbly from the alcohol and the lack of sleep. Unfocused. "You shouldn't have done that."

"Neither should you."

"You're right. It was a mistake."

"A mistake."

"That's right."

"Like an accident."

Mary was speaking in a flat monotone that was freaking me out. "Not an accident, a mistake."

"A mistake," she repeated.

"Yes, Mary. Will you keep it to yourself?"

"Why should I?"

"Because I'm asking you to. I thought we were friends."

"Friends. Ha!"

She took a step toward me. I felt a shiver of fear. "I don't know what I ever did to you."

"You don't? Why am I not surprised?"

Mary stepped closer.

"What are you doing? Why are you holding that paddle?"

"For protection," Mary said, and then she swung.

	Amanda	Margaux	Ryan	Mary	Kate & Liddie	Sean
9:00 p.m.	Lantern ceremony	Lantern ceremony	Lantern ceremony			
10:00 p.m.	On the Island	On the Island		On the Island		Crash boat
11:00 p.m.	Back Beach	Back Beach	Back Beach	On the Island		
Midnight	Back Beach		Back Beach			
1:00 a.m.	Back Beach		Camp			Back Beach
2:00 a.m.	Back Beach		Camp			Back Beach
3:00 a.m.	Back Beach					Back Beach
4:00 a.m.	Back Beach			Back Beach	Swimming	Back Beach/ Rows Amanda
5:00 a.m.	In boat	Searches for A.	Camp/ Boat Beach	On the Island	Camp	Rows Amanda
6:00 a.m.	Secret Beach		Secret Beach		Secret Beach	

Margaux

One Year Later

Margaux saved Cinnamon. She couldn't reach Mary, though she tried. The flames were too quick. She'd singed her hair and burned her hand in the process, but she'd made it to Cinnamon's stall and dragged her out, terrified. She stood with her on the other side of the road, waiting for the distant wail of the fire trucks that got there too late.

Ryan had smelled the smoke and organized as many people as he could into a makeshift fire brigade. But a couple of garden hoses and the tins of water from outside each cabin were powerless against a raft of hay for kindling and an old wooden structure.

It was ruled an accident. Margaux didn't say anything different. Mary had gone up to the barn to make sure her horse was okay when the thunder started. Margaux was there to close her car window that she'd left open and had gotten to the barn right as the fire took hold. Mary had been trying to light something, that much was clear. Maybe the power had gone out, and she was trying to light one of the oil lamps that hung on the wall.

That was the public story, but Margaux had told the family everything after she'd gone to Magog to retrieve Sean. They'd agreed to keep it all in the family and had decided that Mary's piece of the property would go to Sean. Swift had arranged everything. And now, it was a year later, another Labor Day weekend, another memorial. There'd been a barn raising earlier in the summer. Camp was well insured. And thanks to its incorporation and the sale of 49 percent of the shares to the lifers, it was well funded. There hadn't been much time for changes this summer, but plans were in the works. The original charm would be maintained, but the tennis court would be resurfaced and doubled in size. Some new cabins would be built and the lodge expanded. Fifty more kids each session would make the place nicely profitable.

They'd voted unanimously to put Kate in charge. Margaux had stayed in the French Teacher's Cabin for the summer, and Ryan and Kerry's older girls had spent their first summer at Macaw, much to the frustration of their youngest sister. Liddie and Owen had come to visit when Owen's touring schedule permitted. They'd even had a special bonfire, Owen and Margaux playing all the old favorites on their guitars, their voices blending nicely.

Margaux had given her notice at school after a year of avoiding Mark in the break room. She wasn't sure what she wanted to do next. She thought about helping Kate run camp for a while. Or maybe she'd concentrate on her music, dust off some of the dreams she'd shelved. If Owen could make it, why not her? She'd spent a lot of time sifting through her mother's trove of photographs. She'd framed some of her favorites and put them up in the lodge. She'd put another set together for a show at a local gallery.

She'd visited Amanda almost daily, asking for forgiveness and understanding of all the ways her family had failed her. They'd all been responsible for the state she was in, in their own way, even though it was Mary who'd struck the blow. There wasn't any way to make it up to her, but still Margaux came, she spoke, she tried.

A few weeks before the twenty-first anniversary of that night, Amanda had started to fade. The doctors couldn't explain it—why now all of a sudden when she'd stayed the same for so long? It happened, sometimes, that way. The machines no longer became enough. Margaux was there with Amanda's parents when she'd stopped breathing altogether. They'd decided before not to try to reverse course. Amanda was long gone, and now she could finally rest. Margaux sat in the room with her long after they'd turned off the machines, counting memories, wishing she could hear that singular laugh one last time as she said, "Come on, Margaux."

But life didn't work like that.

"You ready, Margaux?" Liddie asked her Sunday evening. They were all standing on the dock. Kate and Amy were holding hands. Ryan and Kerry had their arms around their girls. A small flotilla of lanterns stood at their feet. They'd timed it so they'd light them as the sun was about to set.

Margaux held her own lantern, the words she'd written on it her final promise to her sister. That she'd keep what really happened to herself—they all would—so she could be remembered fondly and well.

Three simple words. Her family's motto.

I'll never tell.

ACKNOWLEDGMENTS

It's easy to forget, sometimes, when you're caught up in the writing of a book, how lucky you are to be able to do this again and again. Thankfully, that's what acknowledgments are for!

To my husband, David—for putting up with twelve-plus (writing) years of me tapping away while we watch TV together. And a bunch of other things I won't write down here. Thank you.

To my early readers, Kristina Riggle, Carolyn Ring, and Heather Webb—your insights and critiques were invaluable.

To my editors, Laurie Grassi and Jodi Warshaw—your enthusiasm for this book has been amazing, and it is so much better because of your edits. I am lucky to work with both of you.

To the publishing teams at Lake Union and Simon & Schuster Canada—thank you for creating beautiful books for me, for spreading the word far and wide, and for championing me and my work. A special shout-out to my Canadian publicist, Lauren Morocco, for knocking it out of the park with the publicity for *The Good Liar*, and the sales and marketing team for helping make that book an instant *Globe and Mail* bestseller. And to Kathleen Carter for being with me through three books now.

To my agent, Abby Koons, and the whole team at Park Literary Media—thank you for going to bat for me.

To my writer friends and family—the Fiction Writers Co-op, the Lake Union Authors, Therese Walsh, and Shawn Klomparens. What would I do if I didn't have you to complain to and celebrate with?

To my friends, especially Tasha, Candice, Sara, Christie, Tanya, Lindsay, Stephanie, and Janet—you guys are always there for me when I need you. If I don't say it enough: thank you.

To my readers—thank you for your reviews and notes and messages. Knowing you like my stories is what keeps me going.

And finally, a special thank-you to my old summer family at Camp Wilvaken. While the location of this book will be familiar to those who have spent time at that wonderful camp, please rest assured that the events of this book are entirely fiction, with the exception of the fact that no one ever got any sleep on an overnight on the Island.

Written principally in Jackson Hole, Wyoming; Montreal, Canada; and Puerto Vallarta, Mexico.

I'LL NEVER TELL

CATHERINE McKENZIE

A READING GROUP GUIDE

BOOK CLUB QUESTIONS

1. The MacAllister children gather at Camp Macaw to hear the reading of their father's will. Unbeknownst to them, their father harbored a deep suspicion that Ryan was responsible for Amanda's injuries and wasn't sure if he should inherit the camp or not. What is your opinion of Pete MacAllister's actions? Was it cowardly of him not to address his suspicions with Ryan himself? Do you think he was afraid of something?
2. Pete MacAllister didn't acknowledge that Sean was his son. Do you think he didn't know for certain that Sean was his? Why do you think he kept Sean a secret? Do you think Pete's wife, Ingrid, knew about Sean?

3. Ryan isn't presented as a very likable character at first—he's rough with his sister, motivated by money, and seems to have a dubious past. How did you feel about Ryan? Did your opinion of him change by the end? Why or why not?
4. Margaux seems to be the most well-adjusted of the five MacAllister children. Would you agree with that assessment? Do you think she feels guilty about what happened to Amanda? If so, how might that have affected her and the relationships she has with her family and others?
5. Mary seems to relate better to horses than people. Do you think she actually understands that what she did was wrong? Would she really have stayed quiet about it and let Ryan (or Sean) take the blame?
6. Kate has hidden her homosexuality from most of her family for years, while Liddie dresses in a manner that leads everyone to believe that she is transgender. Why are the twins not open about their real identities with their family members?
7. Sean has been holding on to his Camp Macaw life more than any of the MacAllister children. What is it about the camp that has such a hold over him? Will that change for him now that he knows he's a MacAllister and that Margaux is his half sister?
8. The MacAllisters run a summer camp for children and yet seem somewhat unattached to and uninterested in their own kids (except for Pete's spying adventures, of course). What would it be like to be raised by people whose primary job is to look after other children? Could that have contributed to the MacAllister children's obvious issues?
9. Attending summer camp is often seen as a rite of passage, giving children independence and new skills at key stages.

Does this novel make you reconsider sending your children to summer camp? Did you attend camp? Was it a formative experience for you?

INTERVIEW WITH CATHERINE McKENZIE

This is your ninth novel—congratulations! How do you keep coming up with new ideas?
Thank you! I honestly don't know sometimes. The best way I can describe it is that I have lots of proto-ideas or scenarios floating around in my head, things like: I'd like to set a book at a camp; I'd like to write a reunion book; I'd like to write an Agatha Christie–type closed-circle mystery; I'd like to write about a large family. Then one day those all fused together and the idea for *I'll Never Tell* emerged in my mind, beginning, middle, and end.

Why did you choose a summer camp as the setting for this story?
I spent nine summers at the same camp (and eleven in total at sleep-away camp), so it's kind of ingrained in my DNA. I've always thought it was a unique experience—people have friendships there that don't occur in the "real" world; people are often different at camp from how they are in real life, and that can create intense bonds and emotions. So I've been looking to set a book in a camp for a while and finally had the right story to do it justice (hopefully).

Were the camps you attended similar to Camp Macaw?
I attended several different camps, but Camp Macaw certainly physically resembles the one I spent the most time in, a camp located in the Eastern Townships in Quebec. Camps tend to have a lot of common features though, like a craft shop, a lodge, various beaches, etc.

***I'll Never Tell* explores the various secrets that the MacAllister family keeps from one another. Secrets and lies have been prominent themes in many of your novels (*The Good Liar, Hidden, Fractured*). Why do you keep revisiting them?**
I think everyone has secrets, and I like exploring how keeping them can affect lives under pressure. I also think that all books are about secrets in one way or another.

There are many different characters and perspectives in this novel. How did you keep the various voices distinct, and is it more challenging to write from seven points of view?
It was definitely a challenge—one of the ones I set for myself in the book. But the characters were all clear and distinct to me, and I hope that came through.

Who was the hardest character for you to write?
Probably Mary. She's holding on to important secrets, and structuring her thoughts was sometimes complicated.

Did you have a favorite character?
The twins were fun to write. I like the idea of complete opposites who are also identical.

Was there any special relevance to including the mention of the book *The Secret Garden* in this story?
It's a favorite book of mine from childhood, and it's also a book about secrets and families.

What can you tell us about your next novel?
I'm working on it!

ABOUT THE AUTHOR

Photo © Jason Trott

CATHERINE McKENZIE's *The Good Liar* was a national best-seller. Her previous novels have been translated into multiple languages. A graduate of McGill University, Catherine practices law in Montreal, Quebec, where she was born and raised. Visit her at **www.catherinemckenzie.com** or follow her on Twitter or Instagram **@CEMcKenzie1**.